Sex, SPOOKS & Sauvignon

TRACY WHITWELL

Published by Accent Press Ltd 2017

www.accentpress.co.uk

A paperback original 2017

ISBN 9781786150349
eISBN 9781786150332

Prologue

NORMAL BLOODY JOB

The phone rings six times before he picks up. When he does, there's a clunking sound and some fumbling. Shit, I hope I didn't wake him. Surely it's too early for him to be in bed?

'Hiya? Tanz…? Hiya, sorry, I'm a bit drunk; I fell off the settee.'

Now there's a coincidence, as I'm a little tiddly myself. I don't bother with pleasantries; we phone each other too often for that malarkey.

'Milo, I have to get a normal job. I bombed in that audition and I'm really skint.'

'Oh. I'm so sorry, sweet cheeks… Don't stay in that bastard London for another second. Get on that bastard train and come home and move right next door to me. Gateshead needs you!' His sentences are all one, drawn-out word. He's mullered.

There's another crash. I think he's fallen off the settee again. Milo is always trying to get me to move back to the north-east. Or 'home' as it was for the first nineteen years of my life. But moving back 'home' means defeat in my career. Moving 'home' is everybody knowing my business. Moving 'home' is seeing my parents *all of the time*. Moving 'home' is not bloody happening.

'I can't move back there, Milo. All of my auditions are in London. Anyway, with your writing doing so well, you should be thinking about moving here.'

'How dare you…! (Howairrrrrrooooo.) I am a Geordie, young lady. Unlike you, I refuse to leave my roots behind. I have a laptop, I can email things, I don't have to go to London in person, and I certainly don't need to live among the enemy.'

The enemy being 'southerners'. And the real reason he doesn't move is that he's basically agoraphobic and he would never live more than half an hour away from his mam and her well-stocked drinks cabinet. Milo is a creature of habit, as well as a genius and my best friend. If he carries on drinking the way he does, he will also be dead by the time he's forty-five.

'I'm applying for a job in a shop.'

There's a sharp intake of breath.

'A *shop*?'

'Yes. A fucking shop.'

'You are an *artist*, Tanz. You can't work in a shop.'

'I don't have a choice.'

Suddenly his voice is thick with tears.

'Tanz, you are a trouper. A modern-day hero.'

'I know. Thank you.'

'And, of course, a witch.'

'Don't start on this again.'

'My best friend is a *witch*. You know things.'

'I guess things, Milo. I "gather" things. I have good

powers of deduction.'

'Sherlock Holmes had good powers of deduction. You have special skills, Tanz.'

He's always saying that. Other people have said that. But I'm a normal Geordie girl who's perceptive, and that's it.

There's one final, almighty crash. Sounds like he was sitting on the back of the settee and it toppled over backwards. The line goes dead. He'll probably fall asleep like that.

I am not a bloody witch.

SUNDAYS ARE SO ROTTEN

So I open my eyes and it's Sunday morning. Well, it's ten a.m. My mam would say that was nearly lunchtime. I'm still tired. I didn't go out last night, but I had three buckets of Merlot, talked rubbish at Milo over the phone, then watched *The Hairdresser's Husband* again. I love that film. Right now I have a jet black cat wrapped around my head. Inka has been licking my hair; it's streaked with damp, and I'm seeping tears the way my washing machine leaks wet foam if a sock gets stuck in the seal. I'm not sobbing. Tears are simply brimming and cascading steadily into my pillow, soaking it, and me, in brine.

Seconds ago I was in a field. The grass was warm and there were daisies. I was in Saltwell Park, a big, sprawling, beautiful place with a lake, ducks, rowing boats, greenery, swings and a fairy castle in the middle of it. I spent my childhood playing there and, just moments ago, I'd been back there with my friend Frank. Repeating his name in my head is enough to wrack a sob. We were eating egg sandwiches by the octopus tree. We were sitting on a red tartan picnic rug and he was laughing at me, smiling his goofy smile, because I was singing a song by The Smiths. He was joining in. It was 'What Difference Does It Make?' All we did was make the jangling sounds of the Johnny Marr guitar riff together.

'Dang-a-dang-a-dang-a-dang-danga-danga-dang-dang...'

Then he grabbed my hand, said, 'You're mental' and I woke up.

Frank died in a stupid car crash three years ago, and he was only thirty-two, so I still get a bit messed up when I see him in a dream. It happens every couple of months. They seem to be getting less frequent, but I always wake up wishing I'd given him the biggest squeezy hug in the world. Sometimes I think he's fooling with me. I never went out with him when he was alive; he was far too fickle, so now he plays hard to get with the whole cuddle thing. Sometimes I hear him talking to me in my head. I know I'm making it up, but it's still nice to hear his voice. I don't want to forget him.

I get up and mooch, then sob on my blood red velvet chair for a good ten minutes, filter coffee in hand, sunshine piercing through the mucky brown slats. I wonder if I should run a feather duster over them as I hiccough. I can multi-task when I weep – it's a talent. I miss Frank a lot, especially when I dream about him, but I am also a neurotic bitch and those blinds need a wipe.

Once I've mopped my face and my frog's eyes have un-swelled, I pull myself out of the misery chair and let in some light. My sitting room's bay window opens on to a teensy front garden and privet hedge two feet away. After that is my street, East View Road, a narrow row of terraced maisonettes, pretty and quaint with walls like paper (I can hear my next door neighbours breathe) and tiny back yards opening out on to each other with low, lichen-covered fences separating one from the next.

I rent it on my own, since the complete bastard I used to love moved out and left me to cover the huge rent, but ended the snide comments about my 'funny shape' and 'awful taste in mirrors'. He was actually much more nasty than that, but that's how petty it got before I eventually told him to get lost. Now I'm wandering about in leggings and a vest top, what passes for jim-jams these days, and pretty much deciding that the best way to cheer myself is to call Elsa. Elsa is my buddy, of sorts, and she's a character. She is so pathetically trend-conscious that she never wears a flat shoe, never gets bigger than a British size eight and always has sunglasses worth more than my car. (Bearing in mind I've owned spoons worth more than my old, but perfectly serviceable, car.)

I call her and she answers on the third ring. Funnily enough, she's another borderline alcoholic but still, most days, gets up to go to the gym before seven a.m. Almost all of my friends are nut-jobs of one kind or another, but she makes me laugh when she's not having life-sapping nervous breakdowns. She sounds groggy.

'Hi, Tanz.'

I hate my name. My mam called me Tania, barely a millimetre behind Annie as the blandest name she could have landed me with. Plus, no middle name. My dad I've forgiven, men are shit with names, but my mam could have had more imagination. Tanz is the only permutation

3

I can stand.

'Hiya. Wild night? You sound tired…'

'Work. A stupid article for *Woman and Home* about housework. I hate housework. And women.'

I laugh.

'You want to meet me for lunch? I'm feeling rotten.'

'What's wrong?'

'Nowt. I just fancy some chips and wine.'

'Well, if you put it that way. Half twelve at Minnie's?'

'Yay! See you then.'

I feel better already. Warm day, and Sunday lunch covered. I will endeavour not to think about Frank being so sweet in my dream. If I don't think, I won't cry.

One good thing is that I can be summery today. It's June and it's lovely out there. As soon as it's not cold I have flip flops welded to my feet. My latest faves are decorated with tarnished silver sequins and butterflies. I slip on my white hippy skirt with a little top. I'm addicted to comfort which is why I refuse to walk down to Minnie's in my best wedges, which will bring me out in blisters in 2.3 seconds. Elsa always looks glam, so I slick on a bit of gloss and layer on the mascara. What I can't do is make myself look tanned. Elsa has olive skin. Naturally, I resemble a bottle of slightly pink milk. Only false tan changes this, but I'm rubbish at applying it. My legs often sport the 'giraffe effect'. Not that I like showing my legs, anyway. I hate my knees.

When I open my front door I'm hit with an unexpected wave of gratitude. The warm air is only part of it. I'm grateful I'm alive and I'm grateful my ex doesn't live here any more. I always throw up some thanks to the gods when I get this feeling. When you moan as much as I do you have to balance the books a bit when you have a moment of clarity.

MINNIE ISN'T MINI

Minnie's isn't mini at all. In fact, it's quite roomy. They prepare lovely, locally sourced food and they stock a few choice wines as well as other kinds of alcohol, all of which I've tried. As I walk in, a scent-wall of hot potatoes, coffee and something sweet and cinnamonish hits me bang in the face. I spot Elsa in the corner, crouching over a large Sunday broadsheet, a lemon pressé already in front of her. The tables are made of thick pine, the walls have hand-painted murals and the chairs are big school chairs. I love it in here and so does most of North London, but the sun seems to have drawn a lot of people out into the fresh air, so it isn't rammed with its usual middle-class families feeding their small children tofu and couscous. Winner.

I plonk myself in front of Elsa. She's reading a piece about fashion. I like clothes, but I don't 'follow fashion'. I've always thought 'fashion' clothes are best modelled by transvestites. Fashion clothes are rarely for five foot four girls with proper hips. Elsa is exactly the same height as me, but has bony shoulders and perfect little boobs. I am jealous of that part of her, but couldn't be bothered to give up bread for the rest of my life to achieve her build. Elsa has dark circles under her beautiful eyes. She has a dusky complexion and navy blue irises; I have seen men buckle at the sight of her. I give her arm a pat.

'Hey, handsome.'

She's wearing a lemon sundress with white rosebuds on it. I know without looking it will fall slightly below the knee. She hates her knees, too.

'Hi. I look like shit, don't I?'

'Elsa, you have never looked like shit in your life…'

'I couldn't sleep again last night. I had to turn the lamp on – and the radio.'

I have an 'on and off' terror of the dark. Sometimes I have to leave on my fairy lights for comfort. I've always had an uncomfortable relationship with being alone at night. I have been addicted to old-school horror films and magazines about murderers for as long as I can remember and yet I'm often afraid of turning off the light. Ridiculous, but I feel her pain.

'Maybe you're stressed about something?'

'It's my flat, it creeps me out.'

She is always stressed out about something. Mostly money. The waitress arrives. She's petite and Spanish with a nice open smile. I think she's younger than us. I'm hitting that point where all of the waitresses in Crouch End are younger than me. I don't want to think about what that means.

I feel carnivorous. Usually I have a baked potato with houmous. Today I want gammon, egg and skin-on fries. Elsa, who's a vegetarian, tries not to look disgusted and orders a mushroom risotto. Our waitress, Maria, grins when I ask for a large glass of white. She already knows which I'll have. If I have red it's the Merlot, I don't care how common that makes me, white is always Sauvignon Blanc. Minnie's stocks one from Chile and it's bloody lovely. Elsa orders a glass of champagne with a drop of elderflower. Elsa barely survives after rent, so much of her wage goes on credit card bills, but she still lives like she's married to Denzel Washington. I use this example because she's completely besotted with Denzel Washington and that's probably why she doesn't last five minutes with anyone she dates.

'Why did you move in there if it creeps you out?'

'I didn't realise until it got dark, did I? It's a nice place by day, it feels like a garret in Paris, but at night my bedroom makes me feel sick.'

She looks exhausted enough for me to feel sorry for her.

Our drinks arrive and after a chink of glasses and a slurp (a sip for her, she never slurps) she prods me.

'So what about this new job, then?'

A good-looking lad with longish hair and carefully distressed jeans passes by as I shrug. He's headed for the counter. Looks like a new barman. I force my eyes back towards Elsa. I'm such a lech.

'I'm starting tomorrow. It's only part-time and if I get that telly job I'll be out of there within the week.'

I've been an actress for years, but jobs have been very rare over the past eighteen months. I sold my flat twelve months ago and have been renting and living on the meagre profit since. My savings won't last forever, though, and a girl has to eat.

'Come on, then. Tell me about it.'

'It's Mystery Pot up the road. I went in to get some joss sticks and saw a sign saying they needed someone to work on the till. They've got tarot readers, apparently. I have to book appointments in and all that. I asked this woman about the job – Maggie – she owns the place. She looks evil but was friendly enough. Weirdly, she offered me a trial after about five minutes. Says she wants more time with her horse.'

'And what's the telly job?'

'Oh, it's massive. Every actress in London will have their claws out for it. I don't even know why I bothered auditioning: there were six other actresses there when I arrived and every one of them was off the telly and posh. Why would they want a broad Geordie who gets no work?'

'You never know.'

'I think I do.'

'Well, good luck for tomorrow. It might be fun.'

Acting is becoming an expensive hobby. The amount of people chasing so few jobs is ridiculous. I've thought of retraining, putting my degree, and brain, to some use but the only other job I fancy is a forensic profiler and that would mean another two hundred years of study. For now, shop work will have to tide me over. I glance at the long-haired bloke again. He's about twenty-five. I remind myself that that is *ten years* younger than me. I like his mouth. I take another slug of wine. As our food arrives, Elsa looks suddenly serious.

'If any of the readers at that place are good, give me a call will you and I'll book in? It might help me work out

10

what to do next with my life.'

I'm surprised by this.

'OK...'

As I raise my fork the new lad at the bar presses a button behind him. A familiar guitar riff kicks in. Suddenly the speaker beside us pumps out the slightly too loud intro to 'What Difference Does It Make?' by The Smiths. And to Elsa's utter bamboozlement I burst into tears.

Very funny, Frank.

THE SHOP THAT SMELLS
OF HIPPIES

I used to be a Goth when I was a teenager – Bauhaus and black clothes and big boots with skulls on them – just before I graduated to being a full-on rock chick. I love music and I also love the paranormal, so I should feel right at home in a new age shop. And the thing is, I do quite like crystals and the smell of patchouli. I'm interested in spirituality, I'm interested in the power of thought, I'm interested in many things, but, I have a huge suspicion of anything that garners a following and generates money and claims to be 'a way of life'.

As soon as something spiritual becomes a business my palms begin to itch. It's how I feel about religion, too. There is something beautiful about having a faith that helps you to lead a good life and be kind to other people. But once it turns into a big gang, with rules and leaders and money and the threat of punishment or eternal damnation if you get something *wrong*, I get very uncomfortable. Gangs always have bullies, don't they? So at five to nine, clutching a huge Starbucks coffee that I shouldn't be squandering my dwindling savings on, I approach the green door of Mystery Pot, feeling more than a little freaked out.

Maggie is waiting for me and has evidently just opened up. She wears a caramel-coloured jacket and slacks, has immaculate, permed, grey hair and looks like a Tory MP's mother. She hands me the keys and nods.

'I've written down all of the rules for locking up and cashing up and the float is already in there.'

She took me through these things when she offered me a week's trial, but I'm glad she's written it down. She has a chilly, carefully cultivated voice and a pointy face, but her eyes aren't cold. Again, I wonder why on earth she owns a shop like this. With her clipped tones you would expect her to introduce herself as an executive of The Pony Club. Still, judge not, lest ye be judged. To her credit she doesn't hang about long and seems happy enough that I'm wearing my black polo neck, tight jeans and old knee-high, wedged boots (it's a bit chilly today). I thought I might be expected to wear some kind of hippy attire, as befits the shop, but obviously not. She tells me the reader today will be Sheila, she'll be here by ten, and hands me a feather duster on the way out.

I'm left standing there with some god-awful, plinky-plonky hippy shop music seeping out of the old CD player in the corner. It's not that loud, but yesterday's one glass of wine at Minnie's turned into five, as a huge debate ensued on whether you can be obsessed with shoes and still be considered a serious person. I like Elsa, but sometimes when I'm drunk I despair of her hatred of talking about anything deep because she finds it vulgar and her terrified refusal to think about anything to do with death.

Death is my default subject of conversation while drinking. Now my head is experiencing the 'plinks' as tiny darts of glass go straight into my amygdala and I wonder if it's supposed to sound like angel tears falling from heaven or something, because if so, it's failing miserably.

As I poke the duster at a giant amethyst that looks like a magic cave, the first customer of the day floats in like Nosferatu. He's a young man, he's wearing a cape, and he stops dramatically in the middle of the shop, smiles and regards me like a museum exhibit. He's only about twenty, but has a crop of thin, receding hair that frames his huge domed forehead eerily.

'Erm. Hello...'

He bows.

'I'm Antony. How *are* you?'

He extends his hand; I tremulously offer my own and he kisses it. There's a touch of froth at the corners of his wide mouth. I really don't need this.

'And you are?'

'I'm Tanz.'

'Hellooo Tanz, you're going to adore it here.'

He motions around the shop like it's the land of plenty. I'm not sure what to say. He has very, very wide-spaced grey eyes under that dome of a forehead. I think on my feet, taking an almost imperceptible step back from him.

'Did you have a nice weekend, Antony?'

'Oh, yes. Yes, thank you, I did. I'm an alchemist, you see, and I took a client of mine to the Valley of the Kings.

We went into the great chamber of Tutankhamun's tomb and I held a quartz crystal in the air and, after several incantations, it turned into a pure diamond! It was wonderful…'

Fuckety fuck. The hairs on the back of my neck have started to wave about like anemones. This is exactly what I expected from this kind of shop. Nutters. I smile encouragingly while wondering how I can run faster than the wind without seeming rude. I'm tempted to ask if he is jet-lagged from the flight back from Egypt, but I think he might detect my disbelief and produce some kind of ceremonial dagger from the folds of that crazy cape and jab it into my lung.

Never has the sound of a door opening been more welcome.

The woman who's just entered is wearing a long, maroon, leather jacket – the kind you see in charity shops. She's got shoulder length hair, bleached white, and she's wearing quite a lot of gemstone jewellery. There's a ruby on her finger (presumably fake) the size of my fist. I want to get down on the floor and kiss the soles of her golden sandals, though her toenails aren't the best I've seen. She smiles at the alchemist and nods at me.

'Hello. Are you Tanz?'

I nod and wave.

'Hiya love, I'm Sheila. Hello Antony, are you chatting up the staff again?'

She has a cheeky London twang. He giggles like a girl and puts his hand to his foamy mouth.

'God no, Sheila, I'm behaving impeccably, aren't I, Tanz? I was just relaying some of my latest adventures.

I've had a wonderful weekend in the Valley of the Kings…'

'Nice. Jet-lagged?'

'A little. But I have a special crystal, given to me by my godmother, that stops the exhaustion.' He lifts his disproportionately large hand back to his face and places his finger on his lips. 'But don't go on about that or everyone will want one!' He turns on his heel, back towards the door. 'Must fly my darlings… more packing to do!'

When he's gone, I look to Sheila who smiles. She's late fifties, has good teeth and lots of lines around her eyes. I'll bet she smokes. I gave up a long time ago; ageing my face when I'm trying to get telly jobs is a very bad idea. I like her lop-sided smile. She holds out a bejewelled hand, obviously noting my anxiety.

'Don't mind Antony. He's actually a very intelligent boy. A few problems, though.'

'I noticed. He told me he turned a crystal into a diamond in King Tut's tomb. Who would leave him alone in a famous tomb to cast spells?'

Sheila shakes her head.

'He does like to embellish, but he's only a danger to himself. He's been rushed to hospital three times in the last two months, you know.'

'Oh shit.'

'Pills and drink twice and last time it was his wrists. His little fantasies are part of a bigger picture.'

'That's awful.'

She moves towards the back room.

'Anyway, his godmother is taking him to Italy

tomorrow so he won't be bothering us for a while! Now, I've just got to light my candles and take my coat off love.'

She has a much more earthy voice than I would have expected. She doesn't have the slow, deliberate speech pattern that comes straight from Victorian séances. I've always thought that if you have the 'gift' you shouldn't have to speak like you're on Mogadon, and she doesn't. She smells of cigarette smoke (knew it!) and strong perfume. It's not the cheap stuff. I have a great nose for perfume; I reckon it's Samsara. Her nail varnish is peeling. It's green.

The last time I had a reading it was out of curiosity and the reader was a young lass. She was pretty and well dressed and she came across as a frustrated performer. I left certain she was full of shit. I fed her far too much information, she was quite negative and I felt duped for a week. I've always believed there was 'something else'; I just don't quite know what it is.

There's a huge crash from the back room and an expletive. I follow the noise. Inside there's a little table with two chairs facing each other across it. Sheila has put a pretty cloth on it, spread some gemstones about and laid down her cards. On one shelf a candle and an incense cone burn. Two holes in the wall show where the other shelf was, until about a minute ago. Now it's on the floor with a surprisingly unscathed CD player next to it. Sheila is clutching her knee.

'Ow. The bloody shelf's loose. I caught it with my shoulder and it came out of the wall.'

We decide not to push the shelf back in, in case it falls

off again. Her knee is bruised, but not broken. I offer to make her a cup of tea, which she is very thankful about. I wonder if she lives with anybody: she seems touched by such a tiny kindness. When she's ensconced in her room, with her cuppa, I check the diary. She has five readings booked already. Blimey. There's only room for two more half hour slots, the rest are hours and already taken. I decide I'll call Elsa later; I think I may have found her a good one.

The phone rings and a nervous-sounding lady called Rita asks for a reading with Sheila. She snaps up a half hour. I peep round the door and tell Sheila, who emits a big, throaty monster of a chuckle.

'Rita would come every bloody day if she was allowed. I only let her visit once a month, though. I'm not her therapist.' She pronounces it 'ferapist'. She chuckles again. 'Well, if she's coming in I might be up for a day of people making problems where there are none.'

'How come?'

'Well, she's a lovely lady, but there's nothing actually wrong with her life, she just wants to talk. And you often find when you're doing a whole day of readings that they start to follow a pattern. The 'problems' follow a theme. Some days you'll get six people who just need assurance. Another day it'll be all kinds of relationship nonsense; another, God forbid, it'll all be odd and dark.'

My ears prick up like nosy meerkats. Anything to do with scary stuff and I'm interested. But the door has opened behind me and I know it's time for Sheila's first customer. Blast.

The man is short, Chinese and very quiet. He wanders

into the room that's barely bigger than a stock cupboard with a blissful look on his face and Sheila closes the door behind him. I would really like to be a fly on the wall in there. This is a good sign. Maybe I might like working here after all, despite the nutters and the hangover. I've taken some aspirin, I have a mug of coffee in front of me, a book to read between customers and a colleague who gets 'odd and dark' people in.

Yes. This could be OK.

'HOME SWEET HOME' TIME

I always like the drive up north. There are two reasons for this:

1) I passed my driving test when I was twenty-eight, so the novelty of the freedom that this fast-moving, albeit old and cranky, piece of metal affords me as I pop up the motorway, howling along to my favourite CDs, still thrills me – especially since I've been single and not answerable to anyone else.

2) Newcastle is still one of the best places in the whole world, and seeing as I travelled all over the world as an actress before it all went tits up, I know what I'm talking about. Theatres, cinemas, museums, art installations, music venues, poetry nights, pubs with character, gorgeous old buildings, history, lovely hotels. I could be a tour guide up there. The countryside is beautiful, the nearby beaches are white and unspoiled (and mostly chilly) and the people are *hilarious*.

Like anywhere else it has its problems, but Newcastle and its next door neighbour Gateshead contain my family, many of my old friends and a huge barrel of nostalgia from my upbringing and teenage years. In the old days when I couldn't drive and I went off to 'that London' to college, one of the biggest thrills of my existence would be my first sight of the Tyne Bridge from the train (the train I could ill afford on my student grant but couldn't resist catching every fortnight.) As it approached Central Station in Newcastle, I would draw an excited breath, knowing I could soon alight and make my way to the nightlife – nightlife that I didn't really leave behind until I reached my thirties.

By the time my thirties came, I had a car and a man who didn't like me driving off up north to see friends all the time. I had budget restraints and worries and confidence issues and all of the other baggage that seems to get worse instead of better if you don't handle it right. This, of course, was compounded by the fact that I was an actress and my bloke was jealous. He didn't admit it, but in retrospect I realised he was, and by the time we split up I had shown up at enough auditions looking haggard and argued-out for the rot to have kicked in. This was the price I paid for staying with someone I loved, but who was wrong for me. Now, even though we split up months and months ago, there's a feeling that acting is taking a rest from me because I let it down.

Still, being single and out of the loop also means I can drive off to my mam and dad's house whenever I've got a couple of free days, throw my diet in the air by eating white bread fish-finger sandwiches and fall asleep in the room I grew up in, or, better, on my mate Milo's spare single futon, usually rolling drunk. My parents live in a very cute two up two down (we moved there when I was eleven and they made my brother's room into a bathroom when he eventually moved out) and they have a fat, but lovely, dog called Zorro. Zorro has so many breeds mixed up in him it's impossible to guess his lineage, though the black fur around his eyes which makes him look masked and earned him his moniker could well be a German Shepherd thing.

As soon as I walk through the front door my mam looks up from her newspaper, lips pursed.

'Your nanna's hurt her leg. Your dad's had to go along. She's not been off the phone all day. She only banged it.'

My mam and my nanna are still vying for who gets the most attention from my dad. Primarily because he doesn't pay anyone any attention apart from the dog. He has a shed. He really does. He goes out there and closes the door, in between tending his tomatoes in the green house and walking Zorro. What with all of that and his work hours, no one sees him much. I suffer from being in the unfortunate position of 'exactly in the middle' of the two feisty northern women in this triangle. My mam feels, rightly, aggrieved that my nanna wanted my dad to marry someone 'important' (like a secretary) and made her feel bad when they were courting. My nanna is furious that she's old and doesn't get enough visitors. Even though she gets visitors most days. I feel sorry for my nanna because she's eighty-two, but I also feel sorry for my mam because she's kind and nice, really. These two have built up such a wall of niggling grievances over the years that all approaches to the subject have to be handled with extreme caution. I hate that it's the first thing that's mentioned, so I go for the easiest riposte.

'She always moaning, you know that, Mam. Why are you letting her upset you?'

I am blatantly ignoring the fact that my mam can moan for England. She could probably represent the Earth in a Universal Grumbling Competition. Sometimes I catch myself complaining about some rubbish or other and I'm mortified. I do not want this to be what I'm remembered for. How many people I sent to sleep, miserable, from listening to my woes. I give my mam a slightly awkward hug. She's four foot six and was never really one for cuddling. I do it anyway because I convince myself she likes it really, in a spiky, not-into-physical-contact kind of way.

She asks if I want a cup of tea. I hate tea and haven't had a cup since I was eight. I used to have a milky one because it was nice to dunk biscuits in. My mam knows this, but it's a Geordie default to offer a cup of tea. My parents drink about twelve mugs of Tetley's a day. They even drink it with hot meals which I find utterly perverse. That's what wine's for, isn't it? My mam used to be a cleaner and my dad works in a factory. In their world only alcoholics and unutterably well-to-do folk drink wine with their dinner.

I look at my mam sitting there with her big eyes and tiny doll's mouth and suddenly feel sorry for her. She had a very hard childhood, hasn't got the most romantic marriage and could probably do without continued sniping from an old lady who isn't even her own mother (who, by the way, wasn't exactly Mary Poppins either). I go and pour her a cuppa from the pot and make myself an instant coffee. I can't bear the stuff, but I'll sip a bit of it black, just to be sociable. I perch on one of the new two-seater sofas that appear to be made of concrete and change the inflammatory subject from nanna to Mystery Pot.

My mam is very proud of the fact I am an actress and have been on TV and she is still absolutely furious with my ex, Blake, on whom she totally blames my drop in confidence and waning career. The only way to avoid the inevitable diatribe when I speak of my career is to quickly convince her that I love working at the shop. For her, the work ethic is strong, so ultimately she'd rather I was at the shop than nowhere and she listens with interest as I tell her about Sheila.

'She sounds like your Nanna Lily.'

'Nanna who?'

As far as I know I had a great Nanna Eve, a Nanna Betty, a Great-Nanna Mary and I have my current sole surviving Nanna Marge. I didn't know anything about a Lily.

'Oh, she was your Nanna Betty's mam. Your great-grandmother. She died a long time before you were born, when I was young.'

'So how does she sound like Sheila?'

'Did I not tell you? She was a well-known medium in Birtley. People used to come from all over for readings.'

Cogs whir in my head. I'm sure I have a vague recollection of hearing this before, but I don't recall any details.

'Your nanna, my mam, didn't agree with it so we didn't talk about it. Your nanna saw some very strange things when she grew up. Shadows wandering around the house, a little girl in old-fashioned clothes standing at the top of the stairs… She was terrified to go out to the toilet at night. Said she wet the bed sometimes she was so scared.'

'You never told me this before, Mam. What else did Nanna Betty say?'

'Not a lot, we weren't exactly close were we?'

True, we didn't see much of Nanna Betty when we were growing up. You don't question it when you're young. Later on, after she'd passed away, I just assumed she'd been a loner.

'One thing I do remember clearly from when I was three or four was that Lily dressed in a fitted coat and she smoked like a chimney. And she used to wear a lot of rings. I remember thinking she must be very rich to have so much jewellery. Turns out people gave her stuff in lieu of payment. Jewellery, food vouchers, all sorts. She was a right character. Well that's what me mam said just before she died, when we were getting on a bit better.'

Funny how my mam didn't get on with her mother, but she still gets a lost look when she mentions her being dead. That's why I try hard with my mam. We're very different, but she's done her best and I don't want her to disappear into the ether thinking I didn't like her. This is despite the fact she once swung at my head with a packet of oven chips and only missed me by a whisker.

'Mam, have you never seen any ghosts or anything over the years? Isn't mediumship supposed to be passed down in families?'

My accent always becomes stronger when I'm with my

26

mother. And I start murdering my grammar, just like she does. She is suddenly uncharacteristically quiet.

'What? What, Mam?'

'Nothing.'

'Nothing what?'

'I sometimes have dreams.'

'Eh?'

My little mam looks distinctly uncomfortable. I can't believe this. Nobody tells me anything. She said she 'felt' things once, but I thought she was talking about 'mother's intuition'. I didn't believe her, anyway. I was fifteen, your parents are nothing but idiots when you're fifteen. Now I'm all ears.

'You know, when you dream something will happen and then when you wake up it really does?'

'No! No, I don't know. How come you're telling me this now, when I'm 35? Why haven't I always known this? What do you dream?'

'All sorts. I don't like to talk about it.'

'You don't like to *talk* about it? But you have now. You've got to give me an example.'

She looks ill at ease, but eventually replies.

'I dreamt my dad phoned me at seven o'clock in the morning and said goodbye on the day he had his stroke. The Andrews Sisters were playing in the background. He said he was going dancing.'

My little mam's eyes are filling up. I'm shocked.

'He used to love dancing with me mam when they were young.'

'Why didn't you say you had that dream at the time? That's so sad and amazing.'

27

'I don't like to talk about it because I don't dream anything you can change. Like when your brother was attacked on holiday. I tried to tell him not to go and he thought I was being difficult. So I didn't tell him what I'd dreamt because it would have just upset him if I had. And maybe if he wasn't attacked there, he'd have been attacked somewhere else. If you can't change anything it's useless having it, I think.'

'Wow. You dreamt it would happen?'

Incredible. And that was quite a philosophical statement for my mam. I like her right now. The middle of my forehead feels weird, though. It feels strange when I'm talking to Sheila, too. Working at the shop has been pretty interesting so far, though it can get a bit boring when there aren't many customers. Talking to Sheila is an eye opener. She believes a hundred per cent in what she does and she doesn't give a fuck what anyone else thinks. She worked two days this week. The other reader is a bloke called Martin. He's small-framed with worried eyes and a nervous laugh. I get this feeling that he's trying to be more outgoing than he really is and he doesn't get as many bookings as Sheila. Probably because he comes across as a bit depressed. No one wants a reading from someone who's down. Except for other 'down' people. His regulars are all squirrels, like him.

Suddenly my mam tries to launch into another volley about my selfish nanna and how she needs to make the tea in a minute and she doesn't want my dad to be kept late. 'Tea' is what Geordies call 'dinner' and most people have their 'tea' before six o'clock and then have a snack later. She doesn't really *need* to make it right now: no one is

28

doing anything later, unless you count watching the TV all night as doing something, but tradition and habit decree it as 'time to make tea' and she will not vary by even five minutes. Therefore, nanna and her gammy leg are interrupting a vital routine. I refuse to get into this. Especially as I'm socialising at seven o'clock and need a shower. I make my excuses and go upstairs to get my glad rags on.

'When in doubt go out and drink cocktails.'

That's my favourite saying, apart from, 'How did this bottle get so empty?'

SLEEP? NOT LIKELY

When I open my eyes it is pitch black and for a moment I haven't a clue where I am. This often happens when I stay at my parents' house. I've woken up in a bit of a panic. The last thing I saw before I opened my eyes was a noose – a noose swinging from a wooden beam – accompanied by an awful chill through my body, like death itself.

I really have to cut back on the murder magazines.

I don't even know where my phone is to check the time and I'm shivering, despite the fact the duvet is three feet thick and the central heating is on. I take a moment to slow my breathing, reminding myself it was just a nightmare, even though it feels like the devil himself just did a jig on my headstone. As my heart rate goes back to normal, I grope about on the floor, my eyes useless in the absolute darkness afforded by my mam's lime green blackout curtains. Eventually, after plenty of fumbling, I locate my handbag and take out my phone. I groan at the time. Five a.m. As I'm getting further into my thirties I'm finding it harder to sleep the whole night through after a night on the booze. Especially when I mix my drinks. I often wake up criminally early, my head buzzing with all

31

sorts of worries, and it can take a good hour to doze off again. This time, I'm not even sure an hour is going to do it. That noose and the feeling of cold nothingness... it was so real. I try to block it with other thoughts.

Bits of last night flash back at me. The big hug hello between me, Milo and Chris... Milo doesn't like leaving the house much, as he prefers to cocoon himself and write made-up stories for a living. Therefore, he gets pie-eyed before any evening out and this was no exception. He arrived already warmly drunk, with red-wine teeth. Milo never stays with a boyfriend for longer than three weeks as they always want attention and he never wants to give it, so he's usually single. That suits me just fine as we have world-solving chats on the phone several times a week.

As for Chris, he's something to do with computers, I couldn't tell you what. We're not close like I'm close to Milo, but I've known him a long time and I think Milo might still have a crush on him (Milo was two years below us at school), so I don't object to him coming out with us occasionally. He is single at the moment, too. He has eyes like giant chocolate buttons and ladies love to love him. But he's very picky and extremely neurotic when it comes to girls. Sometimes I despair of him, especially when I bother to pick up one of his calls and have to listen for a good hour to his latest tale of agony with yet another weak, strange woman that he should have avoided like double VD.

Last night we'd started off in a nice pub on Pink Lane with a civilised glass of wine for me and Milo and pints for Chris, then eventually found our way to some kind of reggae club, where we'd draped ourselves over big, loungy seats in the chill-out area and talked about relationships and our childhoods and stupid stuff you talk about with people you've known for ages. All the while they'd carried on with their beers and vino and I'd graduated to margarita glasses containing a dangerously blue liquid.

At a late point in the evening, something odd happened. I was chatting with Milo, head bent towards him so he could hear me over the bass – which was so guttural it made my stomach vibrate – when Chris came back from the loo. As he passed I stopped what I was saying and grabbed his hand. He looked down at me and I got closer to his ear and words began to tumble out of my mouth.

'Chris, it's all changing. You're going to get married next year. The girl you'll marry is completely opposite to anyone you've ever had before. She's not some over-glam fool. She's got long hair, it's auburn, she's funny and her name is…'

I thought for a second.

'I think it's Lynn.'

He stared at me. I stared back. What was I bloody saying? He bent down and faced me.

'Who have you been talking to?'

'No one. I just… it just came out.'

He shook his head.

'No wonder Frank used to call you the White Witch.'

I felt a wrench at Frank's name, but I was drunk enough not to indulge it.

'He probably said that because I knew what he was up

33

to before he did. He was clear as a glass of water.'

'Frank once told me he could never get anything past you and that you could see inside people's heads.'

'Did he?' I misted up.

'Anyway, just so you know, I met a girl two weeks ago when they sent me to Manchester for that conference thingy. Her name is Linda. She is exactly how you've described, she is adorable and she takes the piss out of me and I've been having a secret affair by telephone. But I have to say, the chances of me marrying her are slim to zero. So, avaunt thee, evil witch!'

Milo had only caught little snippets of what was going on (thank the Lord, as I don't think he'd appreciate pronouncements of Chris's upcoming nuptials), but he laughed drunkenly at Chris's last sentence and struggled to his hazy, wobbly feet.

'Can I get you another blue concoction, Fenella?'

Chris snorted at the reference.

'Hahahaha. I love Fenella...! "OHHHH, I HATE YEW CHORLLLTON!"'

And thus my out of the blue prediction was side-lined by a ridiculous impression of an animated Welsh witch called Fenella from *Chorlton and the Wheelies*. That's why I love having boys as friends. Uncomplicated.

And now I'm awake at five a.m. with a toy drum beginning to play a samba inside my cranium. I switch on the lamp, reach into my overnight bag to redeem my paracetamol and neck two down with a huge gulp of water, from a tumbler strategically balanced on the Formica bedside table. Only when this is done do I warily allow myself to ponder the whole 'prophecy' business.

I have often been referred to as a witch in my life and I mostly put it down to having good, old-fashioned intuition and (pre-bob) Kate Bush hair. I've always known when there was something not right about a person, if someone was hiding something, or when I was going to hear from a friend. But describing someone's new – and as yet secret – girlfriend to them, even near-as-dammit, their name? That's another level.

I want to call Milo and talk about nooses and being a soothsayer, but he was so sozzled by the time we left the club that I put him to bed and came back to my parents'. If he'd been more alive I would have stayed there and we'd have chatted like we usually do. It usually takes a fair amount to render Milo comatose and tonight it was the final sambuca shot after several buckets of wine that did for him, I reckon.

Despite my best intentions, my head is beginning to whirr. For now, I'll let it. I'll just lie still while the drugs kick in and hope my spinning mind calms down. Four hours of M1-driving madness is not best tackled on three hours' kip and a stinking headache.

I no sooner think this than I begin to fidget and restlessly tug at the duvet. It's going to be a long night, whether I like it or not.

SEX CANNOT BE IGNORED

I'm wandering around Waitrose again. I do a lot of wandering when I'm not working. I came here for some fish to steam, some salad and some broccoli. I should get these from the local fishmonger and the local fruit and veg shop, really. I still might. I often mooch around shops then leave again; it's part of my 'walking to stay fit' drive. If I don't go swimming I walk around for an hour or two. That's my rule.

There's a very good-looking man by the fridges comparing different pots of houmous. (I adore houmous, it features heavily in my life.) He has sandy coloured hair and is wearing a trendy suit. I don't go for suits as a rule, but there's something rebellious about the way he wears it, like he has to put it on for work but he hates to conform so he got Charlie Brooker or Stewart Lee to make it for him. I don't know why I think of these two in particular apart from they're funny men and I fancy them.

I'm having trouble at the moment with my hormones. I haven't had sex since I split up with Blake. Mostly because I was with him so long and it got so nasty that the thought of any more than flirting fills me with terror. It's all very well fancying and being fancied, but I get myself embroiled so quickly once I've taken my clothes off, it's just not worth the risk.

That's what my head tells me, anyway. But my body is rebelling against this by turning me into a caveman every time I spot someone vaguely attractive. Yesterday I almost got on a bus I didn't need to catch because this rather gorgeous Kings of Leon-looking fella, complete with early-days-of-the-band beard, gave me an appreciative smile as I passed the bus stop. For all I know he was gay and enjoying my ensemble – I was wearing a rather becoming arm-cuff with a butterfly on it – but I just can't control my rampantly roving eye any more. Worse than that, I'm not really one for masturbation, it makes me self-conscious. Or it used to. But last week I got cheeky with myself for almost an hour in the bath, thinking of this funny bloke from a dog food advert. Before you knew it I was up to my chin in suds and imagining him living down the road from me and me bumping into him in the corner shop and him unexpectedly knocking at my door after seeing where I lived, while I was taking a shower, and... Well the rest is nobody's business, but I know I'm reaching critical mass when it comes to needing a shag. I have to do something about it; I'm just not sure who the victim will be yet. I certainly don't want to be beholden to a bloke again.

It's crossed my mind I could contact an upmarket escort agency, but let's be honest they might send a minger and you just don't know where they've been, do you? As for vibrators, how do people use them without feeling completely stupid? I think they have a very particular sound. What if my neighbour brings all her friends round to stand with a glass against the wall and snicker at the dildo lady?

I decide to abandon houmous-man and indeed get my greens from the fruit and veg place three doors away, like a responsible local should. As I pass the newspaper stand near the exit I notice a missed call on my phone from Elsa. Damn. Suddenly, I also hear a voice as clear as crystal in my head.

'Call Sheila.'

I stop short and a Lycra-clad lady with a basket and a primped toddler holding her hand walks into me from behind. I apologise, she growls something entitled-sounding and walks off. I reach around inside my brain.

'Sorry?'

'Call Sheila. Go round and see her.'

Fuck. This voice sounds male, but not rough or anything. Friendly. And it's not like that other voice, you know, the one you hear in your head all of the time. Your narrator, which is basically you, putting a spin on everything that happens. (For me, usually a paranoid spin.) This voice is removed from that. It's someone else's voice. Murderers hear voices. As do schizophrenics. I read about murderers all the time. Double fuck. A tiny part of me is excited, the rest of me thinks I may be on some kind of devilish *Candid Camera*. I look around suspiciously. No one is even glancing in my direction.

I pull the phone back out. I took Sheila's number to give to Elsa. Sheila does home readings as well as shop ones. If she reads for Elsa at home, then she'll be able to pocket all of the fee. Seems only fair. I press dial before deciding what to say to her. She picks up almost immediately.

'Hiya, it's Tanz... Er, a voice just told me to come and visit you.'

There's a throaty guffaw down the line.

'Well, you'd better come round then. I just got back from the launderette. You called at a good time.'

Why did she take that so well? The address she has given me is just round the corner. I insist on bringing her something and show up at the front door with a cappuccino for me and a large Americano for her. The building she lives in is stunning. She has a studio flat on the ground floor; she'd already told me this, but nothing has prepared me for what's inside. It's how I always imagined the interior of a gypsy caravan would look, when I had romantic notions of running away with a man with dark curls and a hoop earring who played the fiddle. I truly have lived in a fantasy-land since I was born.

It is, of course, bigger than the inside of a caravan, but it has the same sense of being enclosed by a person's whole being. Every wall, surface and item of furniture seems to be dressed in, or covered by, velvet, silk, flowers, angels, fairies or twinkly lights in gorgeous hues of purple, crimson, burnt orange, ochre, deep blue and scarlet. There is so much stuff, but it all fits and the effect is one of being cushioned from the world in a room filled with softness and beauty. I am well aware of how gay this makes me sound, but sometimes you just have to call a spade a spade and this place rocks.

We sit opposite each other at a table beside the French doors, which lead on to a tiny terrace edged by pots of herbs and small rose bushes. We drink our coffees and I begin to feel a bit wrong for showing up here 'because a voice told me'.

But Sheila just says, 'I had a feeling about you.'

Oo-er. I am in awe of this woman who has people queuing up to hear her wisdom. She's a down-to-earth Londoner, she has roots showing in her blonde hair and she wears cool clothes. She is not some self-important, self-professed mystic, lining her pockets while scaring people into coming back to her every week. 'Dances to a different drum' is how my mam would put it. My mam is only seventeen years older than me which means I often look up to older women who are wise and strong. My mam was always more like a big sister, really. Frank used to say I 'collected new mams'.

I clear my throat. 'What kind of feeling?'

I'm wondering if the coffee is extra strong as I've started to feel dizzy. My forehead has this swimmy feeling, like I'm breathing through it, or I'm a Cyclops and I just opened my one big eye. I actually think I might faint. Sheila looks at me through cigarette smoke.

'Are you OK?'

'Yes, I'm fine. I'm just a bit dizzy.'

She looks around the room then back at me. 'The middle of your forehead, between your eyes?'

I nod and she smiles. 'That's your third eye.'

'Eh?'

'You're clairvoyant, love. Actually, if they're speaking to you, you're clairaudient. It's quite strong in you. Was that the first time you've ever heard a voice?'

Wow.

41

'I think so. I mean, I've always had 'feelings' about things, but that voice was quite distinct.'

'Well, it must be your time to learn. Some people have those voices with them from childhood, some close off from it and open the door again later in life.'

Sceptical is what I'm feeling. Everyone wants to be 'different' don't they? But really... really, I know it's not possible.

'When did you learn?'

'I had it as far back as I can remember. I saw ghosts everywhere. People no one else could see. Think it kept me sane, the madhouse I was brought up in.'

I can't help laughing at the notion of being 'kept sane' by the presence of ghosts. 'I would be terrified if I saw a ghost.'

She nods. 'Probably why you hear them, love. Less scary for you. Lots of psychic people are scared of seeing spirits. Ridiculous, isn't it?'

'It was only once. How can I be psychic? I'm just...'

'One not enough for you?'

She laughs and drinks her coffee.

'Of course love, it could be schizophrenia.'

My eyes goggle and she tuts.

'I'm joking! I know how mental illness affects the aura. You don't have any signs of mental illness. Well, no more than any other normal adult! When a medium or a psychic speaks to another one, or sometimes even just stands next to them, there's a sensation in the forehead, sometimes in the tummy. I get that when I talk to you and I think that's why we've met. You need to develop. You have strong presences with you. I can feel three.'

'Really?'

'They're not revealing themselves to me right now apart from an older lady. She's smiling. She's called Lily. Lots of jewellery. Do you know her?'

I feel a coldness down my spine when she says that. 'That sounds like my Great-Nanna. She was a medium up north.'

'Well she's just stepped forward and given me a nod. She's letting me know that she indeed passed her gift to you. She's widening her hands. I think she's telling me your gift is stronger than hers. She wants you to learn.'

'Tell her thank you. But I don't really think…'

'Tell her yourself!'

'Oh.'

I fix my eyes on the carpet. I'm not sure I want to do this.

'Out loud?'

'Out loud, in your head, it doesn't matter. She's just passing through, anyway. Busy busy.'

I say '*Thank you*' in my head to Nanna Lily. I could swear I hear, '*You're welcome*.' It's very faint. Then it's gone. I jump a little in my seat. Sheila smiles encouragingly at me. I get a teensy rush of excitement. All those times I heard people talking to me, in the past, and I thought I was making it up. Conjuring them up in my head. Could it be? 'How come this is suddenly happening?'

I stop because I've just seen a shadow. It was coming towards me and now it's halted about three feet away. There is no reason for a shadow to be moving about in this room, or the sudden pressure on my head and chest.

My throat has tightened. I just stare. Sheila looks from the place I see the shadow to me and back again.

'You can see him, can't you?'

I swallow. This is mental. 'Him?'

'Yes. Do you see him or feel him?'

'Both. Mostly feel. He's a shadow.' Now I'm panicking.

'Why don't you speak to him?'

Because he's a ghost and I'm scared, you idiot. 'Really?'

'Like I said, out loud, in your head, either works…'

I test it out, speaking with my mind.

'Hello!'

The shadow steps forward. It's like I'm being pushed back in my seat…

'Woah, WOAH! What's happening…?'

'Ask him to step back so it's more comfortable.'

I breathe in and out slowly, then think, *'Can you step back a bit, please? I'm new to this.'*

And he does. I feel him backing off and I'm sure I can 'feel' him laugh. He seems to be excited. I can 'see' him with my mind. Like a character from a film rather than a solid man in front of me. He's around fifty-five, has greying hair and he's wearing a blue cardigan and brown slippers. I take the plunge.

'What's your name?'

'Edward.'

I hear it in my head clearly. He has a gentle voice and is very posh.

'He says he's called Edward! I heard him. He stepped back! Thank you, Edward. I'm Tanz, nice to meet you!'

I can't help speaking out loud to him, I'm so delighted. I'm positive he's clapping his hands. Sheila is suddenly very bright-eyed.

'Well done, Tanz.'

'I can tell what he's wearing. He's got a cardie on; he's got grey hair…'

'And he's wearing his favourite brown slippers?' She finishes with a flourish. The fact Sheila is 'seeing' the same thing is mind-blowing to me. I try speaking with my mind again.

'How come I can see your shadow, Edward?'

'Call me Teddy.'

I feel a thrill when he speaks to me. 'He's told me to call him –'

'Teddy?'

'Yes! Do you know him, Sheila?'

'Of course! He came with the house. It was a grand place before it was split into flats and studios.'

'When did you… pass away… Teddy?'

'Nineteen twenty-seven. I wasn't old, but I had a nice life!'

I can see him in my mind's eye raising one of those old-fashioned champagne glasses. He is wearing a black tuxedo. Then the image is gone again.

'You were very dapper.'

He steps forward. He obviously likes compliments.

'How come I can "see" him as well as feel him, Sheila? I can hardly believe it.'

'I think it's because I see rather than hear. You're picking up on my way of communicating. You'll recognise it from now on if you're on your own.'

45

That puts me in a flap. 'I'll have a heart attack if this happens when I'm on my own.'

I hear Teddy laugh. His voice is clear but small, like he's speaking down a telephone line. Sheila chuckles, too.

'You can close down, Tanz, I'll show you how. You don't have to "see" anything if you don't want to. But I do think you're a natural. And I think you are going to attract help in your development. If you don't want to develop you'll have to block it and hope you can push it away. It may not be easy.'

There's a disturbance in the air where Teddy has been standing. Sheila notices and raises an eyebrow.

'Oh. Our Teddy's not too happy with that thought. He likes you.'

Why am I so utterly thrilled by this? I hear his voice again.

I can help you. There are lots of us that can help you. Just open up and have a chat. There's nothing to be afraid of. Don't block.'

As if I would, now he's put it like that.

46

PETER SUTCLIFFE
AND PAT THE CAT

I've got a lot to think about. The air is so warm I could be abroad. The streets are still quite busy even though it's seven in the evening and all I can think about is talking to a dead fella at Sheila's place. What a lovely man he was. Sheila says he's still around because he likes visiting and not because he's 'stuck'. She says she'll tell me some stories about the 'stuck' ones next time. Amazing.

I can see people looking at me because I've got a stupid grin on my face that I can't wipe off. I'm shaking a bit. I sit on a bench next to Barclays Bank and call Milo. I get his voicemail. He may be visiting his mum. There's no reception at her house and he usually stays late to watch loads of recorded episodes of *Judge Judy* and drink her good gin. I leave a message.

'Milo. I've just been talking to a *ghost*. I shit ye not. I can't believe it. My hands are sweating. I don't know what's going on. Either I've finally lost it or I'm like that bloke off the telly, with the white hair, who keeps channelling evil people with Scouse accents.'

I laugh at my own joke. I sound really manic. I've got to calm down. I'll do myself a mischief if I don't get a grip.

'Anyway. Hope the writing's going well. Let's speak soon. Don't worry if you get this late. We'll talk tomorrow. Big kiss.'

As I stop the call I see there's a voicemail from Elsa. Elsa's a bit crazy so she'll text and call a lot, then not speak to me for six weeks. This must be one of her friendly months. I look through the window of an over-expensive boutique clothes-shop as I listen to the message. There's not a single damn thing in that window that I could wear or that would suit me. Supposedly beige is in fashion. I'd rather stab myself in the eye with a spatula than attempt to wear beige. What's wrong with these people? I'll bet Elsa has a whole bunch of clothes in a shade of beige that looks absolutely fabulous against her tan. Elsa understands trends and would even come out best in a tussle with a pair of stupidly expensive culottes.

She sounds fraught. Says she hasn't slept properly in days and needs to talk to me. Minnie's is about fifty steps away. After everything that has happened I need a glass of wine. I call Elsa. It goes to answer phone. She might be on the Tube with no signal; she might be in some cellar bar off Soho getting smashed with stupidly hip people or she might still be at work, beavering towards a deadline. Who knows? I leave a message and step inside.

The warmth in Minnie's is overpowering this evening, but there's a small empty table with a fan next to it and I grab it. I don't know the smiling girl who comes to take my order, another new one, but she seems sweet enough and I bagsy myself my usual pint of vino and some olives to pick at. I actually fancy cake, but that's not happening. Certainly not at this time of day: it's against the rules.

It strikes me, as I wait for my drink, that I didn't know whose voice it was – the one in Waitrose – that told me to go to Sheila's in the first place. Maybe it was Lily? It sounded male, though. I'm working tomorrow so maybe I can ask Sheila, though I don't want to get on her nerves by talking about this all of the time.

A glass, satisfyingly misted with cold, is placed in front of me. And a plate of olives in chilli oil with warm peasant bread. I'd like to give the bread back, but I've suddenly realised how hungry I am. I bloody love bread anyway, it's my Achilles heel. As I take my first bite a familiar face passes, bearing a tray. It's the barman who put The Smiths on the other day.

He's carrying food to someone; he has his hair tied back and I notice his eyes really are the most extraordinary china blue colour. My eyes are hazel and I have always coveted blue eyes. My dad has blue eyes. As I sneak another glance I'm just in time to see him slide and trip. He manages to save himself the indignity of landing on his backside, but at the expense of the tray. Two bowls of fries and a pot of ketchup go flying and shatter on the wooden floor. Without even thinking my mouth opens.

'Sack the juggler!'

He looks at me. I redden. I have no idea why I just said that. A couple of people giggle and to my eternal relief he breaks into a grin. I get off my chair, grab his tray and begin to pile chips and bits of crockery on there.

'No, no! Let me get that.'

He has a nice accent. Soft Irish. Dublin, I'm guessing.

'I'm the eejit that dropped it.'

He actually said 'eejit'. I look at the floor, point out an incriminating skid of potato.

'You slipped on a chip. There are a few on the floor. Not your fault at all.'

A woman whose toddler is sucking on fried potatoes at the next table has the good grace to look embarrassed.

I grab the handful of napkins he'd been carrying on the tray and wipe up a gobbit of ketchup.

'Will you stop that, really, it's not your job.'

He takes them from me; he has nice strong hands and well-shaped nails. Just then the waitress shows up with a dustpan, brush and damp cloth. Not wanting to get in the way I retake my seat as he explains to two estate agency blokes that new fries are already on their way. He smiles at me as he passes. I grab my magazine, *Serial Killer Monthly*, out of my bag and idly glance at it while guzzling my wine and thinking of those hands.

I am such a sucker for accents, especially Celtic ones, especially Irish. This, added to the fact that I have been dying for a shag for about two months accelerates my drinking speed alarmingly. I have to be careful with my stereotyping. Just because someone is smiley and Irish with twinkling eyes doesn't mean he is naughty and up for anything. Especially with an older woman. There is no guarantee he finds crow's feet attractive/he's single/he's any good at satisfying ravenous Geordies.

Shit. I've finished the glass. How did that happen? The waitress comes back. I now have a choice. Go home and watch the telly or stay here, on my own and drink more, while not-so-surreptitiously sharking after some Irish lad with nice hair.

'Could I have a glass of champagne this time, please? Actually, make it a Kir Royal.'

The waitress smiles again.

'Celebrating tonight?'

'Actually yes, kind of.'

'Is it your birthday?'

Even I'm not sad enough to sit drinking in a bar-café on my own at dinner time on my birthday. (Actually, I did exactly that a month after Blake and I split up, but that was a choice, a statement of liberation – until three of my mates showed up at nine o'clock and we got so pissed I was lucky not to be stretchered out.)

'No. I've just had a good day.'

'Oh, that's really nice.'

I'm not sure what's really nice, but I'm glad she looks so pleased. She goes off to get my drink and I attempt to immerse myself in the story of a man who killed many, many women because he couldn't maintain an erection and hated them for it. All of his sexual fantasies were about tying women up and pleasuring himself as he strangled them to death. I usually find this stuff compulsive reading, but you know what, this has been a fantastic, life-changing day and the magazine is in serious danger of bringing down the mood. I close it as the next drink arrives, just in time for Irish boy to pass after delivering fresh chips. He stops, glances down and stoops closer to my ear.

'My uncle hitched a lift from Peter Sutcliffe's best

51

mate once. After he'd been caught. His mate said Peter was a really nice bloke, no one could believe he did it.'

He walks off. I am so impressed. If I had the choice between having a drink with Johnny Depp's best mate or Peter Sutcliffe's, there'd be no contest and *that* is saying something. Come to think of it, given the choice of spending a couple of hours with Johnny Depp or visiting Peter Sutcliffe, I would be hard pushed to choose. What the hell does that say about me?

I hope it says I'm not as shallow as other actresses. But it could also mean I'm a potential killer. You read about it a lot, murderers who were obsessed by other murderers, with the technicalities and psychology of killers. I've been reading about this stuff since my nanna introduced me to her collection of *Crime and Punishment* magazines. She was a total one-off, my nanna – still is. Because of her I'm obsessed with murder and expensive perfumes. It doesn't matter how full my credit card is, how much I need to find my rent, if the Coco Chanel runs out I have to replace it or I'm all over the shop.

I'm painfully aware that if I stay in Minnie's much longer I'm going to look like a lonely old cow with no home to go to. Especially now that I'm not reading, just sitting here, drinking champagne like my mam drinks builders' tea. I wish I was more ladylike sometimes.

My head is a bit spinny. I've only had two drinks, but I've also only had two small pieces of bread and some olives to eat in the last six hours. I am tempted to have fries and more drink, but I am too self-conscious to do it. As I'm dithering a text arrives. It's Elsa saying she's getting the Tube and will call me in twenty-five minutes if she's dropping in at Minnie's. A second later another Kir Royal arrives at the table. I'm about to protest when the waitress motions towards the bar.

'It's from Pat. He says you deserve it.'

She leans forward conspiratorially.

'I think he likes you.'

She leaves again. I am rooted. What are you supposed to do when someone sends a drink over and you need some food to soak it up? Will I look like a wanker if I order something? Like I'm expecting that for free, too? As if he's a mind reader he stops at the table and places down more olives and bread.

'I have never had a customer jump out of their seat and try to help me clear up a mess before. Thank you for that.'

This is the second time I've blushed today. I never blush. I've blushed at most five times since I was twenty.

'Thought you might appreciate a little nibble with it.'

Seems that my stereotyping was bang on. This lad is trouble. He winks and wanders off. I don't always like winks. Granddads wink. But this wink doesn't annoy me. This wink is a cheeky chappy wink and I can't help but forgive cheeky chappies.

'Erm?'

He looks back. I motion to him. He returns to the table.

'Yes, madam?'

The drink has loosened me up.

'I can't sit here and drink another drink on my own. I'll look like a prostitute.'

He stifles a snigger.

'We don't get a lot of prostitutes in here as far as I know, madam, and they usually show a bit more cleavage

53

than you are right now.'

I am wearing a little sparkly purple jumper with a denim mini skirt, leggings and my trusty flip flops. I see his point.

'I have come here in my day wear. Casual is all the rage.'

'It's nice.'

'I wasn't fishing… I… Can't you come and sit here for a bit so I don't look pathetic? The murder magazine isn't cutting it tonight and my mate might be on her way so I can't leave yet.'

'Much as I'd like to, I'd get the sack if I sat down. But they can't sack me for chatting at the bar.'

He motions to a high stool at the little bar. He picks up the olives and my drink. I follow him with my jacket and bag. Usually I would be self-conscious, but I've had a giant glass of white and I'm on my second Kir Royal. Sod it. I feel a little less stupid now. People drinking on their own should prop up the bar.

'I'm Pat, by the way.'

I don't bother telling him I already know this and I hold out my hand. 'I'm Tanz. Nice to meet you, Pat. Thank you for… this.' I dip some bread in the spicy oil and take a bite. I'm famished. 'I can't believe your uncle met Peter Sutcliffe's best mate!'

'Yeah. He was a lorry driver, same as Sutcliffe. Said he was really shocked, like. Said you wouldn't meet a more mild-mannered man.'

'You find that a lot. These blokes who are the most disturbed are the best at seeming unassuming and nice. Funnily enough though, where men see another bloke

54

being agreeable, women know better. Female neighbours and colleagues and such like, often say that they were a bit disconcerted by a killer. They say he made them feel uncomfortable, but they couldn't tell why. Something about the way he'd look at them.'

'Jeez. You know a worrying amount about murderers. My mum's like that about blood and guts. She watches everything she can about accidents and the ambulance service on TV. I prefer a nice film myself!'

He pronounces it as 'fillum'. Where I come from the pronunciation is very similar, but not half as sexy. He's tall and he has a strong, regal nose. He's quick to smile and I doubt bar work is his final calling.

'How come you've ended up in London with that accent?'

He shrugs and wipes the bar. 'I realised I didn't like my career choice so I'm starting again. Fancied bumming around the world. I started here to get more money together. My sister lives up the road so I decided to stay in her spare room and save up a couple more hundred then go travelling for a year.'

'Wow. When are you off?'

'Jeez, are you trying to get rid of me already?'

'You're kidding me, not if I'm getting free champagne.'

'What do you do?'

I hate that question. If I say actress, they immediately ask what I've done. As soon as I tell them it's TV some people turn into idiots. I know how horrid that sounds, but you do definitely become interesting in the wrong way if there's the remotest possibility that you might be a 'celebrity'. Other people immediately assume you're a knob. Others still are nice, but want to talk about it all night. But if I don't say actress, what do I say?

'I'm sometimes an actress. Right now I work in a shop.'

'Crouch End is full of actresses, isn't it? There was one in here the other night. Supposed to be famous, but I don't watch TV so I'd never seen her before in my life. She started off a right snobby cow then got sozzled and Marina over there had to prise her off me with a crow bar. What shop is it?'

I think I wanted him to be more impressed. I'm a mass of contradictions. I'm well aware of this.

'It's Mystery Pot; it's just up at –'

'Oh, I know it. My sister loves that place. There's this woman there who does the cards, gets it bang on every time apparently. My sister keeps trying to persuade me to get them done, but I'm scared.'

So his sister's met Sheila, then.

'Scared?'

'I'm not sure I wanna know, you know? Does it help to know something awful's going to happen before it happens?'

'Why on earth would it be something awful?'

I look at him and suddenly something clicks in my head. A little ball of fire ignites and the café seems to go completely still. He's drying a glass. I touch his hand.

'You've lost someone, haven't you? Someone close? And it's changed everything? It's a man. He says you needed to get away from the sadness at home. You've done the right thing.'

He's staring at me with utter shock on his face. Fuck. I've blown it now.

'What? How did you…?'

'I'm so sorry. I should keep my gob muzzled.' I now feel like crying. There's such sadness there, I can feel it and I've gone and poked a stick at it. He looks like a lost toddler.

'No it's… Jeez… My dad died last year.'

'Ohhh, that's terrible. I'm sorry to bring it up.'

'It was terrible. Especially for mum. I've escaped and she's trapped there with the memories. But how could you know that?'

'I didn't. I don't. I just said what I felt.' I don't want to say any more but I know I have to. It's there, pushing at me. 'I just have to tell you, press upon you, you've done the right thing. Your mum was worried sick that you'd lost your dad when you were so young. You could have reacted very badly. But now you're doing something positive. And he approves too, I can feel it so strongly.'

He's still staring, but he doesn't look as sceptical as I thought he might.

'I'm not that young.'

I get up off the seat.

'Can you guard my drink while I go to the loo?'

SOME ARE STUCK AND SOME ARE VISITING

I need to hide for a minute. He's bound to think I'm a crackpot now. Men do not take kindly to spooky shenanigans; I don't know many males who believe in this kind of thing and I don't want everyone to think I'm one of those eccentric mentalists who wear billowing kaftans and coloured Birkenstocks and claim to know where Grandma Olivia hid her wedding ring before she died. Why couldn't I have just had a nice flirt and gone home?

Still, I got it right didn't I? I 'felt' something and I was right. Maybe I've helped him a little, even if I have freaked him out. I sense a buzz in the pit of my stomach, like a couple of hawk-moths are dancing in there. A small part of me, that I'm trying to repress, keeps saying the same thing, 'You've always felt you were different and now you know why'. And I can't help breathing the tiniest exhalation of relief.

After I've hidden for as long as possible without seeming weird, I comb my hair, replace my lip-gloss and decide to take myself off home and tell Elsa to meet me there if she still wants to see me. Today has gone on long enough.

As I push open the door I find myself blocked by the waiting frame of Pat. He takes my arm and guides me towards another door. I find myself outside in a tiny yard. The sky is darkening and a wall lamp is casting watery light down the painted white bricks and onto a couple of plastic chairs. He motions me to one seat and he takes the other beside me. He pulls out cigarettes and gestures around the tiny space.

'The smoking room.'

He offers me one. They're Marlboro Menthols. I like a menthol, especially when I've had a drink.

'I started smoking when Dad died. I'm such a wuss, I only like the mint ones.'

'Me too.'

'Good. We can be wusses together.'

He lights mine first, his hand shaking a little. He lights his, and leaves it in his mouth as he takes the band out of his hair, which falls in waves around his face, then pushes it back again and re-ties it. He then takes a long drag and slowly blows out the smoke.

'I have no idea how you just did that. I've been thinking about my dad all day. I don't like to tell my sister because it makes her cry. You've totally spaced me out. How did you... know?'

'I don't know how I know. This is all new to me. I don't really *know* anything. I just suddenly get a feeling and I say it aloud. My friend does that stuff for a living. She says it's like being a vessel.'

This cigarette is making me fuzzy. I look at him again.

He is shaken up. I can see it. My gob opens again.

'You're doing the right thing, you know. Your sister is comforted by you staying with her. Your mam has other family and friends. She will find a light at the end of the tunnel.'

I smoke, feeling a strange beating in my chest. There's one more thing to say...

'Your dad always knew you were going to travel and now you're on your way. He's very proud. Did he used to call you Pat Cat or Pat the cat?'

His intake of breath is sharp. Again I wonder if I should just shut up.

'That's what he called me all right. Pat the cat. I was always sneaking in and out of my window. I'm glad he's proud.'

'Why wouldn't he be?'

I feel like his dad's clapping. That's all he wanted to say. I immediately feel his presence less strongly. He's made his point.

Pat stares into space. There's something very personal about sharing these things with a stranger. It makes me feel protective of him. I want to wrap my arms around him like I'm his mam.

'I didn't know witches drank cocktails.'

This breaks a slightly awkward silence nicely.

'I'm no ordinary witch.'

'I'm not being funny, but can we go for a drink somewhere when I finish my shift? I reckon I'm too stirred up to go home straight away?'

As he asks, my mobile goes off. I remember Elsa. I grab it out of my bag. Sure enough, it's her.

'Sorry Pat, just a sec.'

A very uptight voice greets me. 'Where are you? I'm in Minnie's. You're not here?'

'Sorry, Elsa. Give me a minute, I'll be right out, I thought you were going to text from the station?'

'I did! Then I jumped in a cab. I hate buses.'

She clicks off. I check my phone. There's a text. I didn't hear it come.

'Pat, I'm so sorry. My friend is out there, she's upset about something, I've got to go and talk to her. Maybe we can chat later?'

'You're a proper Agony Aunt, aren't you?'

Before I can think he's got his arms around me and is giving me the sweetest hug.

'Thank you. You have no idea.'

He smells divine. Cologne, fresh cigarette smoke and man. It's been a long time since I've been this close to a hottie. Plus, I just saw him at his most vulnerable. I breathe him in, like some kind of filthy old perv. This hug is lasting too long now. I don't want to take advantage of a situation that's stacked so majorly in my favour. I just gave him something he desperately needed. I think about pulling away.

All at once he puts his lips on mine. Lovely, warm, juicy lips. Grateful or attracted? I don't bloody care. I absolutely should not be doing this. If he opens his mouth, I am toast. I have to gather myself and get to Elsa or she'll kick off. I stop, pull away gently and smile.

'You're welcome.'

When I walk back in, I'm quivering. Even my jaw is trembling. Christ almighty. Talk about conflict of interests. I don't think giving messages to strangers is supposed to make me horny, but then I doubt everyone I give a message to will be as sexy as Pat.

THERE'S A GHOST IN
MY HOUSE

Elsa is sitting by the bar. I have never seen such dark rings around her eyes. Apart from when she's smudged lots of glittery black eyeliner around them, of course. She's effortlessly rocking a floor length black maxi dress and tasteful silver jewellery, but she looks ill at ease and miserable. I go to her and give her a hug. So very different from the one I just broke away from. This one is testy and her energy is as grey as the circles around her eyes.

'Have you ordered a drink?'

She scowls. 'No, I haven't. There's no one bloody serving.'

Just then Pat appears and she moodily orders the biggest glass they have of Pouilly-Fumé. The most expensive wine they have, of course.

'Another Kir Royal?'

Her shocked eyes whip across to meet mine. 'You've been drinking champagne?'

'Just fancied a change.'

'How long have you been here?'

'I don't know. An hour or two.'

'Hmmm. Lady of leisure.'

I don't think she means to be a cow, but she knows I miss my career and the money that came with it. Criticising me because I haven't been working today is like criticising a bloke with a broken leg for not joining in his usual football game. I decide to let it pass this once, but next time…

Pat puts the drinks in front of us pronto and I thank him as he casts a disapproving eye over Elsa.

We sit at the table I was at in the first place and in a role reversal of last time we were here, Elsa starts to cry. I'm not sure I've ever seen Elsa weep. I've seen her eyes filled with tears of rage and I've seen her at her weakest when she was mugged by some low-life who punched her for good measure. But this. This is tired crying. This is the crying you did when you were five and you had been running about in the park for hours and you suddenly felt emotional and drained and didn't know why. My mam used to call it 'tired temper'. My dad didn't call it anything. He'd just scoop me up and put me on his knee with his arm around me until it stopped.

'What's going on, mate? Has something happened?'

She nods then dabs around her eyes with a tissue from her bag. Her mascara remains perfect. 'Don't laugh. There's something going on in my flat.'

'The oppressive thing, still?'

She takes a huge slug of wine. 'I haven't slept properly since I moved in. The only good night's sleep I have is when I've had a full bottle of wine before bed. But I can't do that all of the time, I'll be a bloody barrel. And anyway, not even that always works. If I do nod off I get woken up at three fifty-five a.m. no matter what. Every single day. It's bloody killing me. Tanz, there's something in my bedroom and it won't go away.'

The hairs go up on the back of my neck. Sheila taught me this thing for 'protection' earlier. I have to visualise a warm light around me apparently, protecting me from anything harmful or ill-intentioned. I attempt to do it now. I imagine an orangey light rushing through me, expelling any negativity, then surround myself with brightness, like a neon force field. I can almost see the dark fog around Elsa.

'Are you talking about a ghost, Elsa?'

She slumps and shrugs. 'I know that makes me sound like an idiot, but I don't know what else to call it.'

'You don't sound like an idiot. What's it doing?'

She looks pitifully grateful that I'm not mocking her. 'It's not so bad in the daytime. The flat just feels a bit claustrophobic, like I'm not the only one there. It's not threatening really, though I don't write there on my day off any more, I go to Costa round the corner with my laptop. But at night, when I get in, I feel positively unwelcome. I go into the bedroom and it feels cold, even with the heating on. I keep the light on and put the TV on in there for company, but it still feels awful, like something bad is going to happen. Most nights I start feeling as though I can't breathe. I can't get comfy at all and I feel like I'm being watched. Then if I eventually do nod off, at three fifty-five a.m., almost to the second, I jump out of my skin and wake up scared. Then I wind up lying on the sofa, which is too lumpy to sleep on.'

She takes another gulp of wine and I ignore my Kir. I really have had enough to drink now.

'I'm sorry to whinge, Tanz, but I'm terrified of going to bed. I don't like being there any more and I signed a year's lease. What can I do? Can your friend at the shop help? Does she know anything about ghosts?'

I don't know if Sheila can help. I don't see why not, though. She was about to tell me about spirits that are 'stuck'. I wonder...

'Let me call her right now.'

I scroll through for Sheila's number. A lifetime of watching Hammer movies and idolising Vincent Price, Peter Cushing and Christopher Lee has definitely left an impression on me. This kind of thing really excites me.

Sheila picks up, eventually.

'Sorry love, I was having a fag and watching a Cary Grant film, *Arsenic and Old Lace*, do you know it?'

'Oh my God, are you kidding me? It's one of the best films ever made. Plus, it's got Peter Lorre in it.'

'I know. Well I couldn't find the pause button, it took me a while.'

'That's OK. I'm sorry to disturb you.'

'You're not. That was great today. I've never met such a natural.'

I'm over the moon she thinks so. In other circumstances I'd tell her about Pat and his dad. The edited version, of course, without the thoroughly inappropriate lust at the end. But I don't want Elsa to know. It's my little secret for now.

'Look, Sheila, I'll be quick. I'm with Elsa, you know the friend I told you about, the one who wanted to call you

68

for a reading?'

'Oh yes. The one who puts make-up on to go to the gym?'

'Hmmm. *Anyway*, she's got a bit of a problem with her flat. There's something, probably someone, in there and they're stopping her from sleeping. They're making the whole atmosphere rotten, basically, and she gets woken up at the same time in the middle of the night, every night.'

'Right. Well, first off, have you protected yourself?'

'Yeah. A few minutes ago.'

'OK, have a delve.'

'A what?'

'You're sitting with her now, are you?'

'Yep.'

Elsa is sinking the rest of her wine, looking intrigued.

'When you put down the telephone, have a delve. Think about her flat and feel about for any kind of energy you can pick up through Elsa. You'll get an idea of who's in there. We can pop over there after work tomorrow if she wants? We should be able to sort it, unless it turns out to be 'complicated'. I reckon you'll be a dab hand at ghost-busting!'

Suddenly I'm visualising Bill Murray with his backpack on and a laser beam coming out of his outsized spook gun.

'Wow. Thanks, Sheila. Just a sec.' I look to Elsa who's dying to know what's going on. 'Are you around tomorrow evening at sixish?'

'I can be.'

'Good. Sheila, that's fine. Let's do it!'

'Good girl. See you tomorrow.'

I wink at Elsa.

'What? What did she say?'

'We're going to come and ghost-bust your house tomorrow!'

'Really? I mean, how can you help? Isn't it a specialised thing?'

'Sheila's going to teach me. Just a second, I want to try something. Sit still.'

I sit still myself, look at Elsa, then 'feel about' with my mind. Looking for a clue as to what's going on. Two things come to me. It's an old lady in Elsa's flat and she is angry and confused. Plus, she's not evil, she's scared. Interesting.

'You're being haunted by an old lady. She's terrified and she's angry.'

Elsa almost jumps out of the seat. She glares at me with absolute alarm. 'Please don't, I have to go back there tonight. How can you possibly know that? That's the last thing I want to hear. I'm bricking it as it is.'

'Elsa, I have a very nice sofa bed. Don't go back there. Stay at mine. Even if you have to get a cab to yours early in the morning for clothes and stuff for work, you'll still get more sleep at mine than yours.'

I've never seen her look more grateful.

'You are a life saver.'

'Shut up.'

'No, really. Who the hell else could I go to with a 'haunting' problem and they'd know what to do? How exactly do you *know* that about the old lady, though? I mean, anyone else would think I was mentally ill.'

'You are mentally ill. Anyway, I'm not sure what's going to happen. I may be awful at the whole spirit-clearing thing.'

'Well whatever happens, you'll be less scared than I am.'

Elsa glances at the bar. 'That surfy-looking barman keeps looking over here. Do you know him?'

'Oh, not really, we were just having a chat earlier. Nice lad.'

Her eyes narrow. 'Nice lad? He can't take his eyes off you. Is there something you want to tell me?'

'No.'

'He's quite handsome, isn't he?'

'Yeah. He's cute, I suppose.'

'Cute, my arse. He's gorgeous. Isn't it time you dipped your toe back in the water?'

'Errm. No. I can't be bothered with it all.'

Elsa yawns like a lion. 'Tanz, I'm sorry to be a pain, but I'm dying on my feet here, that wine's gone straight to my head. Could we maybe…?'

'Of course.'

I wave Elsa's tenner away when Marina brings the bill. I pay with my groaning credit card and as I'm slipping on my jacket, Pat approaches and hands me a square of paper.

'Let's go for that drink some time, if you fancy it?'

Then the cheeky blighter kisses me on the cheek. I want him to kiss me on the mouth, but that's not prudent. Elsa is looking at me smugly, not without a little envy. Like many pretty women she's used to being the centre of attention with attractive blokes. My looks are interesting rather than beautiful and I'm not as skinny as Elsa, so I always feel like her ungainly chubby sister when we go out. This is a new situation.

We use her tenner to get a cab. We should walk, it's not that far, but both of us are tired. Once inside I rustle up crudités and houmous, which I quickly realise is not sufficiently mopping up the drink so I add a few rounds of toast.

As I put the duvet on the pull-out sofa bed and she gratefully curls up under it, she peeks out and smiles. 'You've got to call him, Tanz. Or I will.'

'Stop it. Let's just concentrate on sorting your flat. God knows what's going to happen there.'

She's almost asleep before I finish my sentence. It's probably the carbs. Usually Elsa treats bread the same way she treats tramps and beggars. Like their existence makes her sick. She doesn't mean to be horrible to tramps and beggars incidentally, she is just mortified by uncleanliness and she assumes that they are filthy. I leave on my cherub lights and put a glass of water on the table next to her. I think of leaving the TV on, but I reckon she'll be fine.

I can't believe it's only ten thirty. It feels like I just lived a forty-hour day. It should be at least six a.m. I programme Pat's number into my phone, not because I think I'll call him, but because at least I won't lose it if it's in there. I'm always losing things. It amazes me that after a day of revelation like today I can still be thinking with my loins. I push thoughts of his lovely mouth out of my mind.

As I clamber into bed my phone rings. I pick up.

'Hello, is this Rentaghost?'

'Hiya Milo.'

'HIYA MILO? Mrs "I have no powers, I am not a witch!". Spill the beans. I want details of the undead and I want them now…'

I can't help laughing.

Looks like my day's not quite over yet.

FIND THE LOVE

I don't get to talk to Sheila much at work because she's booked out the whole day. Talk about Mrs Popular. Today's theme seems to be rude, toffee-nosed idiots who want to be told their lives have meaning when they don't. Sheila slaps my hand when I tell her this.

'We're all looking for meaning, love. Some people are rude because they're scared.'

'So what. They're still rude. Wankers.'

Just then another leather-faced rich woman troupes in, in ill-advised, spike-heeled boots, white skinnies and obvious hair extensions. I'd usually think this rocked on a sixty-year-old if she didn't look at me like I was dog poo. I always wonder where well-off people get the idea that they can be as horrible as they want from. It seems to be worse in people who used to be poor then acquired money; their taste is laughable and they stink of condescension. Anyway, this one has a huge stain on her aerobicised, sixty-year-old arse and I'm not telling her. She is also the colour of beef gravy. She doesn't look tanned, she looks barbecued.

As the door closes on her grubby bottom, I recall Elsa

leaving my place via taxi at seven a.m. with a smile on her face. She'd slept like a baby and was feeling relieved that someone was going to (try to) help. Funnily enough, after my chat with Milo I'd not slept quite so well. I'd woken up near dawn convinced I'd heard a long, drawn out scream. But when I checked on Elsa she was out like a light. It was only when I heard a car horn outside (who beeps their horn at four in the bloody morning?) that I thought maybe that was what had got into my dreams. It took a while to shake off the creeps, though.

At lunchtime Sheila manages quickly to explain about spirits who come back to visit as and when they please, as opposed to poor lost souls who don't/won't leave for whatever reason. The latter need guidance and help, whereas the former may have a lot to teach us. God, this stuff is interesting.

Turns out she's done a few 'clearings', or 'ghost-busts' as she prefers to call them. I've noticed that Sheila finds humour in spiritual stuff, which is probably why so many people come back to her for readings. She doesn't take herself too seriously and she's down-to-earth and truthful. When I ask how she got into this business, she just repeats that her childhood was shocking and if she hadn't had her 'other friends' she may not have survived it with her sanity intact.

When I ask about her mam she just spins her finger next to her temple and chirps, 'Cuckoo, cuckoo, cuckoo!'

And now we're in my car, which is looking more sorry for itself than usual as some idiot knocked a dent in the door while I was parked outside my house, and drove off without leaving a note. This is the norm for London, but it still riles me. When you're already skint you can do without it.

'What if I can't feel anything?'

Sheila snorts. 'How can you not feel anything? You only had to concentrate a tiny bit last night to discover it was an old woman and what her state of mind was. I think you're more likely to need to protect yourself from feeling too much. You're obviously very sensitive.'

'If I'm so sensitive, how come I only found out about all of this now? Why haven't I been doing this for years?'

'You have.'

I think back to all of the times in my life I've 'known' something and called it 'instinct'. The most glaring one was the day I turned up for school when I was eight years old and my form teacher wasn't in class. He was a funny, clever man, we all adored him, and I'd never known him not to be there before the students arrived. My instinct was that it was too cold in the room, unearthly cold. There was a stillness. An absence that I felt but couldn't vocalise. Basically, as soon as I walked into that classroom I knew that our teacher was dead. Ten minutes later it was announced in assembly that he'd died of a heart attack the night before.

Afterwards, I told myself it was a conclusion I'd come to because he wasn't in the classroom when he should have been. But that's quite a leap. Teacher late, therefore dead. Things like that have always happened to me and I've put it down to educated guesses. Now I'm not so sure. It seems to be the truth that if you're not looking for something you don't see it. Maybe I always 'knew' stuff. I just didn't recognise what was happening.

The traffic on the way to Elsa's is shocking. The roads of London always jam up with cars around teatime. I ask Sheila to pick some music and she rifles through my little leather CD case. I am chuffed when she hands me *Led Zeppelin II. The Brown Bomber*. I chuck it on and go straight to 'What Is And What Should Never Be'. It's just perfect driving music, cranked up on a bright evening. Sheila knows the words.

We pass the journey happily enough, singing at the tops of our voices and making inappropriately sexual comments about the members of various rock bands who were just *gorgeous* in the 1970s and that Sheila was old enough to have seen live in their heyday.

It's only as we get a couple of streets away from Elsa's flat that the merriment suddenly dries up and the atmosphere in my Peugeot becomes a lot more sober. I switch off the music.

'Why do I suddenly feel like shit? Do you feel queasy?'

'You're picking up on the energy in the flat. You're picking up on the lady we've come to meet.'

Fucking hell. Frightening. It's all very well loving the concept of all of this, but now it's real and I'm going to have to face something that has scared the bejesus out of me since I was little... a troublesome, possibly angry spectre.

When we knock, nobody comes. We're there a couple of minutes when Elsa comes haring around the corner scattering apologies like shot-gun pellets. She's been in a coffee shop with her laptop as she didn't want to be home on her own. She shakes Sheila's hand as she's unlocking the door and starts gabbling what she'd already told me last night. As we mount the stairs she throws a smile my way.

'I'm not feeling so messed up today because Tanz took good care of me last night. After taking care of the barman at Minnie's, of course.'

Sheila raises an eyebrow and I roll my eyes and shake my head. Cow.

Soon we're on the top floor and the door is open. Elsa switches on the light then holds back. Wow, she really is scared. Eventually she enters cautiously behind us.

'I'm sorry it's a bit messy. I wasn't around to clear up today.'

I have been in this flat once before. I found it pretty, but quite oppressive. It was sunny and light enough, but I couldn't wait to get out. Now I know why. As I walk through the front door it feels OK, but entering the living/dining area is like walking into an invisible wall. The air is so heavy, it's almost viscous. Sheila nods at me and smiles.

'Feel that?'

'How could I miss it?'

Elsa is standing in the kitchen doorway watching us, not quite sure what to do with herself. Sheila notices her discomfort.

'Why don't you boil the kettle love, while we feel about a bit? The good news is you're not going mad. There's someone here and they're not too happy. We'll have to see what we can do about it.'

'Oh... OK.'

Elsa does as she's told. Which is a distinct novelty.

'Tanz, just concentrate on what you feel. I usually walk about until they make themselves known.'

Sheila goes to the wall with the shabby-chic sofa against it, rests one hand on the faux antique wallpaper and closes her eyes. I'm drawn to the window, overlooking the street, where Elsa keeps her big, old-fashioned school desk. As soon as I reach it, my temples throb and my breath is short. I feel completely dreadful. I close my eyes and I can hear a voice – a raspy, breathless lady. She has longish, wild grey hair. I can see her now in my mind's eye, trying to pin it up in a bun. I recover from the initial shock, closing my mouth with a snap. I decide to speak to her with my mind, so as not to shock Elsa. Again, I feel a little self-conscious.

'Hello there. What's your name?'

'What are you doing in here? Get out. Why are you sitting there? You can't be here. Get out. Get out NOW.'

She sounds very panicked as well as angry. In my mind it looks like she's waving an umbrella. I know it sounds strange, but I can visualise her, rather than see her. Like I have new eyes that are turned inwards. I feel terrible for her. She's angry, but so tiny and frail.

'We're leaving really soon, honest. Is this your place?'

'Of course it is. Why won't you all just leave me alone? Have you seen the walls? Have you seen the state of my bathroom? This is private property.'

Her energy abates like she's stormed off.

I open my eyes. Sheila is watching me. Elsa is back in the doorway not saying anything.

'What did she say, love? I could see her standing over you. She's a spunky little thing, I'll give her that!'

80

'She says it's private property. She was threatening me with her umbrella.'

'I saw it. It was bigger than her!'

'Elsa, you've messed up her bathroom, apparently?'

Elsa moved in with me for a couple of months about five years ago and I can categorically confirm that she's one of the most untidy women I've ever met. My bathroom looked like an explosion in John Lewis every time she took a shower. She only tidies up when there's a possibility she's bringing a man home, then she's like the House Doctor on roller skates. It's bizarre. Why sell yourself as a super housewife if they're only going to find out imminently that you're a total slob?

At this moment Elsa looks mortified and scared. She doesn't like being told she's untidy in the first place, but it's a hundred times worse when it's a dead old lady saying it. I try to give her a reassuring glance. Sheila walks toward the door.

'Let's have a nose in the bedroom now, Tanz. I think that's where we might get some answers.'

Elsa looks at us. 'Should I just stay in here? I've made a pot of coffee.'

'Yes, love. You start without us. We'll be as quick as we can.'

BLUE PETEY

The bedroom is an absolute tip, even by Elsa's standards. There are clothes, belts, shoes, deodorants, a damp towel and half-empty water bottles all over the place. The bed is unmade and the blinds are half-shut. There's also a feeling of confusion and sadness in this room. I look to Sheila, who blows out a puff of air.

'Bingo.'

'This is horrendous. It's a miracle Elsa's slept at all. I'd have nightmares sleeping in here.'

'Me too. It makes me want a ciggie.' For a second she looks longingly towards the door, beyond which is her packet of Regals. Instead she taps my arm and points to the unkempt double bed.

We both go to it and sit down. I close my eyes. Within seconds I am feeling absolute panic and my breath is short again. I regulate my breathing like I did when I went diving off Koh Samui and saw a shark. There's such a desperate feeling in here. Sheila stands. I pat the mattress.

'I think this is where her bed was when she lived here. It may even be the same bed.'

Sheila giggles. 'Christ, I hope not, love.'

Suddenly I can feel the lady beside me, standing to my right. She doesn't like anyone being in this (her) room. But there's something else. I seize on it and speak to her pale, shadow self. *'Please tell me your name. We really want to talk to you. Then we'll go. I promise.'*

She pauses a second, then can't help herself.

'Sarah.'

She's so lonely. It's underneath the panic and the anger. Hollow, desperate, awful loneliness. I speak aloud now, so Sheila can be part of the conversation.

'Sarah. Hello, I'm Tanz and this is Sheila. We just wanted to check on you, that's all. Do you live on your own?'

'Since Len died. Yes, since Len.'

'Your husband?'

'My Len, yes.'

'Do you know when he died?'

She is indignant, the tone changes.

'Of course I know. I'm not batty. First of April 1962. Ten years he's been gone. Still miss him like it was yesterday.'

My heart goes out to her. I look at Sheila.

'She thinks it's 1972.'

'Of course it's 1972, silly girl.'

She must have been a pocket rocket in her time, this one. But her voice is wispy and I guess that she suffered from chest problems of some sort.

'Can you feel the disturbance when she gets mad, Tanz? The air shakes.'

I nod and listen. 'Her breathing doesn't sound so good.'

Sarah thinks I'm talking to her. *'Bad chest. I always have a bad chest. Asthma 'n all. No kids, no one to look after me. It's murder.'*

As soon as she says asthma, I link in. Tiny old lady in a single bed by the window in the dark. She's trying to breathe and she can't. She's coughing and wheezing and her face is changing colour. Now I know what happened. She caught a chill, got a chest infection then died from asphyxiation, fighting to get some oxygen in. Poor lady. As I'm thinking it, Sheila puts her hand to her chest. She's obviously picked up on it, too. Suddenly I feel tearful.

'What a terrible way to go.'

'It feels like she has emphysema or a really bad chest infection, love. She definitely couldn't breathe.'

'She says she had asthma.'

'Bloody hell. Can't imagine that's much fun, Sarah.'

Sarah's reply is sad. *'No, it isn't.'*

'She says it *isn't*, Sheila. Does that mean she still has a chest infection now, even though she's…?'

'Oh yes. If she was lonely for ten years and this place was her only reality, maybe she couldn't let go of it. If she hasn't let go then she's stayed here in exactly the same state as she was when she passed. She only needs a nudge and she'll suddenly realise she doesn't have a bad chest at all.'

The air begins to vibrate as Sheila speaks. Sarah's not having any of this. *'Of course I've got a bad chest, listen to it! It's rattling like my Petey's cage. How can she say I haven't got a bad chest, the stupid woman?'*

I'm intrigued. 'Who's Petey, Sarah?'

'My budgie. That blue budgie out there in the cage. My

*little baby. Who did you think? I'm all he's got, the poor
sweet lamb.'*

Oh my goodness. 'Sheila. She stayed for her budgie.
She's been here forty years because of her bird!'

Even Sheila looks surprised.

Something else occurs to me. 'And I'm going to bet
she died at five to four on the dot. That's why Elsa wakes
up terrified. Oh, boy. Sarah, listen to me, we have to tell
you something…'

I'm not quite sure how to put it. I look to Sheila who
looks back expectantly.

'Do I just explain the situation?'

She nods.

'Sarah. You have to go into the living room and look.
Look properly. Look around you. It's not just the new
wallpaper and furniture. Look where Petey's cage was.
It's not there. Really, it's not. Petey died many years
ago… Petey's gone… and you should be going, too.
Going to see him.'

I feel the vibration in the air again. She doesn't like
this one bit.

*'Don't be ridiculous. Petey's through there. Petey's
fine… Petey's my little lamb… he's –'*

I speak as gently as I can, glancing at Sheila to make
sure I'm not getting this wrong. 'Sarah. You have to
listen. This is horrible. You are living a lonely life in this
place. You feel ill and angry and strangers keep coming
in. The girl that messed up your bathroom lives here now.
And there's somewhere much nicer you could be. Where
you'd feel well and strong and happy. You deserve to feel
wonderful, Sarah, and you could, easily.'

'*What do you mean?*' Sarah sounds hesitant, but at least she's listening.

Suddenly, Sheila speaks. 'Sarah love, look to your left. Go on, look to your left. There's a door opening, isn't there?'

'Who do you see? Who's there?'

All goes still. Faint but clear, I hear it. I hear the anger and the pain drain away from her voice as she says just one word.

'*Len?*'

'That's right, Sarah, your Len's here and he'll take you to Petey. Just walk to him.'

I feel her go. It's nothing dramatic or showy. There's no massive flash of light or crash of thunder. It's like something was here, an energy, and now it's gone. An absence. I look around the room. It's lighter. The oppression has lifted and now it just looks like a messy room. I can't believe it. Was that it?

I turn to Sheila. 'Did we do it?'

She nods. 'Well, that went all right, didn't it? Well done you. All that stuff about a better place she could be in. That's so right. And kind, being kind was exactly right. They're so used to being confused by all the comings and goings over the years that they don't understand. They can't see the wonder that's waiting for them right in front of their faces. You just have to introduce some doubt and they're suddenly open to the possibility that they don't have to stay trapped. That's when I jumped in. Bloody fish to water, you are.'

It was so sudden. Was that truly it?

'Sheila. That was un-be-lievable. Has she really gone?'

'Looks like it.'

I move to leave, but she stops me. Lowers her voice. 'Your friend out there. Is she a depressive?'

'Erm…'

'Come on. She must be to have chosen this place. Or let this place choose her. And this kind of mess, you find it a lot in 'disturbed' rooms. Troubled spirits thrive in mess. She needs to tidy up: it'll help to tidy her head up.'

'OK.'

We go back through to Elsa and tell her the good news. She doesn't look like she knows whether to believe us or not. We explain about the old lady and how she didn't want to move on because of her bird. I decide not to tell her that Sarah died at three fifty-five a.m. precisely in the bedroom, as that might do more harm than good. We promise we saw her move on. I accept a coffee and a biscuit. Ghost-busting has left me gagging for sugar. I adopt my most serious voice.

'Elsa. We're going to drink our coffee and eat most of your expensive biscuits. You are going to get in that bedroom and tidy up. Put all the bottles and cans and used up creams and whatnot in a black bin liner. Shove the dirty clothes in your wash basket and the clean ones in a drawer or the wardrobe or in another bag, I don't care, just do it quickly. By the time we leave, in about twenty-five minutes, I want you to have a tidy room. Sheila says it'll help to keep the place "clear".'

I have to bring Sheila into it. She won't do it just for me. She's so shocked she doesn't speak, then she jumps up.

Sheila chimes in. 'Open the window and burn a nice

smelly candle if you have one 'n all. Can I smoke in here?'

Elsa looks like she might say no, then shrugs.

'How can I refuse after what you just did? Smoke by the open window if you don't mind.'

She throws open the window to the street, goes to the kitchen then tentatively enters her bedroom with bin bags and a box of matches. She runs back in for a second.

'Thank you so much. Both of you.'

Then she's off again.

I can't believe she's doing as I told her. Nobody ever does what I tell them. Sheila goes to the window, face thoughtful. We hear a lot of rummaging from Elsa's room.

'That was impressive, love. What you did in there. I hardly had to say a thing. Your first time. You just got it.'

'I don't know about that, I just felt awful for her, being so unhappy. She was in the kind of trap you see living people in all of the time. Still, at least she was dead and could move on!'

Sheila emits one of her dirty laughs. 'True enough.'

Sheila looks like she's sucking on a stick of nectar rather than a cigarette right now. 'Just so you know, you can't talk them all down that easily. You get some right buggers. Evil so and so's in life and still evil so and so's in death. But she wasn't evil, she was just a lonely old lady who was worried about her bird. God bless her. Best not to talk about her right now, though. Or think too much about it. She's only just gone over; we don't want to bring her back!'

I wonder if my admiration is too apparent? I'm buzzing again. What just happened was awesome and

Sheila is my new hero. Still, I do have one unanswered question.

'How did you know that she should look to her left? When it was time to go?'

She sucks again on her nectar stick. 'When you know you've got to them, made them doubt or hope, close your eyes and visualise where they're standing. You'll see a pinprick of light somewhere, or a door opening. It'll just appear in your mind. In Sarah's case, maybe she imagined she would 'go to heaven' through a door when she was a child so that's what appeared. Sometimes you see someone waiting to accompany them, sometimes they spot someone through the porthole and tell you who it is. They usually sound happy about it and they almost always go through. We just help them by soothing their fears beforehand. What a lovely job, eh?'

'Sure is.'

And it really is. When I go and check on Elsa twenty minutes later it's already a different room. She has piled her dirty clothes into one bag and her clean clothes into another, and wedged them into the wardrobe. The shoes have gone on their shoe rack and the rubbish has left the room in another bag. Now the floor is cleared the room looks bigger. She has switched on the make-up lights around her mirror, lit a Jo Malone candle, probably a freebie from one of her freelance jobs, and she's straightened the duvet. The open window has let in fresh air and the candle smells great. I call in Sheila. Neither of us believes how different a room can look in such a short time. Elsa's cheeks are pink.

'It feels different.'

Sheila nods and hands her some crystals from her bag.

'Wash these under the cold tap and don't carry them next to coins. They should help with negativity, especially the haematite. Don't dwell too much on what just happened: we want to let Sarah get settled wherever she is. Chances are she'd not want to return here in a month of Sundays, but you don't want to call any unwanted energy back. Keep the windows open for a bit and I'd get some sage tomorrow, light it and take it around the house, carry it into each room and waft the smoke. This should be a new start for you and your flat.'

'Do you want to come back to mine again tonight Elsa? You can if you're not ready to stay here.'

'No. Actually I'd like to tidy up everywhere. Doing the bedroom has got me in the mood. Plus, if I run off again I might be too scared to come back. I need to see if I can sleep here now.'

I admire her spirit. *Spirit*. Geddit?

As we walk down to the car, Sheila winks. 'If she wasn't your friend we'd have had a little wage for that.'

I can't believe anybody gets paid for doing something so gratifying but, on balance, Elsa should have forced Sheila to take some money seeing as it's how she makes her living.

As I start up the car I send a little wish up to Sarah. I hope she's having a lovely time. I visualise her cuddling her husband and feeding her bird. It makes me feel warm.

That night in my dreams there are no nooses or screams. I just see a quiet wood filled with bluebells. I love bluebells.

THE PHONE-CALL OF FORTUNE

Inka, so called because she's the blackest, shiniest cat you'll ever see, is sitting on my lap, purring like a truck. It is noon and I've only been up an hour as I was reading my book. It's a tarot card book I picked up in a charity shop. Talk about God providing (if you believe in any of the gods). Fifty pence it was. The brand new ones in Mystery Pot cost eleven pounds.

I can't be spending that kind of money right now as my savings are dwindling fast. In fact, in another week or two I will have reached the end of the wire when it comes to cash flow, so I am now limiting myself to one crushingly expensive, shop-bought coffee a day when I'm at work (I simply love a large soya cappuccino with a sugar free shot of hazelnut – who doesn't?) and I stick to home-brewed coffee on the days I'm not working. Today I'm not working. I'm also shockingly bored by this book. Sheila says I should check how good I am with the cards. She recommended the Ryder Waites, but they didn't inspire me. I've seen the deck I want. They're called Medieval Scapinis and they are the bomb. I'm just not sure I can justify the expense.

I'm toying with putting on a repeat of *Homes Under the Hammer* when my phone pings. It's a major novel of a text from Elsa. She usually texts rather than phones if she's freelancing from an office. She says the last few nights she's slept like a baby, one of them on no alcohol at all. She's followed instructions and also set out more candles around the place, dusted and cleaned the whole flat and added *flowers*. (I can't help wondering if we gave her a personality transplant by accident. I mean Elsa, buying flowers? Really?) She says it feels much more comfy now and she's less stressed. I text back that I'm happy for her and would love to see her for a catch-up sometime soon.

Just as I'm sending it my home phone rings. I usually wait for the answer phone to kick in, in case some idiot is trying to sell me double flamin' glazing, but I take a chance and pick it up.

'Tanz! All right?'

The booming tones of Bill. Six foot four, blond, piercing green eyes, Glaswegian, funny, my agent and – crucially – gay. (So many of my friends are gay. A blessing of being in the entertainment industry.) He is engaged to my other agent, handsome, sensitive, equally hilarious Joe, who stands half a foot shorter than his man but has the spirit of a tiger.

Even though I've had only one audition in the past three months, I would never leave them. I know how horrid the acting world is at the moment and I know my past victories in 'the business' are now nothing compared to pouting, frivolous females who are younger, still considered up-and-coming and who managed to get a few of their lines right in *Hollyoaks*.

I really cannot compete in a world of vacuous celebrity consumerism. I could now prove myself as an actress a million times over and it would make no difference. I have an 'interesting' face, I am not a lover of schmoozing and I live in a universe where sporting massive plastic tits and selling every aspect of your life to the tabloids is pretty much expected. I will never fit into this new world order.

'Hiya Bill, how are you?'

'Not as good as you're about to be. You know the Snow-bar ad?'

How could I forget? A fortnight ago they had me pretending to be a liberated housewife in the imaginary snow, doing a silly dance to some awful song about their new chocolate bar. To be fair, they let me taste one and it wasn't appalling. Then they kept me hanging on until three days ago, when they announced that unfortunately I'd got down to the last two, but they'd 'gone in a different direction', i.e. away from me towards some other lucky cow.

'Of course. The bastards.'

'Not so fast! "The bastards" would now like to offer you the part, as their first choice just broke her foot in a pothole. Apparently she thought it was a little puddle. Compound fracture, can't walk. So now they need to go back to their other and, of course, superior choice.'

'Oh my God! Oh my God, Bill. When?'

'Flying to Spain tomorrow. Is your passport in order darlin'?'

'Of course!'

'Money's three hundred a day for two days plus travel, plus they're offering you a three grand buy-out. Means you don't get repeat fees, but it's three thousand upfront. It's pretty rubbish compared to the old days, but deals are getting tighter and it's better than some. Good news is they'll pay it as soon as the ad is showing and they expect to have the first burst out in four weeks.'

'Aaaaggghhhh. Three grand in four weeks' time would be MARVELLOUS!'

'Well done, darlin'. I'll email all the details now and speak to you later. Bon voyage!'

I cannot believe it. I hug Inka and kiss the top of her head. Her purring now sounds like rain thrumming on a tin roof. She would sit on me all day if I let her.

I have been completely bricking it as to how to pay my credit card bill along with everything else and still afford my rent. This job has bought me a few months' grace if I rein in the spending, do my three days a week in the shop and stop treating myself to enormous vases of wine at Minnie's.

Minnie's. I still haven't called Patrick. I assume he's Patrick if he's Pat.

I decide to have a bath to celebrate getting my job. I will shave my legs and armpits, put some super-strength conditioner in my hair and slather myself in cocoa butter cream. Then I'll go for a big walk in the drizzle with my ladybird umbrella up.

But before all of that I shall send a little text. Today I landed a job. Tomorrow I will be on an aeroplane, I will do a minimal amount of work and will return knowing I shall not have to scrape for pennies for the time being. That deserves a treat. I shall text Pat and ask how he's feeling and maybe he'll text me back. That would be nice.

As I turn on the bath taps, not four minutes after texting him, he calls. I was not expecting that.

'Hello, is that the Wicked Witch of the West?'

'No, it's not. I'm the Lovely Witch of the North-East, thank you very much.'

'Oh, forget it then. I prefer bad witches.'

'Ha.'

'How are you, Geordie girl?'

'I'm OK thanks, better than OK actually. I've just been saved from a life in the workhouse.'

'How come?'

'I got a job. One of those humiliating adverts that make you look an absolute twat in front of the nation. But beggars can't be choosers and now I can keep my Skybox for another fortnight.'

He doesn't so much laugh as rumble. His laugh is like a rock-fall. 'Well, I've got the night off. Are you coming for a wee drinkie to celebrate?'

God, his accent is delicious.

'Are you old enough to drink, Pat?'

'You cheeky mare. I'm nearly twenty-seven, I'm positively ancient. Have you still got your own teeth?'

'Hoy!'

He rumbles again. 'How old are you? Please don't ask me to guess. I'm rubbish at ages.'

I am surprisingly reticent about my age. I still have to tell casting agents I'm thirty-three. Well I don't have to, but I do it anyway because they have no imagination. The closer you are to thirty, the closer you are to still being young. The further away you are the more fucked up it all is. Forty is supposedly a desert for actresses. That's why I don't want to be relying on acting as a career by then. It's too demeaning and embarrassing. Either that or I have to become some kind of unlikely movie star. The thought of that doesn't even attract me. To live in those heightened realms you have to pretty much leave reality behind – in a bad way.

'I'm at the back end of thirty-five. I am officially ancient.'

'You're officially sexy. Where should we meet and what time?'

I ignore the compliment.

'I've got a flight at noon tomorrow and I have to pack and stuff, so how about six-thirtyish so I can get home early? I really need a proper night's sleep if I can.'

'OK... I know a nice cocktail place on the way up to Muswell Hill. It opened a fortnight ago. It's called Purple Haze. It's relaxed, it's got sofas, the drinks are ace and it's not Minnie's. What do you think?'

I like the fact he didn't leave the choice to me.

'Yeah, cool. Purple Haze, six-thirty.'

'See ya then.'

I can't believe how easy that was. What a thoroughly nice bloke he is. I can imagine him travelling the world, making friends wherever he goes, having women falling in love with him and him barely noticing, just surfing and hanging and living in the now. Young person's malarkey. Even at this juncture, in my mid-thirties with no ties and no kids, I've started to feel time ticking. Getting too old to do 'young' things.

My cousin Kel is my age and she has a daughter. She loves her and she loves her husband, but she says the ticking is even worse when you give birth because suddenly your life is mapped out, as a carer for another person. Until her daughter's old enough to fly the nest, Kel can't go out when she feels like it and she can't just take off on holiday when the mood takes her. She can't go dancing and sleep in till noon or go to music festivals or pop down the pub for a chat without thinking of the welfare of her child. The babysitters, the finances, the preparation, and the worry while she's out that something may go wrong…

Kel says she'll be going on fifty by the time the responsibility is lessened and that terrifies her. At one point she was as adventure-loving as me. Now she says she's making her new adventure with her family, but sometimes she feels trapped. She reckons that's why parents become alcoholics. A bottle of chardonnay a night lessens the burden. She's only half joking. But I'm also an alcoholic and I am child-free. Probably for ever.

A DIRTY MARTINI

There is no way I should be taking so long to get ready. I'm going for a drink with a good-looking lad. I know this, but last time he saw me I was not dressed up so I don't see why I'm making such a song and dance about it now. There are clothes all over my bed like I'm in a chick flick. I don't like chick flicks and I don't want to be a flamin' girl about this. I'm only going for a cocktail.

'*Bollocks.*'

That is not me. That is a voice in my head. These days it's hard to tell what is the voice of paranoia and what is the voice of 'another'. But this sounds suspiciously like 'another'. One that starts to laugh.

'*You don't just want to go for a drink and you shouldn't do, either. Get back in the saddle, lass, and enjoy. You take things far too seriously.*'

I'm not sure about voices in my head taking the piss out of me.

'*Who is this?*'

'*Someone who wants you to have fun. Wear something that makes you feel happy, put a comb through your hair and get yourself out there. If you don't at least kiss him, you'll have me to answer to. Byeeee.'*

The voice has gone. Perhaps I made it up. But what it said was quite right. I am not auditioning to be Pat's wife. I'm going to have a chat and exercise my flirt muscle. Good. I pick out a little black dress with red roses on it, team it with black leggings, shiny red flip flops with a wedge and a slash of lip-gloss.

My hair is actually my favourite thing about myself. It's a simple bob-type style and if I blow dry it with my round brush, or give it a little straighten with my ceramics, it goes shiny and behaves itself. It's dark brown, but I'm sprouting the odd white hair now. It's one of the only things I'm not worried about. You categorically cannot stop your hair going grey. And so far I've only got about three of the wriggly, albino buggers so I refuse to be bothered. That's what hair dye is for. I'll probably grow it really long when I'm older and be an eccentric Bohemian. I'll wear lilac flowers in my white hair and chic long shirts with well-cut trousers and comfy but pretty shoes. (Old people have terrifying feet. If mine stay nice I'll wear flip flops till I die.)

I think about death and getting older more than anyone else I know. Every single day. I always have, since I was tiny. Every new wrinkle, no matter how small, every dry patch on my elbow or heel, every bit of me that's less lean, sends me into a flurry of terrified conjecture. And it's not just the physical stuff. I wonder how I'll feel as my family peel away. I wonder how I'll be when I'm effectively an orphan and have to grow up. When my friends and acquaintances become full stops. Will I have to stay here on this planet, becoming more and more

102

alone, every new death like a grandfather clock clanging a funeral march in my heart? Or, perish the thought, will I be one of the first ones to go?

It's morbid, I know and I really wish I could forget about it. It's part of why I sometimes get depressed (most actors are depressives, apparently). Wine helps. Music helps. Live gigs make me happy, as does dancing. But I have to learn to live my life without suddenly being brought up short in Tesco behind an ancient old biddy who's struggling along, my eyes brimming with tears at the thought that my world is about to become a series of horrible losses and degenerations.

Life has already started the process with the disappearance of some of my grandparents and Frank, lovely Frank, who should still be here. That's probably why I'm so delighted by this latest development. A curveball. Completely inexplicable vibrations in my world. It's occurred to me that I have accepted this ghostly stuff very easily; maybe because I need it more than most.

I grab a red pashmina I picked up in Bangkok, which looks much more expensive than it was, and give myself a spray of Chanel. I look in the mirror. I look colourful and not too try-hard. That'll do.

I arrive at Purple Haze feeling pleasantly warmed up after a fifteen-minute stroll. I've not really looked at the place before, but they've made it nice. It has huge windows and Mediterranean blue paintwork and, to my delight, the window frames are rimmed with multi-coloured tube lighting, like Christmas. I brace myself for the inevitable sixty second shyness of entering a bar alone, which is ridiculous considering how many countries I have visited on my own. I walk in and glance around at the pleasant mosaic and harlequin tiled bar, with a funky cocktail counter and a little stage, presumably for live performances. Small ones. There's a guitar and microphone stand already set up. We're in for a treat later.

Pat is at the bar. He turns as I walk in. I am exactly on time which is a fluke as I'm usually running late. He's got on a linen shirt, sort of off-white. His hair is coming out of its binding and he's grinning his head off, as is the barman. They must have been sharing a joke. He looks very happy and relaxed. I can't help but smile back. He waves. I head up to the bar. He puts his hand on my back, kisses me on the cheek and gives me a cocktail list.

'You look great.'

'Thanks.'

'Now... I'm starting with a Brazilian mojito and I'm paying tonight. No arguments. What would you like?'

I glance down and spot two of my favourite things – raspberries and vodka. 'I'll have a raspberry mint martini.'

'Cool.'

My concoction looks like a stabbed dinosaur. The green stuff is apparently peppermint liqueur. This place opens at six so it's just us and a man in a tricorn hat so far. This is Crouch End so people in interesting apparel aren't unusual. The barman is in a very expensive T-shirt and has carefully ruffled hair. North London contains a lot of people who try not to look like they've tried very hard when they patently have. And there's nothing wrong with that. I have always lacked the knack of looking effortlessly expensive but cool. There's too much of a geek fighting to get out.

I am led to a big brown sofa near the window. We both sit, but not too close. When he kissed my cheek he smelled of washing powder and whatever that great cologne is he has. Amber and musk. I love smells. They remind me of people as much as songs do. Because my dad would give us a hug when he came home from the pub when we were really young, I've also always adored the smell of beer and cigarette smoke on a man's breath, which must put me in a fan club of one.

Our drinks are icy and clinky.

'So, how have you been since I went all "I see dead people" on you?'

He laughs into his mojito and has to wipe his mouth with the back of his hand.

'I have to say, you completely and utterly freaked me out.'

'Oh no!'

'In a good way. I was really looking forward to carrying on the conversation. Until your snobby friend showed up.'

'Snobby? She's not snobby.'

'Oh, she so is. She snapped her fingers at Marina the other week; she's lucky they didn't get broken off!'

This doesn't surprise me as much as it should. Elsa has a streak of Princess Margaret in her. She can be a bit grand. Her dad is a hotshot artist, big on praise but short on money. She grew up in Edinburgh in a nice house, but he spent more than he made on impressing people so they had to sell it. He treats her mother like shit and cheats on

105

her constantly. Elsa hasn't got a clue how to be normal. Her dad taught her that she was a cut above everyone else and she finds it very hard to see otherwise. Sometimes being her friend is a pain in the arse.

'I so wanted to talk to you more. But in a way it was good because I went back to my sister's instead and we talked about Dad and it was great. It's lifted something that had been eating at me.'

'That's brilliant.'

'Yes, it is. It turns out I'm the one they've all been worried about, Mum included. They all seem to think I'm twelve.'

'Aren't you?'

'Shut up! What about you? Did you sort her out? She was looking very sorry for herself.'

'She's fine now. There was an old lady ghost in her house. I went round with my friend Sheila the next night and we had a chat with her and she moved on.'

He literally gawps. 'You had a chat with a ghost and she moved on?'

I nod.

'I tell you, you're certainly not a boring conversationalist. Last time I went for a drink with a girl she gave me her full manicure history. I tried to strangle myself to death with my scarf and she didn't even notice. Do you want another drink? The first one seems to have evaporated.'

'Ooops. So it has. Sorry.'

'Don't be sorry, mine's done the same. Nerves.'

I cannot imagine this lad being nervous, *ever*, so I roll my eyes and he giggles.

'You're not paying all night.' I take out my purse with my 'don't mess with me' look and he takes it straight off me and puts it back in my bag.

'I got paid today. Plus, you did me a big favour the other night, you know? Please. Let me get a few in. Same again or new one?'

'I think I want another one of these, even if it does look like a car crash on the moon. Thank you.'

It occurs to me that I'm not the slightest bit jumpy now. He's interested and interesting, this place is cool and I don't have any fatal diseases that I know of. That is enough for anyone, isn't it?

When he gets back he listens with rapt attention to the whole saga of Sarah and her budgie and laughs his head off at the messy bathroom and the umbrella waving. When I finish he shakes his head.

'You do know, don't you, that there are many people you could tell this story to and they would immediately have you committed?'

'Yup. Including Mam. Even though it's in her blood she still thinks it's dangerous nonsense. When anything like that happens to her, she pretends it hasn't, apparently. And that's my own mother. Other people might think I'm trying to be one of those lot...'

'Who?'

'You know, those mediums on the telly, telling people what they need to hear to feel better. And those ones who are suddenly overtaken by murderous ghosts on camera. They look like mentalists. Vaudeville acts. I don't even know what it is that I'm doing. I'm channelling something, but I don't like the word psychic and I'm not sure what the right word should be.'

'Well, whatever it is, you're very good at it. My sister will probably accost you in the shop soon. She's absolutely gagging to hear if Dad's got anything to say to her. I told her to leave you alone, but I'm not sure I can stop her. She *loves* all of that stuff.'

This scares me. I hope she comes in on one of my days off. 'So, how are the travel plans going?'

His eyes light up. 'Not long now.'

Turns out he's starting his trip in Thailand, one of my favourite places in the world. I feel a stab of jealousy, as I miss it with all of my heart, but simply can't afford to go back right now. In an attempt to smother my envy, I tell him beaches and islands to visit and the best huts to stay in. After Thailand he's going to Australia, then he'll 'work backwards', whatever that means. He really is an intrepid little soul. He pats my knee, moving in a little closer.

'And what about you, jumping on a plane tomorrow to go to work like you're Kate Adie or something?'

'Hardly! I'm off to shoot an awful advert. The money's a bloody godsend, though, and I'm going to be in a nice hotel for a night so I'm quite excited. There's a lovely pool there so I can have a swim and a sauna.'

'You do know, now you've sold it to me like that it's going to be a fucking nightmare, don't you?'

He's made me laugh again. He has the same bleak sense of superstition that I have. Geordies are remarkably superstitious. My mam once said we had Irish in our blood. It would make sense.

'Well, I will be dancing around in fake snow in a warm

place, pretending it's chilly, which might be weird but I doubt you could call it a "fucking nightmare". What might be more of a nightmare is remembering the crazy dance I did at the audition and replicating it in high heels and a dress in snow made of polystyrene or whatever.'

'Jeez. I would pay to see that!' He looks to the bar and nods then looks back at me. 'I just did something a bit James Bond. He just asked if we wanted another and I nodded yes without asking you. Sorry, am I a presumptuous wanker?'

'Not if you're paying.'

'Good. Oh look.'

I follow his eyes to the tiny stage. The man in the tricorn hat, who I admire greatly for the selection of highwaymen frock coats that he wears to do his shopping in Budgens, is working on his laptop a table away. Pat is out of his seat and heading for the stage. I'm a music fan, but I really don't want to be serenaded on the guitar. There's something a bit pre-planned about gestures like that. But he doesn't pick up the guitar. He goes to the mic stand and takes up a – what is it? Next thing I know, I'm hearing the harmonica solo from 'Isn't She Lovely?'. Stevie bloody Wonder. And he's awesome. I'm a bit embarrassed, but also totally impressed. It doesn't last very long, but it's fantastic. Mr Tricorn smiles mysteriously to himself, then gets on with his computer business. Pat puts the harmonica back where he found it and runs up to the bar to get the drinks.

I watch him as he approaches the table once more. He is basically a big, beautiful kid. Everything he does has energy. I am not eyeing him up as a potential boyfriend, I don't want one of those, but I like how much fun he is. He didn't get up there to show off, he got up there because he felt like it. As he places the cocktails down I am full of admiration for him.

'You are very talented.'

'My uncle taught me the harmonica. I've got a couple of them. Did I look like a massive eejit up there?'

Before I have time to think too hard, I bend forward and kiss him on the lips.

'No you did not. You looked great.'

He obviously doesn't need any more encouragement, as he puts his glass down, takes my face in both of his hands and kisses me for rather longer than I kissed him. The fact that he's so at ease about everything is very refreshing. The fact I have been longing to get it on with someone for ages immediately wreaks havoc on my body. I want him to push me down on this sofa right this minute and crush me into the cushions. He certainly knows how to kiss. The confidence of youth.

I wish I didn't keep thinking about his age – he's only eight years younger than me – but the stress of my last relationship and the intermittent worry about money has taken the sheen off my once devil-may-care attitude. Also, ever since I turned thirty-five I've felt different, like I crossed a line into new territory. My friends with kids tell me that I will feel as though I've gone up a generation if/when I have a child. I will feel older and I will feel tired. Another reason I don't want one. My own mother told me not to have a child unless I really, really have to. It's one of the only progressive opinions she has ever voiced. In most other ways she's like a maidservant from

1764 who just accidentally wandered into the future and is still slightly shell-shocked by what's going on.

Every time I come up for air from kissing Pat I want to kiss him again. The teenage joy of snogging someone passionately and not having to think or talk is a heady one. Eventually it's him that stops, heaves a huge theatrical sigh and picks up his drink.

'Is it me, or did it someone switch the heating up *very high*?'

'No. I think it's quite cool in here.'

'So that's what it's like kissing a witch.' He reaches forward, gives me another peck and grins. 'I like it.'

'Well, that's a relief.'

He looks at his hands for a minute. Oh. That must be him being serious or shy or something. When he looks at me, his eyes are more bold than shy.

'I'm going away soon.'

'I know.'

'We met under very extraordinary circumstances.'

'I know. I was there.'

'I don't want to insult you or anything…'

'Go on.'

What the bloody hell is he going to say?

'Do you live alone?'

'I live with my cat. I am a cat lady.'

'Makes sense, I'll bet it's a black cat.'

'OK, so Inka happens to be black. What of it?'

'Do you have a boyfriend?'

I snicker. The word boyfriend sounds so old-fashioned in his accent. 'No. I wouldn't have kissed you if I did.'

'Very commendable. And a great relief.'

111

'Oh yes?' I'm now knocking back my third cocktail, I have just shared a hot-as-jalapeño kiss with this vision before me and I love a bit of badinage.

'Tanz, I'm well aware you are a good person, I don't think you're a pushover, or a girl of ill repute, but I was wondering if you'd take me home? Like soon. Like after this drink? I can get us some vodka or something on the way. I'm not always so pushy, but life is literally too fucking short and you are literally too tasty.'

Another time I would be self-righteously furious at being asked less than an hour into a date to take someone home *like a hooker*. I have a definite chronology for how I do things and what he's hinting at is *at least* a month in. Or it was last time I dated. But these circumstances are extraordinary. He has taken my breath away in as much as I'm now scared to death while being speechless with desire. He's laid his cards on the table and it's up to me. Any doubt either way is eradicated when he kisses me softly then puts his forehead to mine.

'Please don't be insulted. Say no if I've made you uncomfortable.'

I pick up my martini and drain it, then offer him a small wink.

'There's an off-licence two doors away. I like Zubrowka.'

I drape my pashmina and lead him out. The vodka is purchased within three minutes. Like Providence herself is following our every move, a cab with a yellow light shows up and is immediately hailed by Pat.

'It's only a fifteen-minute walk!'

'Which means it's an even shorter drive. Good.'

The journey passes in a blink as we kiss like sixteen-year-olds all the way home. The time between his request at Purple Haze and me fumbling my key into the wonky front door lock is at most twelve minutes.

I take him to the living room and leave him with my iPod while I run to the loo. I am actually quivering. For a second or two I want to climb out of the window and run off. What the hell am I playing at?

'Good girl.'

It's the voice. There, then gone. Like permission. Maybe I really am imagining it. Who cares?

I grab two glasses and orange juice 'from concentrate' out of my fridge and go to the living room, where Pat has lit my reading lamp and put on some nice background tunes from a collection on my iPod called 'Kick back and breathe it out'.

'Great room. Welcoming.'

I look round, glad I tidied up today. It's small, but the walls are clean white and the carpet is that hemp stuff, with a nice Indian rug on top. I have things from my travels dotted around, a Buddha here, a silk wall hanging there, a bodhrán hanging over the fireplace and a blue Tanglewood guitar on a stand. I don't play the guitar very well, but I like to have it around. I also have a banjo in my bedroom that I can play a bit better.

I pour us both a large vodka, then add the cold juice. Pat takes my drink from me and puts it down on the reading table with his own. This time when he kisses me, it's more dangerous, as there are no witnesses to behave in front of. This, however, does not render him all thumbs. He pulls me towards him on my futon settee with the cheap woollen throw and kisses my mouth then buries his face in my hair, so I can feel his breath on my neck. Those dextrous hands with the clean nails cradle my rib cage as he whispers in my ear.

'I've not really liked anyone for ages. Now I'm feeling very, very naughty.'

'You are very, very naughty.'

I can't believe how much I want to bypass ceremony and rip off his clothes. Seven months of being a nun has rendered me an animal. I try to keep myself in check, but as I kiss him again his hands move upwards. I have to hold my breath as he manoeuvres to my breasts. Suddenly he turns me and drags me towards him quite forcefully so I'm straddling him and peels down the straps of my dress until it has been pushed to my waist. Now he's virtually face to face with my strapless bra. With a wicked smile and another kiss, he reaches his hand inside and begins to stroke my nipple with his palm.

That is as much as I can take. I grab the bottom of his linen shirt and rip it over his head. His chest is dappled with fine, sandy hairs and he has strong arms and the kind of flat, muscled belly you see on young men before the beer begins to fill it out. I rub my hands over him, like I'm considering the purchase of a shiny new stallion. My lack of shyness is astounding to me. His lack of shyness, less so.

He reaches round like an expert and releases the catch on my bra and takes my nipple in his mouth as his hand massages the other. *Oh my Goooddd…*! I take this for as long as I can then pull him onto the floor and undo his jeans. I don't care if missionary is supposed to be a boring position, I just want this man naked and on top of me. I manage to wriggle out of my leggings and the rest of my dress, and after loosening his jeans I push them and his pants down and off with my feet.

Now the only thing between us is a pair of functional, black M&S knickers. I reach down and grip him and am gratified by how happy he obviously is to be here. Ecstatic, judging by how hard he is. His gasp is followed by a hand reaching down and stroking me through my underwear. Slowly, while kissing me, his fingers slip inside. As I arch into his hand I am hit by two sensations, one of falling backwards into a pitch black abyss and another of the skin being rubbed off my back by the rough carpet. Next thing, Pat sits up, hand still in my knickers, and reaches into his coat on the sofa. This is awkward to say the least so he removes his hand and sorts through the wallet until he finds what he's looking for. A condom. Good lad.

'Hope you don't mind, I always carry a few in here.'

'No, I'm glad, I don't even know if I have any, any more.'

He quickly puts it on. Expertly puts it on, in fact.

'Come up here, gorgeous, I loved what you were doing before.'

He sits back up on the sofa, and I climb up his body until I'm straddling him again and can lower myself onto him. His groan is as unselfconscious as mine. As we move together he sucks on my nipples before our mouths meld together and then we both begin to move faster and soon I can't tell what's happening any more. All I know is I can't stop grinding and I'm mewling like a kitten and he's gasping into my shoulder and then… and then…

With one last yelp, the world suddenly goes quiet and still in my head and I'm riding a surge of white light. A thunderous firework explodes. Or actually, maybe, I just orgasm. Pat is seconds behind me.

We stay in that position for a while, until I reluctantly climb off to retrieve our drinks. As we sip, we kiss and touch and drink some more.

'You wanted an early night, didn't you?'

'Yes, I did, but it doesn't seem quite so important now.'

The smell of his skin is like a drug to me after such a drought. He lightly brushes my bare breast with his fingertip and pushes me back on the sofa. Putting his drink on the floor, he dips the finger into the cool liquid and slips it between my legs.

'That's good. Because I'm not finished with you yet.'

My eyes close as his tongue follows the path of his finger.

GHOST PERVERT

Half an hour into my flight, the plane has risen above the grey clouds and the sky is all blue with wisps of white candy floss. I have a gin and slim in front of me and I am running on two hours' sleep. If that. My eyes keep closing of their own accord then popping open again like broken shutters.

Every time they close I have flashbacks to last night and have to stifle another embarrassed yet smug smile. It just didn't stop. That Mills and Boon bullshit about melting into each other and making love all night has suddenly taken on a whole new perspective. Apart from it was more like eating each other alive, like starving kids with a vat of Ben and Jerry's, all night.

After the first time, we played with each other like naughty children for hours. Every time it seemed we were sated and needed to sleep, something would set us off again and another hour would be gone. Eventually at about five a.m. we realised we were too wired to sleep so I pulled out the futon settee into a bed and put the kettle on. Soon we were snuggling up with the duvet on our knees, eating a box of wafer thin chocolate mints from the

99p shop with big mugs of camomile tea, and watching *Manhattan Murder Mystery*. I did not expect Pat to like Woody Allen, but he was captivated. When the film finished we managed to snatch our meagre sleep ration, and then it was nine o'clock and I had packing to do.

Were it not for the absence of any more condoms I think Pat would have tried for another cheeky one before he left, but I begged for mercy as I would be late and I needed a bath. With no real other option, we embraced and he trooped off home with a spring in his step like he'd just had an early night and ten hours' kip. Never had sex been so welcome for me, or so bloody great.

At this moment I am torn between being a bit loved up and a bit excited that there are so many others out there who could be as good, or perish the thought, even *better* at it than Pat.

That sounds greedy, doesn't it? Before I was with Blake, last night would not have been possible. I would have written myself off as a grade one slut for capitulating too easily and would have needed to hear he was in love with me soon after our first time, to justify it. Looking back, fuck that. What an idiot I was. An ocean of need. Now I'm well aware that Pat's an Irish dynamo, but he's going away and that's probably why I'm happy to have fun... and contemplate fun with others. Slut schmut.

I'm very thankful that the seat next to me is empty. I pull up the armrest to give myself more room and snuggle into my cushion. I begin to doze. As I fall into a deeper sleep, the steady roar of the aeroplane's engines and the air-con mingle and become the sound of the sea.

I open my eyes.

I'm in a verdant garden outside one of those villas with white walls and tropical flowers growing up a trellis that you see on holiday. Ahead, over a low stone wall, is a beach and the sea. Miles of it. It is just perfect. I'm sitting on a canvas chair by a metal and glass table. The sky is bluer than blue and I feel utterly peaceful. Suddenly I can hear music. Ridiculous music: 'Ernie (The Fastest Milkman in the West)' by Benny Hill. What the...? That's when I notice there's another canvas chair a few feet away and it's not empty.

Frank! Of course it's bloody Frank.

'Frank, what's with the soundtrack? Is this your theme tune?'

He's sniggering his head off. What a clown.

Frank always liked the sunshine; that's why I usually dream about him in the sun. His brown eyes with the green flecks are bright with mirth. His hair is sticking up all over the place as it always was. He's wearing cut-off jeans just above his tanned knees and a bright Hawaiian shirt that is only half buttoned up. He looks well. Unlike other times, I know this is a dream.

'How are you?'

'How are you, you mad cow?'

'Same as usual.'

He picks up his seat, brings it closer to mine. He takes my hand. 'I need to tell you something, witchy woman...'

I glory in the fact I can feel his warm hand in mine. I can really feel it.

'What's happening now, what you're doing with your life, it's the right thing.'

Did he just say something serious?

119

'What, talking to dead people or having sex with young men?'

He cracks up. 'BOTH! Look. You always had great instincts about other people, but you were always ridiculously shit when it came to yourself. I'm going to help you.'

'How?'

'None of your beeswax. All you need to know is, there are certain people that only a girl like you is qualified to help. I'll help you to help them! You're going to have a ball.'

I can feel myself getting tearful. I know it's a dream, but this meeting feels more 'real' than all of the others put together. And I feel I'm going to wake up soon. *Boo*. 'You've never told me... how you are... what it was like to die?'

He wrinkles his nose. 'I didn't die. It only looks like it from where you're standing. I'm good. I'm fine. I only ever feel sad when I see my mam or my mates upset.'

'We miss you. A bit.'

He laughs. 'Well stop it. I'm here. I'm always here. Just give me a shout.'

'That's easy for you to say.'

'I've been trying to get through to you, Tanz. I'm always talking to you. You just have to open your ears, the ones inside! Anyway, congratulations on your latest piece of high art. Dancing like a fool in front of a TV crew and a sex maniac.'

'A *what*?'

He sniggers again and puts his finger to his lips.

'Look, you can take the piss out of my rubbish acting

jobs all you like, but I'm going to need to make money somehow while I'm hobnobbing with your dead mates.'

'Still so touchy! I've been talking to you for ages, you know, you just didn't know it was me.'

I'm rather indignant at this. 'Was that you telling me to grab Pat?'

'What of it? Didn't it do you good?'

'That's not the point, you massive pervert.'

Right now I'm not in a dream with a dead bloke, I'm in a nice holiday garden with my mate Frank. Who's irritating me, like he always did. And before you know it, he hugs me. The first hug since he died. We hug like we used to and he smells the same. That's when I burst into tears.

'This crying for me has to stop, Tanz. I don't know what you're bleating for anyway, you were a total bitch to me when I was alive.'

I slap him and I sob and I hug.

'Listen, you've got some interesting days ahead, I'll be about, OK? Oh, and shag Pat again before he leaves, that lad has *stamina*.'

I wipe my snotty nose on my sleeve. *'You were watching?'*

His laughter is infectious. 'I have better things to do, thank you very much.'

I hug him again, just because I can.

Then a siren goes off. My head whips round to find where it's coming from and suddenly it's dark and I'm opening my eyes and I'm on an aeroplane with the seat-belt light flashing and an alarm telling me to buckle up.

For the first time in a long time I haven't woken up

crying from a Frank dream. I've woken up thinking of him just as my friend, not my dead friend. I feel stronger. But my arms feel empty.

APPARENTLY I NEED A BROOMSTICK

The hotel is lovely, not that I do much exploring. I have a costume fitting at four p.m., so I lie down on the big bed with the whiter than white sheets and catch another (dreamless) hour of sleep. As I drift I can hear people swimming in the outside pool, laughing and splashing and enjoying the heat. It's a night shoot so I get to stay until noon tomorrow. I will definitely have a swim and a little sunbathe if it's like this in the morning.

It feels like I've only blinked when the alarm goes off on my phone and I have to meet the driver downstairs. This is one of those modern hotels, all glass and chrome and marble, that let in a lot of light. Some people say they're impersonal, but I love the space and the cleanliness. Everything is just so, which is quite different to how I usually live. How can anyone not love another human being cleaning for them? Despite my own grungy flat, I do worship a spotless bathroom.

The driver is a very tanned older man with distinguished grey hair, white at the temples, who flashes

123

glistening Mr Ed teeth at me as he opens the back door of his air-conditioned, silver car. The air conditioning purrs as we drive and I marvel at how refreshed and calm I feel. Boy, I must have needed that nookie. Usually I need my sleep or I'm a monster. Not today – though, of course, my two super-naps and a hug from Frank must have helped. This place is stunning. I like its greenery; it's lush but exotic. There's a smell in the air; I wonder if it's some kind of herb that grows here? It smells like a sweet shop, as opposed to London, which often smells like a sweatshop.

Soon we pull in to a villa. This, my driver informs me, is where the first advert is already shooting. The ad is in two parts: the first in glorious holiday sunshine, the second in the night in the snow. That's because there are two new chocolate bars – Sun-bars and Snow-bars. Clever, eh? Both coconut based. I think the only difference between the two sweets is the sun one is covered in milk chocolate and has bits of candied fruit in the coconut, and the snow one has darker chocolate and is creamier and tastes of cinnamon or something more Christmassy. The creator's imaginative powers were obviously boundless.

Because they secured this place to shoot the sunshine scenes today, they decided, almost definitely on financial grounds, to hire next door's garden which doesn't have a pool, to fill with fake snow for the night shoot. This suits me down to the ground as I don't have to shiver my tits off in a dress and shoes in the Pyrenees, but I don't envy the prop department who have to deck the garden out and make it look like flamin' Lapland.

The living room is open-plan with Swedish furniture and a large, carved wooden statue of an Indian brave with full headdress in the corner. I like him very much. The costume lady is called Zannah, is about fifty and has dyed her curls an orangey red that I find very funky and tell her so. She's smiley, with a gap in her front teeth, and her English is perfect. She shows me the wraparound dress and the shoes I have to wear. So far so bland, as it always is with adverts. I try the dress in the bathroom and it fits. Thank God.

There's nothing more annoying to wardrobe mistresses than actresses who underestimate their dress size. It happens all the time, especially with women who aren't twenty any more and refuse to acknowledge their expanding waistline and widening hips. I found out myself the hard way; it's easier to stay skinny at twenty than at thirty and I can imagine it's even worse at forty.

As I'm chatting to Zannah about today's shoot and cheekily gleaning titbits of gossip about the gorgeous, but hopelessly hysterical, blonde actress playing one half of the sunshine couple, I spot someone approaching us in my peripheral vision. And out of nowhere I feel a stab of fear. I turn my head a little, while still chatting, to get a better idea of who it is. I can make out a mass of long, dark, bushy hair with grey streaks and loose black clothing, but not much else as the sun streaming through the window behind her is strong. As she reaches us, Zannah touches her arm and nods towards me.

'Tanz, this is Bayana. She's your make-up artist. She speaks very little English, but I can translate anything important that she has to say to you.'

Bayana has very prominent eyes with black irises. Her skin is dark and she has a large, well-formed mouth. She isn't slim, but she suits her size and she is staring at me. Really gazing intently. I think she was looking at me like this all the way across the room which is why she freaked me out. Never have I seen anyone who looks more like a witch. A real, in-your-face witch who knows what you're thinking. She doesn't look very friendly. I don't like it.

She reaches out her hand and I go to shake it with my right hand, but she shakes her head.

'Other one, please.'

Her voice is deep and heavily accented. I glance at Zannah, who smiles encouragingly, and I hold out my left hand. Bayana takes it and looks at my palm. When she smiles she looks like she might eat me. Or maybe I'm only thinking this because she scares me. She points at a line on the right-hand side of my palm, beneath the gap between my pinkie and my wedding (ha!) finger. It runs pretty much to my wrist. She says something to Zannah in Spanish, who gabbles something back. Damn, my French A-level is useless in this situation. I make a mental note to learn Spanish, pronto. Zannah raises an eyebrow.

'Bayana says you are Romany.'

'Sorry?'

'Your bloodline. Romany gypsy, that's where you get your gift from. You're a medium, no?'

Those hairs on the back of my neck are up again. Bayana speaks more, while Zannah listens and nods a lot. Bayana traces the line with her index finger, pointing out little crosses on the main track. I have never looked at my hand in this way before, never noticed these crosses, faint but not invisible.

'She says you are frightened of your gift and these crosses are the times you have avoided it and maybe will again. But eventually you will accept it and it will be a great time of learning for you. This is your medium line. Not everyone has one. She knew as soon as she saw you, you had it. She is also Romany.'

Bayana nods at me. She's not so much evil-looking as full-on. English people do not stare at strangers this intently. Her smile is seeming less sinister now. I look back at my hand, amazed.

'How does she know all of this?'

'You... are very good... you help people.'

Bayana speaks so falteringly in English compared with her machine gun Spanish. Her voice is rich, masculine. Again, she speaks to Zannah who translates.

'She says you have a teacher on earth, which is good, but you have even better teachers in spirit. You need to trust yourself. She says you have interesting times ahead. She also says you should get the cards you wanted to buy. Play with them. It will help you connect. You know what she means?'

I'm incredulous. The centre of my forehead has gone haywire. Bayana is the real deal. More than me, more than Sheila even. I bet she's never been scared of her gift. And if she's to be believed I am *Romany*. The joy!

I thank her. Zannah then tells me that Bayana will be giving me natural make-up and a little coral lippy to compliment the dress, which is navy.

Just then, a man walks in. He is good-looking in that plastic, actor-who-looks-after-himself way and he's about forty-five. He has sun-bleached red hair and a smattering of freckles. He's posh as hell and uses it to comedic effect.

'Hello, Tanz. I'm Rog. Flew in yesterday and paid for an extra night so I could get a bit of sun.'

He ignores my proffered hand and kisses me lavishly on both cheeks.

'Coco Chanel. Very nice.'

'Thank you. Are redheads supposed to sunbathe?'

'Oh, I'm not one of those blue-skinned gingers. I'm more of a bronze, really! I like your accent. Reminds me of college. The Geordie girls were always a lot of fun.'

I'll bet they were.

He looks around him towards the garden doors, through which stand the crew, about to go for another take. I can't see the actors, but I know they're out there. Something akin to fear crosses Rog's face. I wonder if he's nervous about shooting the ad later. He doesn't seem the nervous type.

Roger is an old-school womaniser; you can tell a mile off. I find this kind of man quite amusing. Mostly because they're as clear as tap water and they love hanging out with the ladies. The trick with the Rogers of this world is to have a laugh with them, but never, *ever* fall for their patter. They are incorrigible and shift their favours around like pieces on a chessboard. Their stories are great, but if you actually get in any way sucked in they will run like hares and leave you weeping into your brandy. So many of my friends have been fooled by this kind of man and I've had to delve deep to find any reserve of polite sympathy, because mostly I could see it coming from the

128

millisecond I was introduced to them.

When he stands next to Zannah and gives her a squeeze they look like a pair of Duracell batteries. Two copper tops. I've always fancied redheads, but this one I'll be giving a miss. Zannah smiles indulgently at him. Bayana looks him up and down once, then dismisses him and looks back at me. She leads me off towards her make-up table. When we're out of earshot she takes my hand again, but doesn't examine it. She frowns then smiles straight at me. Like the weather suddenly brightening after grey skies. She nods.

'Darkness come. Not worry. Protected.'

I seem to recall hearing this kind of thing before, in about two hundred horror films, just before something terrible happened. I feel a twinge of dread.

'You will have a lot of new experiences when you back in England! Romany witch. Very nice... Now, try this...'

And that's the last she speaks of it. She slaps a coat of lippy on me. It doesn't look terrible.

'Yes, good.'

I like her better now, apart from the 'darkness come' bit. And I'll have to do that protection thingy that Sheila taught me because I'm feeling a little light headed from the force of nature that is Bayana. I want to ask her more questions, but her English is pretty terrible. So instead I surreptitiously watch her out of the corner of my eye when she's not gawping at me. I wonder what she sees that makes her stare? I do hope it's not the evil eye floating above my head. Though, to be fair, she did say I was protected.

Soon I'm back in the purring silver car with Mr Suave, the driver, and Mr Flirt, the actor. Rog is determined that as we're not called until nine-thirty we should dine together. I would have liked to go for a little wander on my own, maybe pick up some grilled fish somewhere, but he wants us to go 'à deux' and that's that. And it's not like he's unpleasant; he's fine. It's just that I have things to think about, Spanish gypsy witches, ghost protectors and all-night sex with an Irish love god being but three.

Anyway, good as my word, I meet him in front of the hotel after a shower and a change of clothes. He's scrubbed and shiny in a black T-shirt and cargo pants. I get the feeling he's been craving company as he chatters away about the champagne in the hotel and the holiday he had last year where the pool was so big you could swim to a bar on an island in the middle. His stories seem to be peppered with bars. I'm pretty sure he's already partaken of at least one bar today. We walk along the street beside the beach and actually it is wonderful to breathe sweet air while the sea blithely swooshes beside us. It's been a crazy week. It's great to unwind.

Rog takes us to the place he went to the night before. Open-plan, open air (there's an indoor bit, but it seems a shame), good wine list and a waiter that looks like Ryan Gosling. Woof. What is it with me and sexy serving staff? Rog asks if I mind him ordering the wine. I do mind and order him to order Sauvignon Blanc. Because we're on the coast I indulge my fetish for seafood and get some whitebait, grilled octopus and salad. He goes for a large steak. Men always go for steak, it's something to do with their penis, I'm sure of it. The wine is too delicious. I ask

Ryan to get us some tap water to stop me getting squiffy. He smiles and I slip down the chair slightly. Rog is oblivious as he tells the twelfth story about his theatre exploits. Bless.

Surprisingly, Roger admits to having a wife. She is a renowned TV actress and a little younger than him. They have three young children.

'But Tanz, she goes to bed by nine o'clock most nights. We live in the bloody back of beyond. What am I supposed to do after nine? I tell you, I bloody miss Hampstead. She said to me this week, "Rog, why are you doing that stupid advert? We're not that skint!" and I said "Darling, a few grand never goes amiss". But the truth is, there is only so much fun to be had from mopping up milky vomit and goo goo gooing all day long.'

'So why the hell did you have three, then?'

'It was her. She had our first, Aimée, and it was quite good fun and it made her feel all womanly, so she got the bug. Then she went all mother-earth, making chocolate brownies and organic butternut-squash sandwiches and all that. But I can see she's getting bored now. I give her until our youngest, Harry, is two and she'll be "fuck all the voiceovers, I want to be Mrs Famous again". She's on that rowing machine two hours a day as it is, to keep her figure. It's only a matter of time before our nanny gets completely lumbered. But you can't stand in the way of a woman and her ticking womb!'

I can't work out why actors ever have kids. They're the most easily bored, fidgety-minded juveniles on the planet.

'Rog, you have to be supportive. You were evidently bored today, showing up on set early, so being away from home obviously isn't as enthralling as you thought it would be.'

'No, it was great. I could just float about being the man I was before, posho pain-in-the-arse on tour! It's not like I'm ever going to leave them for good, you know. I'm not a total bastard. I just like to remember what it was like years ago, when I was free. There's nothing wrong with that, is there? I didn't ask for three sprogs! I was happy with one.'

'*Roger*! You can't say that. Well, you can, but it's best not to.'

'I know, I know. I'm a shit. But a charming one, don't you think?'

'You're all right.'

'I'm starting to worry that you're impervious to my charms.'

'Worry no more, I absolutely am. Ohhhh, look at the time! I need to clean my teeth and make a phone call to check on my cat sitter.'

'Come on then, let's get the bill you Teflon-hearted Geordie wench.'

NIGHT GAMES

After a thank you to the director, Tom, the wiry chap from Walsall who has provided me with a night in Spain and enough money to settle my nerves for a few months, the actual shoot passes painlessly enough. Obviously I have to dance like a loon, with jazz hands and can-can legs, which tickles Rog and the crew no end, but instead of taking hours and hours like other ads I've shot, this takes a wondrously brief eighty-seven minutes. Rog's close-up takes an extra ten minutes and then we're done.

I'm cock-a-hoop. Last night's exploits are finally taking their toll. I look forward to a glass of wine on my balcony as a sleep-balm, then I shall collapse on my lily-white sheets and snooze to my heart's content. As we sweep into the bar, Rog asks if I'd like a night cap. I tell him I'm bushed and get a glass of vino to take to my room.

'Fair dos, my lady. Pleasant dreams.'

I wonder who he'll chat up in the bar tonight. Probably anyone and everyone until about six a.m. I'm so tired I take the lift. I put on my black lounging trousers and a little white vest and immediately feel comfy. I open my balcony door and sit down on a cosy seat overlooking the pool, which is lit from below and looks like the Blue Lagoon. I can hear crickets and soft chatter. To think last night I was in sex heaven. Well, tonight I am in peace heaven. With the worries I've had over the last year, I'm feeling terrifically grateful again. I offer up my usual little prayer of thanks as my head begins to nod.

I am just drifting off when I hear a tapping. I have no idea what it is. Dazedly, I wonder if someone is doing DIY in the hotel. 'Tap, tap, tap.' Is it coming from my room? 'Tap, tap, tap.' What the hell?

I get up and wander in. There is silence, then the tapping again… Someone is knocking at my door. I open it a crack. And there stands a half sheepish, half beseeching red-haired man brandishing a champagne bucket with a bottle of Perrier-Jouët in it and two crystal flutes.

'Rog?'

'I'm so sorry darling; I know you said you were tired, but you only have one night here and, well… downstairs is a bit of a no-no for me at the mo. Can I just join you on the balcony for a little glass of shampoo then I'll leave you be? Scout's honour.'

Oh God. I don't want company, but I actually feel sorry for him. He looks like a chastened schoolboy. I open the door.

'Oh. You're an angel!'

He heads for the balcony as I wrap an electric blue pashmina around my shoulders. I refuse to put on a bra when I feel so comfy, but I'm not really a show-off-my-nipples kind of gal either, so this will do the trick nicely.

Pashminas are a bit of a compulsion of mine. Apart from the ones I got in Bangkok, I also bought about six of them in different colours last time I went to Canal Street in New York. I couldn't believe how cheap they were. What can I say? I love a bargain.

Rog is already uncorking the champagne when I get out there. Luckily there are two balcony seats and he's making himself very comfy in the other one. He pours the champagne like an expert, remembering to tip the glass. Perrier-Jouët is not exactly the cheapest champagne and I dread to think how much it cost at the hotel bar, but judging by the number of telly programmes his wife has starred in over the years, I'm sure he can afford it. I wonder what she'd say if she could see him now?

The bubbles tickle the back of my throat as I receive the first sparkly hit. It immediately takes the edge off my sleepiness.

'Why was the bar downstairs a no-no?'

He fingers the stem of his champagne flute for a second or two.

'Erm... Do you promise you'll still love me if I tell you?'

He is *such* an actor. I sigh.

'Yes, Rog, I promise.'

'The actress, the one playing Mrs Sun-bar?'

'Yes, I met her briefly this afternoon. Gorgeous-looking blonde with tiny hips and sink-plunger lips.'

'Yes. Her.'

'Well?'

'She's staying at this hotel along with Mr Sun-bar. Who looks a nice-enough chap. Not long out of drama

135

school apparently, still has that sheen of hopeful enthusiasm that gets kicked off you and trodden on by the time you're thirty.'

'Right!'

This business is rife with bitterness. I wonder how Rog feels working in the theatre and doing bit parts in adverts while his wife garners TV fame and fabulous pay packets. I don't know many men who like to be 'kept' by a woman. Apart from my ex, of course, but I'm not going there right now. I'm far too happy today to hark back to that bullshit.

'Anyway, the actress, she's called Ruth. I worked with her on a thing at The Bush about a year back. It was one of those progressive little plays that look like they might be rather profound then turn out to be fucking awful. Our director seemed an able sort of chap until we started rehearsing and it became abundantly clear he didn't know what he was doing. The only upside was Ruth wandering around in the altogether for half of the show every night. I played her lover, she played a maniac. You know how it is, when things go a bit tits up at work... the Dunkirk spirit and all that... we got close.'

'You had an *affair*?'

'An affair? God, no. That's not what it was at all. Harry had just been born and my wife hated my guts. Partly because of the hormones and partly because I'd decided to do the play instead of staying at home. But I always feel so helpless in those first months, it's her and the baby and I'm the spare prick at a wedding. I mean, she's got a nanny to help her, what does she need me for?'

This is why actors shouldn't have kids. But the thing

is, in twenty years I'll bet he's the one who'll be proudly speaking of his brood like they're his own private talent-army. He'll embarrass them by showing up when they go clubbing and will probably attempt to steal his son's girlfriends.

'Your wife probably felt fat and vulnerable, Rog. She probably wanted you to want to be at home.'

'But she's not usually the clingy type, how was I supposed to know that?'

'You could have asked her?'

'I did. She told me not to do the play!'

He refills both of our glasses. Rog is a hilarious car-crash. I wonder if he's aware of it. I reckon he milks it. I think he loves his wife a lot, but wants to be the centre of attention like an adopted three-year-old.

'So what about big-lips Bertha, then? Why are you hiding on my balcony?'

'Oh God. Well... as I said, I played her lover and after she indicated she rather liked being naked in front of me, we took it somewhere a little more private in the last week of the show. Places like the theatre cleaning cupboard, the pub loos, the back of her Mini Cooper – that one was interesting – then finally against a wall down an alley by some rather potent West London bins.'

'All right! I don't need all the details!'

'Sorry, yes, sorry. You're quite prudish for a northerner, aren't you?' He guffaws. 'Anyway, when the show finished and I went back to domestic bliss, I found out that life had quite horrendously mirrored art. She was indeed a young maniac. Spoiled rotten, not used to anyone saying no to her, especially a forty-two-year-old ginger,

137

and totally incapable of taking a bloody hint. Even a hint involving a threatened police protective order.'

'Jesus Christ? You're joking?'

'No. In the fortnight after the show finished she texted me four hundred and twelve times. We were soul mates, we were going to love each other for ever, she was going to be with me whether I liked it or not. By the end of the second week she was going to tell the *Daily Mail* if I didn't come to her flat and "fuck her into next week". By that point I'd pretended to lose my phone and got a new number. I was shitting it and my wife was plunging into despair with post-natal thingummybob. If she'd found out it would have finished us.

'That's when I dropped my old phone in the local duck pond and called my agent. He took Ruth's number and said to leave it with him. Turns out he called her, made himself out to be more important than he was and told her if she breathed a word to anyone about me or my family she would never act in this country again. Her ambition won over her mental illness and I never heard hide nor hair of her until I walked into that villa today and saw her through the window being Mrs bloody Sunshine!'

'That must have been a great moment for you!'

'It was pant-fillingly scary.'

'Did she see you?'

'No, she had her back to me. I very quickly checked my costume then ran off to a little tapas place with my book and kept out of the way. I only wandered back when you were due in as I knew they'd be taking you to the hotel soon after and I wanted a lift. Thank God they were still in the thick of it out there.'

'I hope you've learned your lesson.'

'I don't know. It's all quite exciting, really.'

'Roger, if you really think that, you're an idiot.'

'I like your pashmina, by the way. Isn't it a little warm though, don't you think you should let the air get to your lovely arms?'

'Fuck off. Don't start with me. I told you, I'm impervious.'

'I can't help myself. I'm a sex maniac.'

He winks. Suddenly I remember my dream on the plane, Frank telling me I would spend my time with a sex maniac. I stare at Rog.

'Don't look like that darling, I said a sex maniac, not a bloody rapist.'

'Sorry, no, slipped off there for a minute. Anyway, I'd kung-fu kick you right off this balcony if you were a rapist.'

He guffaws again. I reach over and refill my glass. I think I deserve it after listening to his ridiculous, and let's not forget, self-inflicted miseries.

'Anyway, what happened in the bar, you Class-A fool?'

'Well, here's the thing, I'd just bought the champagne. I was going to call up to your room and try to force you to come back down again.'

'Presumptuous!'

'And that's when I turned and saw Little Miss Sunshine, sitting outside on the lap of Little Mr Sunshine, her pre-pubescent co-star. Looks like she fancied a bit of younger meat this time.'

This phrase tumbles me back onto the rug with Pat last

night. I blink hard to get rid of the pictures that flood my mind. Boy, was he vigorous.

'To avoid embarrassment I briskly made for the lift. I have no idea if she saw me, but I wasn't hanging around to find out.'

He laughs and as he does there is a furious hammering at my hotel room door. My back stiffens.

'Oh lawks! I think I've been hunted down!'

He makes to climb over the balcony. We are five floors up and he is pissed. I grab him and make him sit back down.

'STAY!'

The pounding continues relentlessly.

I stand, and like a condemned witch to the ducking stool, I trudge warily towards the rattling door.

THE PAIN OF BEING ALIVE

I glance back at Rog's owl eyes peeping fearfully over the back of his chair out on the balcony, before I steady myself and open the door. Ruth is in a sarong, tied halter style around her neck to make a slinky dress. (She's one of those girls that doesn't need a bra, the bitch.) It's silk, it's fuchsia and yellow and it shows off her bony shoulders and toned arms to perfection. Her golden hair is swept up and her tawny eyes would be enchanting, were it not for the crazed look and the flustered red nervous patches on both cheeks and her neck.

The moment the door is moving she is hopping around, trying to see past me into the room. She attempts to barge past and, in a move that is entirely out of character for me, I grab her arm and push her. She almost falls backwards and grabs the door frame to steady herself.

'Excuse me, what the fuck do you think you're doing?'

I always lay on my accent thicker when I am angry and/or trying to sound hard. Her mouth opens and closes like a guppy. Then she lets out a cry.

'ROG! ROGER I KNOW YOU'RE IN THERE, YOU BASTARD.'

She has a soft Yorkshire burr. She is radiating energy; it's coming off her like heat. She glares at me, bile and spittle flying. 'Just you wait, you stupid old cow. You think you're special because he came to you? Well, it won't last. He'll dump you and make you feel like shit. Anyway, what kind of slut bangs someone they just met on a job?'

This girl is priceless. Plus, she pouts even when she's apoplectic. I can't help it; I begin to laugh at the absolute cheek of it.

'What are you laughing at? Are you laughing at me?'

She lifts her hand as if to hit me. Suddenly Roger is sweeping up from behind, just as I land a good kick to her left ankle. I am not a violent person and I'm only wearing flip flops, but she *really* shouldn't make assumptions.

'Woah! Woah there.'

Roger grabs her arm as she dramatically falls sideways, after hopping about in agony. What a total cry-baby. I can hear approaching voices. I don't want the management – or indeed anyone – being party to this fiasco so I drag them both inside and close the door. She slumps on the bed, cradling her ankle. I look at my foot – I've split my big toenail. Damn.

Rog stands a little away, afraid she might attack I think. Her eyes dart viper-venom.

'You prick.'

'Now come on.'

'You complete shit. We had something so amazing and you just dumped me out of nowhere. Wouldn't answer my texts, wouldn't speak to me.'

'I'm married, Ruth. I have three kids.'

'You weren't thinking about them much in the back of my car, were you? And it doesn't look like you've been thinking much about them tonight!'

She glances towards the balcony and spies the empty champagne bottle.

'Oh, lovely, a little romantic drinkie before the big deed, is it?' She turns on me, her lip curling. 'Well, just so you know, he's not exactly as big in the pants department as he is in the *mouth* department.'

'Oh, you know what? Can I just fucking clarify? Rog was in here hiding from a mentalist and wasn't on a romantic mission. You might think he's God's gift, but some of us don't get our rocks off shagging married men!'

Her face contorts.

'A *mentalist*?'

'So you don't think it's a teensy bit mental that you just pounded on the door of a stranger and tried to push your way in, screaming and shouting at a man who may or may not be there and that you haven't seen in a year?'

Her anger now seems to be melting into self-pity.

'You told her? About us?'

Rog rolls his eyes. 'There was no "us". We had a few jolly little bunk-ups at the end of a job. Why is that an "us"?'

Well, I have to hand it to him, Rog has a way with words. He may as well have punched her. She begins to sob.

'I'm not a... I'm not a bunk up... Men love me, they fall at my feet. Why? Why wouldn't you answer me?'

143

'I did bloody answer you. I told you it couldn't happen. There was nothing else to say.'

'And then you got that gangster agent to call me. You tried to destroy my career.'

I am horribly tempted to point out that a fringe show and the odd advert is hardly a 'career' to break, but that would just be cruel. Roger is moving from one foot to the other. Obviously Ruth's emotions are freaking him out. I am feeling more respect for his wife by the minute. She must really have to handle him like a big baby. I wonder if I should boot them both out of my room and let them fight it out in the corridor.

'Help her, Tanz.'

A bloody voice in my head.

Why should I help her? She's been curling her lip at me since she came to the door. She called me an old cow. Fuck her.

'Speak to her. She needs you. We'll help.'

I don't know who 'we' would be, but I can't say no. It makes me feel very harumphy, though. I heave a tiny sigh then turn to Rog.

'Can you do me a favour? I'd like a word with, erm, Ruth, on my own, please. Stay by the bar downstairs. I'll call down if we need you for anything, OK?'

I don't take his mobile number as it might make things even stickier with Ruth. The relief on his face is farcical. I just hope he doesn't kiss me – that will not help matters in the slightest. Ruth is confused and reluctant.

'But Rog, I want to talk to yoooooouuu!'

She is still snuffling and her beseeching tone is wrenchingly pathetic. Sometimes I truly wonder what made me want to be an actress. Am I as messed up as these people? Crikey, I hope not.

Rog can't get out of the room quickly enough. His wink is inappropriate, but that's him all over. Ruth sits on the bed, cradling her ankle. I try to sneak a peek at it and through her fingers I spy blood. Ooops. I must have cracked her right on the bone. That'll be how I ripped my nail, then. I go to my suitcase and produce the Zubrowka vodka I purchased from the duty-free on the way here. I then go to the mini bar and fish out my stash of apple juice. In the ice bucket I find a few solitary blocks floating in mostly melt-water. I put them in the flutes, pour generous measures of the vod and top them up with apple juice. I hand one to Ruth and she takes it. I hold mine aloft.

'Here's to your ankle.'

'You kicked me.'

'To be fair you were about to hit me and I hadn't done anything.'

She takes a tentative sip, then a swig. 'What on earth is this?'

'Bison Grass vodka with apple. It's total heaven.'

'It is, actually.' Her amber peepers regard me over her considerably less full glass. 'Were you really just sheltering him from me?'

''Fraid so. He's not the bravest of blokes and I think you scare the shit out of him. I don't know him from Adam.'

'I loved him.'

I remember falling helplessly in love with people I worked with when I first became an actress. I soon learned. She is downing her drink like it's water. She seems to be fighting back tears. I grab her glass and top it up, then sit next to her.

'Can you really love someone you shagged for a week?'

'Yes. I can.'

Peace and stillness. I feel it descending. I put down my drink and look at her. Suddenly I don't see a pouty, slim, spoiled bitch with all the advantages I didn't have. I 'feel' something else coming out of her and I see a person who is struggling.

'There's something wrong with your neck, isn't there?'

'Sorry?'

I steady myself and let the words come. 'Two years ago, maybe a little more, something... something happened to your neck and shoulder and your confidence was shot to pieces. Did you have a crash? You crashed the car. Your boyfriend was with you. You split up not long after.'

She is gaping. I feel bad for her. I feel warmth towards her.

'Then you got the job. A long time later. It was your first proper gig since... your neck... Roger put a smile back on your face, didn't he? And then he ran off. I'm so sorry. You wanted to die, didn't you? Oh, you're too young and beautiful to die. Please tell me you'd never do that now.'

I sense her sadness acutely. My eyes are always welling up, but in this case I think it's justified. She grabs my hand – in shock, I think.

'I did have a car crash. I did. I was with my ex and he

was being horrible to me and I lost concentration and crashed into a lamppost. He was OK, but I got whiplash and I hurt my shoulder. I couldn't move properly for ages and I didn't know if I would act again. When I got that shitty play I was over the moon. Then I met Roger and he was sooo funny. And... I know it's horrible but, because he was older, I thought he'd adore me. I thought he'd help me stop feeling so sad. We were so connected when we... you know. I thought we had a future. I know he's got a wife, but when he spoke to me it was as though I was the only person in the world. I could only assume he wasn't happy in his marriage. Why else would he behave like he was single?'

She stops to draw breath and glugs down another third of a flute of rocket fuel. She is a bit googly-eyed now.

'How did you know about me? Are you... like, a witch?'

'Nah. I can just feel when someone's in pain.' I push a straggly strand of hair behind her ear.

'Can I tell you something, Ruth...?'

'Yes. Of course.'

'What happened with Roger, it was horrible for you. It's understandable you were upset. But I promise you, if you hadn't been in such a vulnerable place you wouldn't have lost it so badly over him.'

'Wouldn't I?'

'He's a handsome, funny bloke, Ruth. But lots of creative blokes are attractive and charismatic. They play with it, like a cat plays with a mouse. It wouldn't matter how gorgeous you were, how sexy, how great the shags were. He wasn't looking for a relationship. He has one of

147

those. He was having an adventure and he wanted to feel good about himself. He picked you because you were the best-looking girl there. If you really want a shot at happiness you have to resist these fellas who offer you the moon and hand you a pebble. When you get older you'll recognise them a mile off.'

'You're so clever.'

She's ever so slightly slurring now.

'Bitter experience, that's all. Rog is not going to leave his wife, and if he did he would expect you to wash his underpants, be a step-mother to his kids and turn a blind eye to his cheating. You are worth a *lot* more than that. And you're too young. Do you understand?'

'Funny. I was just thinking tonight when I saw him, how much more knackered he looks than I remember.'

I grin at her. 'Believe me, that will only get worse. Roger will be selfish for the whole of his life and he will only get more knackered-looking.'

She smiles, can't help herself. I top her up again, much more apple juice than vodka this time. 'I shouldn't have called you an old cow. I'm sorry about that. You're actually quite pretty, I just wanted to make you feel shit. That's horrible, isn't it?'

'Oh, don't give yourself a hard time, I hated you on sight.'

She really giggles now.

'What happened to your co-star? The lovely boy with the quiff?'

The giggling stops abruptly, as she remembers. 'Oh God, poor Freddie. We were getting on so well then I spotted Rog and I just flipped.'

148

'Right. Just a minute.'

I pick up my room phone and call the bar. Within seconds I have Roger on the line. He sounds more pissed than before. He is horribly grateful. I ask if Freddie is with him. He says not. I bid him good night and tell him he is now free to wander off.

Ruth is in the loo so misses the last exchange, which can only be good.

'He must be in his room, Ruth. Do you know the number?'

'612.'

The phone hardly gets the chance to ring before he picks it up.

'Hello Freddie, my name is Tanz and I'm in room 514. Could you possibly come and pick up Ruth? She would like to see you and thinks she might have upset you? She needed to speak to me urgently, but it's all ironed out now and she'd like some company.'

I'm surprised he doesn't knock at the door the minute I put the phone down, he sounds so breathlessly eager. Already enraptured, obviously.

When Ruth returns I give her some water from my bottle and tidy up her mascara.

'Have some fun, Ruth. You don't need to settle down. Shag everyone or shag no one, just don't upset yourself. If it makes you feel better, I know two things. You have a *big* job coming in the next six months and you won't look back.'

She gasps. 'Really?'

'Yes. Absolutely. And the other thing. Your mum. She's sorry. OK? She's sorry. You're all she cares about.'

When the knock comes, I let Freddie in and offer him a Zubrowka and apple. He accepts it, his noble brow creasing at the sight of his lady-love, face like a collapsing balloon, as she sobs again.

Luckily, this time Ruth's tears are not crazy tears. And she's wiping furiously at her eyes.

'I'm so sorry, Freddie, I shouldn't have run off. Don't look at me, I'm like a swollen lizard.'

Freddie wipes her eyes. 'You're beautiful, Ruth, laughing or crying. Like an angel.'

A bit frilly for me, but she's pleased enough. Soon they leave, arm in arm and clutching the rest of my vodka. Hey-ho, it went to a good cause. Before she goes, Ruth writes my phone number on her arm. I don't refuse her, as actually she's quite sweet when she's not trying to smash down my door.

As she hugs me tight, I whisper in her ear. 'Call me when you're in London. We can talk about your mum.'

She hugs me even harder, then they leave.

I jump on my bed like a starfish and lie face down on the cool sheets. Thank CHRIST for that. I can now go to sleep. My phone is in my bag just beside my head. I check it to make sure it's not running out of juice. I've hardly used it so it's fine. There's a text.

You have destroyed me. I am a shell of a man... Same time next week? Pat.

I fall asleep within two seconds.

And once more I dream of bluebells, this time growing on a grave. The gravestone is blank where the name should be. It makes me sad, but it's not scary.

What is *with* these weird dreams?

THE HUMAN WEASEL

I have to work at the shop three days running to make up for my day off. Today Martin is the reader. Martin is basically a small field animal or, actually, a weasel – he has a feral look in his eye and I think he might be holding down a maelstrom of evil resentments within his meek, veiny exterior. The people who trickle in for readings from him seem to be the most odd and damaged of our customers.

I don't really know what I think of Martin. I have many gay friends; they usually love me. Milo says it's because I'm more than a little tragic, the cheeky so and so. But Martin is so weird. I think he dislikes being gay. That must be awful, but how can you possibly be understanding towards the people you're reading for if you hate yourself and everything you stand for? He doesn't wear aftershave or scented deodorant, either. I've been close to him a couple of times and he smells a bit musty. What kind of self-respecting gay man doesn't smell fabulous?

On the subject of smelling nice, yesterday when I got back from the airport Inka had left me a lovely gift on the bed. When I go away for more than a day, Steve, my neighbour and the only ninety-year-old man I have ever met who introduces himself as 'Steve', keeps an eye out for Inka and lets her come into his house if she's lonely. I don't go away that much these days and, when I do, Inka has the cat flap and the cat feeder with three days' worth of food. Steve provides extras. He used to be a chef in the army. He has a massive old tabby called Compo that Inka tolerates and they hang out in Steve's yard while he potters with his begonias. Despite this, Inka has seen the need to lodge a complaint that I went away. Cat shit on my white duvet cover. *Perfect*. She's such an emotional bitch.

When Martin rolls in he's an hour late and he eyeballs me suspiciously from a chair near the door as he consumes a limp-looking corned-beef sandwich and a packet of plain crisps. He's drinking supermarket brand, full fat cola. No wonder he's so sallow. He notices I have a sealed pack of tarot cards in front of me. This morning I took the plunge and bought the Medieval Scapinis, just as my terrifying, Spanish gypsy make-up artist instructed me to. I'm excited. The first sale of the day was mine, on my poor, overloaded credit card. Luckily I know wages are coming, so I'm allowed to treat myself.

'What are you doing with those?'

He's very softly spoken. He told me a couple of weeks ago that he was born in Luton, though he doesn't have much of an accent. I ask you, who would want to be born in Luton? His mam wants to be ashamed.

'Oh. I just thought I'd get myself a deck, check them out. They're such beautiful cards.'

'It's a lot of money to pay just because you like the

look of them. You're not a reader, are you?'

He smiles. So far, so passive aggressive. Does he think I'm after his job?

'Well, no but, well, actually my great-nanna was a well-known medium back in Gateshead in the old days. She sometimes used the cards and I decided to get a deck for myself, have a little go. Just to see...'

'Well, people presume that anyone can read the cards, you know, and they can't. It takes time and natural ability. But then, with you being an actress you might just be able to blag it, eh?'

Ooooh, get her! Well, that's just made my mind up; after wavering on the subject, it is now certain. Martin is a prick. When I talk to him, I don't get the middle of the head feeling as strongly as when I'm with Sheila. What I do get is slight dizziness and a touch of nausea. Is this how he feels all of the time? Churned up and threatened? Ooof. Well, I wouldn't want to live in his head. And I certainly wouldn't want a reading from him, injecting his horrid energy into my already vulnerable noggin.

I am saved from any more of his snipes by a female dormouse in an anorak and specs, who comes in for Martin's first (and, so far, only) reading of the day. He wipes his margarine hands on his dark navy cable-knit cardigan and leads her through, having not lit any candles or put a cloth on the table. Horses for courses, I suppose.

When the door is safely shut I strip off the cellophane and take out the deck. The cards run smoothly through my hands. They are so beautiful. There are many tarot decks and each reader has a different preference, but every time I've looked through the catalogue this one has jumped out at me. I also adore the Russian St Petersburg deck to look at, but it's very black and stylised, so even though it's pretty I'm fairly sure I wouldn't be able to read with it. I'd just want to stare at it, like I would a book of ornate fairy tales in Urdu. Sheila told me I'd be attracted to the right deck for me and looking at these gold embossed beauties I feel a stirring in the pit of my stomach. I want to give them a go.

I call Sheila. She's in her house smoking a fag, I can hear her dragging on it. I'm not sure smoking should be a hobby.

'I'm glad you bought them, love. I think it's always good to explore the different avenues.'

'As soon as I felt them in my hands I got all excited. The book felt so technical, but...'

'Oh, throw that bloody book away, Tanz. You don't need it. You're very intuitive, obviously, so studying the book will hinder you. There's nothing wrong with knowing the traditional meanings of the cards, but it's not the first thing you should do. You feel excited because you're exercising a new muscle. Every time there's a new chance to "play" your subconscious is going to jump up and celebrate. You should get every customer who comes in the shop to draw a card. Tell them it's a little freebie. Get them to turn it, and say the first thing that you "see". I don't mean look at a card with a king on it and say, "you're going to be King of bloody England", but say what you feel. You'll be surprised, darlin'. You know you're ready, so just enjoy yourself.'

Actually, if it's for free I think I am ready. It's not like they'll be losing anything by taking a card from me.

'But Martin's here, he might get all arsey.'

'Oh, him. Has he got no readings again?'

'He's got one. She's in there now. Really small woman with massive jam-jar glasses and a crew cut.'

'I know the one. Nice enough, shy, looks like a miniature Rose West?'

I can't help a little snigger. Being a serial killer buff I always appreciate a murderer gag. 'She does, actually. But without the excessive pie eating. Anyway, he seemed to be hinting I was after his job before. If I start pulling cards out left, right and centre he's going to have a cow.'

'If he doesn't pull his socks up he won't have a job there anyway. Maggie's furious with him. He's supposed to show up at ten in case people drop in for readings. He usually casually wanders in at noon, gets bored and disappears at three. He did that the other day and missed out on two late readings. She doesn't actually make that much from the shop and she doesn't take a huge amount from our fee either, but she likes things just so, does Maggie, and he is going to blow it big time if he doesn't buck his ideas up. He's lucky to be there at all.'

'Do you think he hates women?'

'I think he hates everybody, bless him. He just needs a boyfriend and a personality transplant.'

She's so right.

'Look, he'll be finished in a minute so I'd better go. Thanks, Sheils. I'll give it a bash. I'll call you tonight.'

'OK darlin'... Oh, wait, just before you go... I think we've got another bust if you fancy it? Sounds like a lively one. Angry ghost throwing things about.'

'Holy moly, you're kidding me? Throwing things?

How exciting. Ring you later.'

Two or three minutes pass as I leaf through the cards, marvelling at the detail. Suddenly I hear the squeak of the door and look up to see Martin's head poking out.

'We'll be in here another thirty minutes; she's decided she wants the full hour, OK?'

He's less unfriendly when he's pleased.

'Brilliant. OK, Martin.'

When he's gone, the front door pings and a girl walks in. I say girl, she's around twenty-eight. Is that a girl or a lady? Anyway, she's younger than me with striking caramel skin and eyes like a saucy panther. She heads straight over to the counter to look at the gemstone jewellery that Maggie stocks behind glass. A lot of it is that generic 'magic crystal hanging from black leather thong' kind of stuff, but certain people seem to love it. There are also leather bracelets with runes on them in a basket next to me. She starts to look through them. I nod.

'Would you like to pick a card? Just to see what today's got in store for you?'

She eyeballs me, looking for the hard sell.

'Don't worry, there's no charge, I'm just practising.'

'OK then.'

She reaches for a card and hands it to me. I turn it over. The Queen of Swords. A clever woman who looks very lonely to me. Private.

'You've got to stop waiting for this David bloke. He's hurt you one too many times. You're hanging on to your pain so that you don't have to let anyone else in.'

Blimey. Where did that come from? The girl blinks. I blink. I hope to God there is a David or I'm going to look such an idiot.

'How did you do that?'

I shrug; I'm as confused as she is. There's a seat by the till and she sits on it, staring at me like I'm an alien. People do tend to stare at me much more since I started doing this. It's disconcerting.

'I just felt it.'

Tears spring to the corners of her eyes, but she quickly quells them. 'You're right. He's been a nightmare. It's taken me ages to believe he's wrong for me, but he is. He rang this morning, being nice, to confuse me again. I almost fell for it. I almost invited him over. Instead I came out of the house for a walk to clear my head. I've never been in this shop in my life. How did you know his name?'

She's very well spoken. A nice, sensible young woman.

'I have no idea how I knew. I think you'd have thought I was just reaching, otherwise, so I was given his name. You don't usually believe in this stuff, I reckon. Oh, and another thing... the man from abroad... the one who bought you flowers. You don't fancy him so don't encourage it. There's someone else on the horizon, just be patient.'

She honks a laugh. 'Oh my days! How do you *do* that? You're right, I don't fancy him, but he's so persistent I was thinking of having a date with him just to be nice.'

'I think he may be a bit needy. Be polite, tell him you're not ready. Let him fade out. If you kiss him or give him any other green light you will never get rid of him.'

She touches my arm. 'That's amazing. He has been

157

very over-keen.'

'If you have to, tell him you and this David got back together. But, of course, don't actually do it. You already know what David's about, you've just been scared of having no one. Well that won't happen. Go on holiday or something, have a rest and come back ready to conquer the world! Right, reading over.'

She shakes her head. She has short afro hair and now that she's relaxed, a ready smile. 'I never heard of a fortune teller knowing *names*.'

'Oh, I'm not a fortune teller. I'm a Romany gypsy.' I can't help saying it: it makes me so proud. 'I couldn't tell you your fortune if you offered me a million quid.'

'Well, you are amazing. Thank you so much. I feel like I should give you something.'

'Don't be daft, I was just practising.'

She stands up, takes a card from the counter with the shop number on it. 'Who do I ask for if I want a reading?'

'I'm Tanz, but I'm not a reader here. I just work on the till.'

'Well, that's just ridiculous. I'm Juliette, by the way.'

'Lovely to meet you, Juliette. Now go forth and book a holiday.'

'You know what, I might just do that. I've wanted a weekend spa break for ever! I'll be seeing you again. Thank you so much.'

'No bother.'

As soon as she's gone I send a text. *Milo. I have become a friggin' JEDI. Call you later x*

I'm in shock. It's getting easier. I don't know how, but I just open my gob and this information pours through.

There's a pressure in my chest and I have to let it spill out as it arrives. It's actually a great, if dizzying, feeling. Only thing is, I didn't read from the card, I just looked at it and said the first thing that came into my head. Oh well, it worked out OK, didn't it?

As I'm musing, out jumps teeny Rose West followed by Martin. She seems fairly alarmed, but she pays and thanks Martin in her dormouse voice, before beating a retreat. He's looking very pleased with himself.

'I'm off for a coffee, do you want anything?'

I go into my purse and hand him a few coins.

'Yes please, I want a bottle of water and a banana.'

He heads off and I sit down. Like Sheila taught me, I do a closing off exercise, just so I can 'come down'. I'm hoping the banana and water will help. What I really want is cake, but I always want cake. I made some wheat-free damp gingerbread this week and already had a big chunk with a coffee for breakfast. My hips can't afford any more cushioning, so a banana it must be. I'd like to call Sheila and tell her what happened, but then the door opens again. I jump a bit when I look up. It's Pat.

He's wearing a slim-fitting grey sweater with a pale blue shirt underneath. He looks stunning. He is with a woman. She is thirty-two or so and looks just like him so I'm assuming it's his sister, unless he's one of those freaks who fancies people who look exactly like him. He raises an eyebrow at me and mouths 'sorry' as she approaches. Her smile is as big as a cheese. She dresses conservatively, but is wearing a magic crystal thong necklace. A rose quartz, it looks like. I really hope she hasn't come here for some amazing psychic experience because I'm not a performing monkey and I don't do well under pressure. Well I don't think I do, this has only been happening for about five minutes. I'm not even a novice. I'm a pre-novice.

I smile back because it's only polite. She actually looks crackers.

'Hello, Tanz. I'm Pat's sister, Caitlin. Nice to meet you.'

I put out my hand to shake hers. It's damp. She's nervous. Oh God, she is expecting something. Just then Martin returns and passes me the water and banana. He goes through the back to the loo. I am trapped like a whale on a beach. I have no idea what she knows about me and Pat. The sex. *Fuck*.

'Hey Caitlin, how are you? Hey, Pat.'

'Hello, Tanz. My insane sister decided she wanted to come and disturb you so I thought I'd come along with her. As a buffer of some sort.'

'Pat!' Her voice and accent are sharper than his. 'I just wanted to thank you for what you did for Pat. It's really made a difference for him, hasn't it?'

I'm ready to hysterically shout out, 'What, my best blow job?', but am completely sure it won't be as funny if I say it out loud. Pat has composed a face of pure innocence so is probably on the same filthy track as me.

'Yes, you cheered me up no end.'

I bite my bottom lip. 'Thank you, but really it was nothing to do with me, I just said it! Bless your dad, he's the one to thank.'

Caitlin looks extremely vulnerable as soon as I mention her dad. I feel so bad that I can't tune in to people

160

as and when. I'm sure if she had just walked in this shop as a stranger it might have been different, but now I'm nervous.

'He was a great man, our dad, wasn't he, Pat?'

'He had his moments.' He puts a protective arm around her.

'Anyway, Tanz, I was hoping... well, wondering, if you do readings or meetings... you know, for that kind of stuff? I would love to get some kind of idea of... how he is...?'

Oh Christ.

'Errm. Well, the thing is, it seems to come to me quite randomly. I'm new to this so I'm not sure how much I can force it.'

Martin is now hovering near the kitchen door, bobbing his head around. Is he expecting me to recommend him? What a knob he is. I point down at the deck in front of me.

'See these? I just bought them today and I'm getting people to pull a card out from the deck so I can give them a mini overview. Would you like to choose a card anyway? Just to see how your day is going to go? Then another time, in private, we can have a glass of vino and see what happens?'

You don't have to be psychic to see how much this girl is grieving for her dad. God help me the day I lose a parent. I sincerely hope if I get her alone I'll be able to tune in. Pat steps back and inspects some amethyst 'caves' just to give us a bit of space. He's such a canny lad. Martin gives me the evils for not mentioning him. I ignore him.

'That would be wonderful. Thank you. I didn't really

think you'd be able to do it now while you're working.'

She sounds disappointed; she thought exactly that.

'Here, I'll shuffle these, then you can just pull one out and turn it over for me.'

She does and it's the Eight of Cups. I lean forward so this information is between me and her. It isn't about her dad, but I say it anyway.

'This is about your relationships.'

Her face falls.

'You've always, I feel, handed out too much. Always given too much love with not enough return. Now that's changing. The change has gone on these past six months and there's someone who wants to be by your side all of the time. But you've not been sure...'

She nods uncertainly. Looks at the counter in front of me.

'There is someone. I've not been in the best shape. He says he wants us to move in together, but I don't know. Sometimes he's too nice.'

'It feels like a good move, Caitlin. If you're ready, of course. He's being nice because he understands. Madly enough, I can hear a song playing in my head as I think about him. Is he a funny bloke?'

'He is quite funny! What's the song?'

I giggle because it's so daft. I hardly want to say it. 'Erm. I don't know if you know it. It's by a guy called Joe Dolce and called "Shaddap You Face". I can hear it playing in my head... La la la la laaa, HEY, la la la la la... The whole chorus, actually...'

I know I'm not the best singer on the planet, but I'm not prepared for Caitlin's reaction at all. Or Pat's. She bursts into tears and he starts to laugh hysterically. She then starts to laugh as she's crying. Martin looks at us all like we're dangerous lunatics.

'What? What?'

She wipes her nose on some raggy tissue. 'It's just… that's… that was…'

Pat comes back to her and wraps his arm around her. 'My dad used to sing that to her every time she got moody. It was a running gag in the house. Eventually we all sang it. She found it really annoying, didn't you, Sis?'

She still can't get words out, she's a mess. I speak up once more.

'Did he have a laugh like a fog horn?'

Pat laughs again. 'Jeez, he certainly did.'

'Well, I can hear it.' And I can. How amazing.

Pat shakes his head at me, winks and looks down at his sister who is attempting to rally.

'He does – did. Laugh like a klaxon going off! When Pat told me what you'd said to him, about Dad, I was so, so happy for him. But… God forgive me… I was also jealous. I wanted to know he was watching over me too… I've felt so lost.'

I lay my hand over hers; I can't help it. 'Of course he's watching over you. He's still laughing incidentally. He finds himself hilarious. He approves of this bloke, Caitlin, that's all I can tell you. He wants you to be happy… He's sorry you're sad.'

'Is he? Oh God. I'll try. It's so hard when I miss him so much.'

'He's around all of you. You can do that, it seems, be in lots of places at once when you… pass over. You want to talk to him, just talk. He'll always hear.'

She really is a wreck about this. She needs to go home. I'm not sure how good it'll be for business if people come in and find a sobbing woman by the till. Pat squeezes her.

'You see! Now come on, let's go home and have a nice whiskey.'

'I can't, I promised to go into work.'

'Sis, you look like you just got pounded by a runaway tractor. Phone in, take some time off. They take the piss anyway.'

As he's speaking the door opens and in marches Juliette, my other card-turner. She's brandishing a huge bunch of flowers.

'If you won't let me pay you then I shall give you a gift!'

'Oh my gosh, these are gorgeous. You didn't have to do this!'

'I most certainly did.'

Just then she catches sight of the tear-stained, blotchy face of Caitlin. 'You too?' She shakes her head at me, mock annoyed. 'Do you make everyone cry who comes in here?'

She turns back to Caitlin. 'Are you OK? She's great, isn't she?'

Caitlin nods, clutching her tissue. Pat answers for her. 'She certainly is!'

Juliette looks at him for precisely three seconds longer than necessary then gathers herself.

'Anyway, this is not the last you've heard of me. You made my day. I've booked a spa. I'm running back to get a bag together. Fuck men!'

I snort. 'Thank you, Juliette.'

She's already gone. I beam. Never a dull moment.

Pat takes his sister's arm. 'Right, this one needs to go home.'

'I'm not a child.'

But she's weeping again. She'll need to cry this one out for the rest of the day, probably. I am so relieved I had something to tell her.

'Thank you so much, Tanz. I didn't even know how much I needed to hear that.'

'You're so welcome, Cait. I'm sure I'll bump into you on the High Street now that I know who you are.'

Pat crosses to my side of the counter and kisses my cheek. I react immediately to the smell of him. He whispers, 'Call you later, after my shift.'

Then he's off with his sister, who leans into him like the walking wounded. I sit back down on my seat and open my water. I am now knackered, but also buzzing. I take a swig and peel back my banana. I am so hungry. A voice shocks me.

'Well. *Somebody's* popular.'

I'd forgotten about Martin. He is sitting in the reading room with the door open so he can spy on me. He is a glaring, malevolent weasel-man.

ANGRY SPOOKS R US

After a swiftly bolted plate of salad and steamed cod at home, I have a quick conversation with Milo, who is climbing the walls with anxiety because he has a script-writing deadline, one that will prove he can write for a TV show he detests, God bless him.

'My head's exploding, Tanz. I hate every single character in the show and the producer is a massive knobhead.'

'You're not a knobhead, though, Milo. You are a total genius. You can do it. Think of the money, think of the fact that once you get that job you can finance your own projects!'

'I know you're right, but I'm eating my own feet here.'

'Have a glass of wine, clear your head of everything else, then write the first thing you think of. That's what you said works best.'

'I know, I know. I'm just panicking.'

'I have every faith in you.'

'Stop it, you'll have me sobbing here.'

Twenty minutes later and I've surrendered into the arms of Purple Haze and a raspberry mint martini with

Sheila.

Tonight she has outdone herself, wearing a multi-coloured shirt, black dress pants, a long gothic cardigan and rings on most of her fingers. The scent of Samsara greets me before she does. Sheila always looks fantastic. I can only hope I look equally cool when I'm older. She opts for an espresso martini. I love them too, but the caffeine sends me doolally at night. We sit at a high table with bar stools and I'm amused to see tricorn man is there in a different frock coat, once more beavering away at his laptop. He gives me the tiniest of nods as I look his way. I nod back.

I fill Sheila in on the day's adventures.

'Bloody hell, if you didn't believe you were made for this before then you must do now, love.'

'I'm not a natural reader, though. I turn over a card and then I just say stuff.'

'That is a natural reader! The cards basically facilitate your connection. Cards and their placing on the table can be consulted if someone is shut off or blocking you. Then you can take clues from the spread itself. The cards are a conduit, it's you tuning in that really does the trick. And you did brilliantly today. You couldn't have asked spirit for more.'

It's funny; Sheila says 'spirit', but I don't define it in my head like that. I think of it just as people I'm chatting to. If I go all airy fairy about it, I don't believe it myself. I don't know what else to call it, though. Spirit, angel, guide…? I usually go for silly terms like 'spooks' instead. I wonder if that's just me making the whole situation manageable by taking the piss? Whichever way I look at it, something *very* weird happened again today. Whatever it is I'm doing, I'm getting quite good at it. Sheila sips her martini and gets a Baileys cream moustache.

'You know Tanz, you could try other stuff, see what you're most comfortable with. I like the cards, I'm at home with them. But if they don't rock your boat…'

'It's not that they don't rock my boat, they're beautiful. It's just I seem to get the information in my head anyway, and if I then look at the card, it's a little bit distracting. I start looking at the pictures for extra stuff. It sort of makes it less pure.'

'Then try psychometry.'

'Huh?'

'Holding an object in your hand, something belonging to the subject, like a ring or a watch. It helps you tune into them better, but you're not reading the object, just using it to get closer to the subject because it's filled with their energy.'

This seems rather exciting.

'It sounds as if the cards worked fine for you today, but if they don't make you totally comfortable then find something else. You know you've got the ability, so it's trial and error with what helps you hone it. Some people use runes, some use crystals.'

'Some are just lying and are totally rubbish!'

'Are you talking about Martin, by any chance?'

'Might be. To be fair, I have no idea if he's any good as I've not had a reading from him. And midget Rose West had a whole hour today instead of half an hour.'

'Yes, but she may have felt she had to. Or she might fancy him. You know how crazy some people are. She

169

might have missed the fact he's gay as the hills.'

'Ewwww. And the fact he's totally creepy. Why did Maggie employ him?'

'He can be a laugh when he's not depressed. But his readings have completely died off because he's stopped bothering to charm the customers. I actually think he's potentially good if he would just try harder to care.'

'Look, I know people who are depressed, half of my mates are, most of my family are and I can have TERRIBLE downers, but it doesn't mean you need to be a wanker, does it?'

'No it doesn't, love.'

Suddenly I remember the other cause of my excitement. 'Oh, I forgot. The ghost-bust! Spill, spill!'

A bald man walks onto the little stage and begins to play the acoustic guitar. Luckily he's not too loud, but he does have a voice like a cockney Demis Roussos, which sets me off giggling. We are sitting on the other side of a large mirrored pillar so he doesn't see, thank God.

'Oooo, yes. One of those fluke recommendations. Friend of a friend. A woman who's having problems in her bungalow. She rang and she sounded bloody awful. Really beaten down. She said she'd explain properly when we got there. I said yes, provisionally, depending on you. Obviously she's supposed to pay us, but... well, she didn't sound well off, put it that way. It's usually sixty quid an hour plus a forty pound consultation fee. Do you think that's bad?'

I'm not sure what to say. I don't like charging people for a natural gift, but ghost-busting is exhausting. And Sheila knows better than me about these things.

'If that's the going rate. Plus it is a specialist job. I've heard of people doing exorcisms who charge thousands.'

'Tanz, they're leeches. But we've all got to dispense with this, "I don't like taking a fee" nonsense. It's meant to be an exchange of energies, you know? That's where that girl who gave you the flowers had it right. You can't do it for nothing, especially if you've got nothing in the first place. It's still a job at the end of the day.'

Sheila's already told me her husband was a grade one abuser. She has a permanently damaged knee because of one of his beatings. Apparently he was a handsome, rich crack-pot from the same kind of background as her. He made the money through dubious means and after a year together he became more and more possessive and turned violent. When she escaped and divorced him she didn't even try for the big house they shared or the cars or anything. There was no point. All she wanted was enough to buy her studio flat, and even he couldn't say no to that, as it was so piffling compared to what she was entitled to. Everything else – bills, council tax, food, little luxuries – they all come out of what she earns as a tarot reader and sometime ghost-buster. She doesn't claim anything, she doesn't bother anybody, and she'd rather have her fags, her films and her tipple than any bloke. That's what she says and I believe her. She doesn't even bother looking at men now; she reckons she's had her fill and I don't blame her. It is a shame though, because she's smokin'. And I don't just mean the ciggies.

'Anyway, I was thinking of this weekend – Saturday if possible because I'm at the shop on Sunday.'

'Cool. I'm in.'

'Goody. I'll call her later.'

I don't intend to stay out late tonight, as I'm in the shop with Sheila tomorrow so I'll be up vaguely early. But I do want another one of these cocktails. Sheila gets another espresso martini. I have no idea how she'll sleep; she must be impervious to caffeine. We settle into a different couple of seats right at the back of Purple Haze, close to the exit and as far as you can get from the music. I am very curious about ghost-busting. It is depicted in such a sinister way in films, but last time we did it, it felt kind. I want to know if it's ever sinister.

Sheila thinks. 'It's always for the best when I do it. I don't think people call me in when there's no problem. Some people rub along fine with whoever is sharing their building, but if there's a disturbance, you usually find that the spirit really does need to move on. The ones that aren't so much fun are the ones that are staying in one place, reliving something awful. I found one of those when I was asked by a guard at Pentonville Prison to come and look at the flat he lived in. He was feeling ill in there and it was affecting his wellbeing. He was also getting scared. A big thing for such a tough bloke to admit.

The flat linked on to the jail and as soon as I walked in I felt sick. The horrible feeling was coming from the bedroom. That directly linked on to a part of the prison where prisoners were hanged, before the death penalty was abolished. I went into the bedroom and the first thing I noticed was how bloody messy it was. I mean a total tip. The bloke in question said afterwards he hadn't noticed what a tip it'd become. That happens a lot with disturbed entities, you find them in grossly messy rooms. It makes them feel comfortable.'

The hairs on the back of my neck are on end. This often happens when I'm around Sheila. I wipe my hand over them and sup my cocktail.

'So, I put the feelers out in the bedroom and I found someone all right, but he was very difficult to pin down. He was faceless. It was as if as a personality he didn't exist. All he was – and I saw this because for a short while it was like I became him – was a messed-up soul who would empty his mind of who he was and let in a much darker and colder force when he killed. I saw my own hands around a young girl's neck, then that vision disappeared and I saw a large knife in my hand, coming down towards an older woman in a kitchen. I could see the kettle! It was the most awful, chilling feeling, to have emptied all humanity from myself for those moments, and I soon blocked what I was getting from him. It was too poisonous. He had been hanged, that much was certain. And his spirit was very difficult to get rid of. I tried to be kind towards him, but it was a struggle. He eventually left, but I was bloody sickened for days. That wasn't nice.'

'Ohh. I'm not so sure about that kind of bust.'

'I thought you were obsessed with murderers?'

'Not dead ones that won't fuck off.'

If I don't leave after this drink it's going to get messy. A brisk walk home, soon, methinks. And a soak in the bath.

A LITTLE BIT OF WHAT YOU FANCY

When I get home, I make myself a camomile tea and run a bath. Inka is all over me as soon as I get through the door. Because she rarely gets out her claws, I sometimes drape her around my neck when I'm moving about the flat. She loves this. The funniest thing about my closeness with Inka is that I'm allergic to cats. Only slightly now, as I've become more used to her, but I still sometimes wake up with a wheezy cough and I get the odd rash on my inner wrist, too. But it's a very small price to pay for so much love. And make no bones, animals know their stuff when it comes to love.

My bath, complete with bubbles, an expensively scented candle I pilfered from Elsa's stash and my big white shower cap with red dots on it to protect my already clean and nicely coiffed hair, is the stuff of legend. I breathe out the day and go quiet for ten minutes. Today's shenanigans were quite mind-blowing in retrospect. I send out some thanks for what I was able to do. I'm not sure who I'm thanking so I thank the Universe, which pretty much covers all bases. Of course, being a dark-minded Geordie lass, there's a part of my brain that keeps reminding me 'If you don't know how you do it, then it could just as easily disappear'. I ignore the voice of my own paranoia. So what? Right now it hasn't disappeared and I am so happy to have a new thing to learn. Or, rather, hone.

I am dried, balmed, pyjama'd and under my (clean) white duvet with a book when my telephone rings. It's exactly eleven p.m.

'Are you in the house, favourite witch?'

That accent, that voice.

'How many witches do you know?'

'Loads. Oh sorry, no, wait a minute, that's *bitches*. I only know one *witch*!'

The lad makes me laugh, what can I say?

'Can I call around for a cup of tea, please?'

I panic a little. Am I now going to have to get back up and put some bloody foundation on?

'I'm already in bed, with no make-up, in my pjs.'

'Last time I was at your flat I left you with no make-up and your hair standing on end, wearing an old Super Furry Animals T-shirt with holes in it.'

That is true.

'And I liked it.'

'Pervert.'

'You've got two minutes to make me a cup of tea. I'm nearly there.'

Cheeky sod.

The milk smells a bit suspicious so I make him a vanilla chai; that's what he had last time and he said he liked it. I hate the stuff so it was lurking at the back of my cupboard. I'm a straight peppermint or camomile girl when I'm not tanking up on caffeine. I've just poured the water on the bag when he knocks. He's wearing the same clothes as this afternoon and he gives me a warm hug on the doorstep.

En route to the kitchen I reach in to switch on the living room light. He stops my hand with his own.

'Where were you when I called?'

I hand him his tea and lead him to my room, which admittedly looks very cosy with the little bedside lamp, twinkling lights and plumped duvet.

'Can I be really cheeky and sit on the other side of the bed? Then you can go straight back to where you were before and when I let myself out you can just fall asleep like you were going to?'

I think for a second. It sounds sensible, but also dangerous considering what went on last time he was here. But seeing as I've already let him in without my war-paint and in my checked pyjamas, I've already broken several of my own golden rules. So I shrug and stop thinking.

'OK. But behave, I have to be up for the shop.'

'Sure thing.'

He slips off his shoes and climbs up next to me. I'm inside and he's on the duvet.

'Do you realise you have broken my sister? She is basically a jelly in jeans.'

'I'm sorry about that, Pat. She's obviously a bit fragile.'

He looks knackered, I notice.

'That's one word for it. I'm pleased, to be honest. She really needed to hear something and boy, did you deliver. That song. I have no idea how you did it, but getting that song, it sent her into another dimension. Unless you are the best guesser on the planet, your powers just hit the jackpot.'

'I looked on psychic Google, it told me everything about her.'

He laughs. I don't. Something has been niggling me. 'Pat, I've been thinking. This "getting messages" thing. I'm wondering if it's maybe not some kind of telepathy? Picking up on what people need to hear and on the memories of departed loved ones and feeding the information back to them, to give them what they need? Does that sound feasible? That it's nothing to do with "spirit" at all?'

'Jeez, deep. Yes, it sounds feasible, but either way it would be a miracle, wouldn't it?'

'I suppose so. But it could just as easily have been telepathy that gave me the Joe Dolce song as your dad, couldn't it?'

'Why do you want to believe it's telepathy?'

'Well it's a bit more scientific than talking to dead people, isn't it?'

'Actually no, not really. Reading minds isn't yet a science, is it? And either way, look how it helped my sister. You're a legend for giving her that hope.'

Pat was so gentle with Caitlin this afternoon. So understanding. It hadn't occurred to me before now how much he probably has to play 'big brother' to his elder sister.

'You're a really nice person, aren't you?'

He wrinkles his nose. 'I'm just a normal lad getting on with shit. You're the nice person.'

He kisses me. It's not the urgent, passionate crazy kissing from the other night. It's slower and deeper than that. And he doesn't make a move to do anything else. I try to resist, but I'm afraid I can't help myself. Without breaking the kiss for a second I pull the duvet from under him so that he's next to me properly and then cover him again, so we're both underneath it. But even with our arms wrapped around each other and our legs entwined I still can't get close enough to him. I want every bit that can touch him to do so. But not with these stupid bloody clothes between us. He stops the kiss for a moment.

'Aren't I supposed to go so you can get your rest?'

'I don't want you to go. I want you to take your clothes off.'

He kisses me again then begins to push off his sweater.

'Music to my ears.'

Soon my pjs and his shirt, trousers and everything else have followed his sweater onto the floor, and beneath the duvet I have squeezed as close as I can to him, skin on skin, just breathing in his scent as we kiss. This time he doesn't have to locate his wallet as I found two condoms while I was cleaning out my drawers. They are now in my nightstand and with a deft little grab I can have one ready. For someone who didn't want any shenanigans tonight I'm doing a pretty good impression of a wildcat on heat. I suddenly want him inside me as quickly as possible. I drag my nails down his neck, his back and then his buttocks. His bum is a thing of glory, muscular and taut. I

179

can't believe this sexy young thing fancies me.

His fingers dig into my flesh as his mouth explores my neck and he doesn't protest as I slip on the sheath and greedily pull him inside me. Out of nowhere he stops all movement by gripping my backside and clamping me against him. It's bloody torturous. Then he rolls me on my back, pins my arms to the bed and makes the tiniest of thrusts into me, one... two... three...

I find myself biting his shoulder as I sweat and squirm and try not to scream the house down. When it seems I can't take any more, he suddenly sits up against the headboard and drags me up to straddle him, so my eyes are level with his. It's intense with him inside me and his open eyes glinting into mine, but I keep staring straight at him as I move up and down, up and down, and I see his irises darken and feel his ragged breaths on my cheek. In this moment he doesn't seem like a young lad, he's a grown man. A real man who knows what he's about. And right now that man, with that voice and that body and that kind soul, wants me more than any other woman on the planet. And just as I think this, the aforementioned planet explodes.

This time we both collapse into sweaty sleep afterwards, which suits me down to the ground. In fact, I get almost as much sleep as I would have if Pat hadn't shown up here. I wake up before he does and lie snuggled against his back, marvelling at the fact I slept at all. In the old, old days, before Blake, I was no good at having sex with new people, especially one-night stands because I couldn't sleep beside someone I hardly knew. Once finished I'd always make excuses and run off. You'd think men would like this, but they're not as pleased as you'd think when the shoe is on the other foot.

I think it's much more trusting to be asleep next to someone than to have sex with them. This may be linked to me constantly reading about murders. I mean, you could wake up in some garage suspended from the ceiling by winches with an apple shoved up your vagina, and who would know? It just doesn't bear thinking about.

Anyway, after Blake, I promised myself that when my sex drive came back I was going to sample the joys of casual sex. I haven't got very far. Months and months avoiding it then several goes on the same bloke? That's not very casual, is it? But it doesn't mean I have to fall in love, does it? No, it does not.

Suddenly, the young Irish one is stirring. I keep absolutely still. He reaches for his chai, which I suppose isn't quite so horrible as cold coffee, and swills and swallows. Then he turns and pulls me close.

'I know you're awake you bloody actress; I could feel you moving.'

Uh-oh. I can feel him 'moving', too. I glance at the clock over his shoulder. An hour before I have to get up.

Goody.

HOUSE OF THE CD
TERRORIST

When we reach the cottage it is just before noon. It is one of a bunch of run-down little council bungalows that protrude strangely into a field, the last one being surrounded on three sides by scrubby grass. This is the one we're aiming for. It's not horrible or anything, it's just strangely situated.

We set out from London an hour and fifteen minutes ago, armed with takeaway cappuccinos and a raspberry and white chocolate muffin each. Sheila says the sugar is good to have before a ghost-bust, and afterwards as well, so we also bought Skittles and bottles of water for the journey home.

The woman who answers the door looks haggard. She is rotund with straggly hair, straggly slippers and a straggly tent-dress that envelops her breasts and belly and hangs to her knees. Her eyes are tired and her breathing is thick and laboured. She looks so wiped out, I feel like giving her a cuddle. She is called Ann.

When we get inside the hallway, it is dimly lit and the

183

air is heavy. Also, the carpets are aggressively patterned and the walls are a dusty yellow. We follow her to the living room where another, younger, slightly less rotund woman sits at a rickety dining table looking rather nervous. We are directed to a small, patterned green sofa and offered a cup of tea, which both of us decline.

'This is me daughter by the way, Sue.'

Sue smiles and nods and continues to look uncomfortable.

'She doesn't like coming here, do you, Sue? The whole family hate it here, don't they?'

'I wouldn't stay here overnight, I'll tell you that for nothing.'

Sheila grimaces. 'Now that's no good, is it? We'll have to see if we can change that. Ann, love, can you take us through why you brought us here, just so we can get a feel for what's been going on?'

I'm not saying much at this point because I'm putting the feelers out as I listen to them talk. I can tell there's someone else in the bungalow, some heavy presence, but I can't properly pinpoint 'him'. I'm pretty sure I can feel a 'he' though.

'Well. It all started just after my Raymond – Sue's dad – died.'

As she wheezes into an inhaler she points up at a picture on the wall of her hugging a man with dark hair and a widow's peak. He looks sweet. She looks much, much younger.

'When was that?'

'That was five years ago. My health's gone up the Swanee through all of this... I'm telling you, that nasty

184

man is killing me.'

'MUM!'

Sue is evidently horrified by such talk, but Ann certainly doesn't look too healthy.

'Two weeks after the funeral, I was sitting in front of the telly and it was my bedtime, but I couldn't face it because I still wasn't used to sleeping without Raymond. So I put a film on and tried to get some rest in the chair. Anyway, this banging started over my head and kept going all the way around the room, like someone hitting the walls with a toffee hammer. I was terrified. I didn't know what to do because I was on my own, so I started shouting at it to stop. Eventually it did, but from that moment I felt like I was being watched. And every night, if I didn't go to bed at my normal time, the banging would start.'

'Bloody hell, Ann, I'd have made a run for it.'

And I would have done, too. She's braver than me. She shakes her head.

'Where would I have run to? My next door neighbour is older than me, she's eighty and she's almost deaf. I didn't want to go bothering her. Two of the other houses are empty and I don't have a car.'

As she speaks I begin to feel a pressure on my left-hand side.

'Thing is, I stopped wanting to go to bed because you don't want to get undressed if you're being watched – and I definitely was. If that wasn't bad enough, when I did get into bed, the noises would start. They're still going on most nights. I don't know how to describe it, but the closest thing I could compare it to is bottles being rolled

185

in a concrete yard. I'll be falling asleep and suddenly there'll be this noise. It can go on for more than an hour.'

I'm getting a headache on the left-hand side of my head. I look at Sheila who glances back at me and indicates my left-hand side with a quick bob of the head and sideways glance. Boy, he's a strong one.

'Mum. Tell them about the music.'

Ann sighs. 'Yes, that's his latest trick. I can't play my Shania Twain any more, or my Celine Dion. As soon as I put them in, the thing jams. I was beginning to wonder if the stereo was broken, until the first time the CD drawer opened itself back up and Celine Dion flew across the room. He's done that three times.'

'Sorry Ann, but in this case I think he has a point.'

We all laugh at my joke, but it's becoming more and more uncomfortable in the room. Ann is first to acknowledge it out loud.

'The bugger's in here now, isn't he?'

I look around me, feel him coming in even closer. 'Yep. Can you feel that, Sheila?'

'He's not pleased we're here, is he?'

Sue shivers. 'He pushed me over once, that's why I don't come here unless I have to. I've asked Mum if she wants to stay with us for a few weeks, but you don't want to go, do you Mum?'

'No. This was where me and Ray were going to live out our retirement. I'M NOT BEING PUSHED OUT BY YOU, YOU BUGGER!'

The air is palpably shaking, then he's gone. There's a crash from the kitchen. I jump out of my flippin' skin. Ann emits a little rasp and tuts.

'It's my sweeping brush. He pushes it over when he's angry. He sometimes knocks plates off the bench 'n all. I wish I knew what he bloody wanted. He wasn't here when we moved in and now he rules this place. He doesn't like visitors, he won't let me sleep, he knocks on the wall when I'm trying to read. He's a bleedin' nuisance and I'm going to end up in hospital if he doesn't leave me alone. I just want him to go away.'

I'm excited by all of this (and, of course, scared) because he can mess with physical things. I thought that kind of thing was just fairy stories, but obviously not. I look to Sheila again, who gives me the proper nod. Time to go in.

'Right, Ann love, what we need to do is have a look round, just Tanz and me and we can hopefully find out a bit about him. Maybe work out what he wants? If you two just stay there we'll report back to you soon.'

Seeing as a lot of the disturbance is going on in her bedroom, it's the obvious place to go first. We look in on the kitchen en route and see the broom lying on the floor. His energy doesn't seem to be concentrated in there right now, so we pile into her bedroom and perch on her double duvet. The room is dingy, but not messy. This just adds to my impression that he's a strong energy and so is Ann. She is battling to keep her life ordered; he is battling to break her down.

We sit quietly and centre ourselves, waiting for the surge of energy that will signal his presence. Sure enough, it comes. And, to my amazement, I feel him trying to push me back on the bed. I'm so surprised I almost laugh, not because it's funny, but because he is so brazenly sexual.

187

'He's here love, do you feel it?'

'Feel it, he just tried to push me backwards on the bed, the cheeky sod.'

'Bloody hell.'

'Get out.'

It's unmistakable. The voice of an angry man. It immediately strikes me that being scared is pointless and will give him power. I imagine my protection around me.

'He's telling us to get out, Sheils.'

'I thought he might be. Tell me anything else you hear. I can see him pointing to the door. He's a big bloke.'

'I'm glad I can't see his face properly. He sounds very mean.'

'Get out. And get away from my wife.'

'Oh God, Sheils, he's saying she's his wife.'

'Ohhh. He's claimed her, has he? Explains why he turned up after her Raymond died. Still... where did he come from?'

'Who are you? Do you know this isn't your house? And Ann isn't your wife?'

We're both speaking out loud as it makes it easier for both of us to synchronise.

'This is my field, this is where I do my horses. I saw this house and decided to get married and live here. It's on my field! YOU SHOULDN'T BE HERE, I DIDN'T INVITE YOU.'

'He's saying this is his field. He's saying something about horses.'

'Aww, yes. I'm getting horseshoes and hot metal. He's a farrier. I wonder when he worked here?'

'This is MY field.'

His name comes to me suddenly. Thomas. The picture of him in my head puts him straight into a Catherine Cookson drama.

'I think he's from a long time ago, Sheils. He's called Thomas.'

Sheila speaks up authoritatively.

'What year is this, Thomas?'

He snickers unpleasantly. *'Is she stupid? It's 1904. Stupid bitch. Are you both stupid?'*

'God, he's a charmer. He reckons it's 1904. It's not, Thomas, you know. It's not 1904. I think you died then, in 1904. It's 2012 now and this field doesn't belong to you any more.'

'It's 1904 and this is my field and that's my wife and you two better go before I wring your necks!'

He is one furious bloke. Sheila gets the gist without me having to tell her. His energy suddenly sucks out of the room. He's sensing danger, probably. I don't suppose nasty, stuck spooks like him want to be faced with the truth. I suddenly feel sure that he did something terribly wrong in his life and he's afraid.

Sheila has gone very serious. She whispers, 'I'm getting that he mistreated his wife. She died after years of misery. It was natural causes, but she had a horrible time of it. That's why he's still here. Guilt and fear of going to hell. He must have been stuck in this field, then they built the houses and when Ray died and Ann was at her most psychologically weak, he jumped in and claimed her for his own. Ruling her life like he ruled his other wife. If we don't get rid of him he will finish her off, I'm sure of it. She won't have a lot of time left. He's a bloodsucker.'

If anyone knows about abusive men, it's Sheila. No wonder she's picked up on it.

I stand. 'Right, we know his weakness now. Let's get him.'

We straighten the duvet like good, polite girls and go out to the hallway. He is not letting us feel his energy. I go to the kitchen and the bathroom, I look back into the living room where Sue and Ann look back at me, curiously. I wave a jaunty hand then return to the hallway. Sheila shrugs. Then all at once I know. I open the tiny airing cupboard. I get closer, I empty my mind. Then I laugh. I make myself laugh more. Bully the bully, isn't that the way to defeat them?

'Sheila, Thomas – the great big coward – is hiding in a cupboard. Hiding in a little cupboard from two women like a *girl*.'

'I WAS NOT HIDING, YOU STUPID FOOL.'

Do ghosts have a habit of calling people stupid? That's the second time that's happened. A furious whoosh through the air and he has vacated the cupboard and is back in the bedroom. I feel him go.

Sheila winks at me. 'Brilliant.'

We head back into the bedroom and stop in our tracks. We straightened that bed a few minutes ago. Now there's an indentation like someone is sitting there. I feel a mixture of fear and admiration. This is one powerful spook. On instinct I take Sheila's hand. We step forward. It's time to change tone.

'Thomas?'

He doesn't answer.

'Thomas. We haven't come to cause you trouble.

We've come to tell you something.'

'You have nothing I want to hear.'

Sheila introduces a deep calm to her voice. 'Thomas, your wife didn't die because of you. You didn't give her the best time, but she died naturally. You will not go to hell, you will go to her and apologise and she will forgive you because she is peaceful and happy now.'

'My wife is in that room next door!' He doesn't sound so convinced himself, now.

'Sheils, he's saying *Ann's* his wife.'

Sheila takes a deep breath. 'No, she isn't. She is someone else's wife and she will die as surely as yours did if you don't leave her alone. This isn't your home and you have an apology to make. You have got to make your peace or you will be miserable for ever.'

All at once I get a picture in my head of this big man with a mean face falling to the ground in a muddy field, clutching at his chest. I keep my voice calm and low.

'You died in this field, Thomas. Do you remember? A heart attack in this field, in 1904. You have to go and talk to your wife… You have to find peace.'

As I hold Sheila's hand, I see something in my mind's eye. It looks like a treasure chest… the top opens and it has a toy drum in it… and I see this big mean-faced man, and all at once he's shrinking. He shrinks and shrinks and the nasty, lined, mean face gets softer and more innocent until he is a sweet little boy with big eyes and a perfectly pointed chin. He turns to look into the chest and spots the drum. Out of nowhere he climbs into the chest and closes the lid on himself. As it closes the vision fades. And suddenly the room feels empty.

191

Sheila lets go of my hand.

I am shell-shocked and very moved.

'He was a beautiful child.'

'Probably the last time he felt happy.'

'Jesus, Sheila. Was that it? Has he gone?'

'What do you think?'

I put out the 'feelers'. I don't 'reach' exactly – I don't want to pull any energy back – I just tentatively touch around with my senses. I can't find him.

We migrate to the hallway and it's the strangest thing. The sunlight is now illuminating the windowed door panel. There is much more light in here, I'm sure of it. As we walk towards the living room, Ann emerges. She looks at us, one then the other, then nods.

'He's gone, hasn't he? I feel it.'

If anyone would know, it's Ann. She's been tuned in to this bloke for a long time. When she smiles I suddenly see the attractive woman she was before. I just hope she can get her health back and be that again.

As we go to the living room to explain what just happened, I already know that we won't be charging. Sheila is just as soft as me, really. And I can't imagine Ann has a penny. I just hope Thomas finds his peace and that everything gets better for this poor woman.

I know one thing, though, she should paint this place white and change the hallway carpet. It's horrible! I don't want to say that exactly, so I tell her that if she changes the décor it will help her move on. She is grateful for my advice. Sometimes I'm the gift that just keeps on giving.

THE WRATH OF THE WEASEL

Christ, it all kicked off in the shop today.

I came in this morning and did a bit of dusting as usual. Sheila came with me, gloriously clad in a bottle-green velvet jacket and aventurine jewellery, but sauntered off for a coffee as it was still early. At ten o'clock Sheila reappeared, closely followed by Maggie who was looking mighty fucked off. Maggie works on the till several times a week to keep her hand in and she informed us that she had sacked Martin the weasel the day before. I asked why and she told me there had been a complaint.

Turns out that midget Rose West's husband was not happy. Martin had told her her husband was gay and that she needed to escape. Apparently Rose West was completely traumatised – no wonder she looked so weird when she left the shop. Next day, her husband had called to say he would press charges unless Martin was sacked. Which he has been. Now there's a vacancy.

Maggie is quite determined that I should fill the gap.

She is so pushy, like a Yorkshire Terrier, except you can throw a Yorkshire Terrier in a bin and you can't throw Maggie in the bin, worst luck. I wouldn't be in this predicament if Juliette hadn't called the shop within half an hour of the angry, non-gay husband's call to request that I become a reader. She told Maggie that I was the best medium she had ever met. Bless her. She laid it on rather thick though, so now Maggie is determined. She says she doesn't care if I'm a reader, a psychometrist or a hands-on medium, I'm taking Martin's place. And now I'm quite scared Martin will kill me.

I am given a couple of hours to think about it. What does that mean? I'm not sure what Maggie's going to do if after those two hours I say no. Before I can ask Sheila about it, a very laid-back young Jamaican lad walks in off the street and asks for a reading.

Sheila has just taken him to her room and closed the door when, horror of horrors, an irate Martin scoots into the shop, cardigan flapping, half-mast trousers billowing and all guns blazing. Despite which, if I'm brutally honest, he still manages to make fury look a little limp. He accuses me of getting the job on the till to depose him. Hustler that I am. I mean, really, I plotted his downfall, did I? Sometimes I forget, I suppose, that not everyone wants to be a show-off for a living, and his job was probably important to him. But now I'm mad so I inform him that I got the job in the shop because I was skint, and I'm now being kept on because I'm nice to customers and they like me. As for the tarot-reading post, I remind him that I hadn't owned a deck of tarot cards until yesterday.

He calls me a 'total cowbag', bursts into tears, and leaves.

For all of my mouthiness I hate confrontation and I feel sad that he's in such distress. I'm also relieved he didn't murder me; though I'll wait a few days before I truly believe he isn't going to return with a Taser.

As I sit pondering, thumbing through my Scapinis, I get the strangest feeling of dizziness, like I'm whizzing backwards on some godawful funfair ride. It's accompanied by a sudden jab of nausea and it's all I can do not to fall off my chair. Holding on to the counter for balance I take a sip of water from my half-finished bottle and attempt to steady myself, closing my eyes and breathing out for ten.

As I open them again, I glance towards the coffee shop across the road and see a man at a table in the window directly opposite, looking like he's watching me. But he can't be, because he has no face.

'Oh Christ he has no face, it's just a blank oval. FRANKKKK it's a man with no face!'

But Frank doesn't answer and I rub my hands over my eyes, reluctant to believe what they've just shown me. My heart is going like the clappers. When I eventually force myself to look back, I see that it's actually a man with dark, droopy-looking eyes; he does have a face after all and he's getting up out of his seat. The light's bouncing off the café window so it's hard to see much more. Then a lorry stops at the lights outside Mystery Pot and blocks my view. When it moves again the man has gone. I'm so shaken up I rush over to turn the door sign to 'Closed' and put the lock on. Then I go through to the kitchen at the back to make myself a camomile tea. As the kettle boils, I decide ten minutes is a fair amount of time to hide in case the scary man decides to try to pop in for some impromptu shape-shifting.

When Sheila eventually emerges from the reading room she is looking very stern and the laid-back Jamaican lad is distinctly less laid-back. He's as pale as a black man can be and, as he pays, his eyes keep darting to Sheila and away again. There is wonder mingled with fear in those pretty eyes. Before he leaves he almost genuflects.

'Thank you for everything. I'll… I'll be thinking about what you said.'

'You'll do more than that. You know you will. Otherwise you are letting down your mother. Make things right, love, or you'll regret it. I'm warning you.'

I can't believe it. I've not seen this side of Sheila before. He all but runs out of the place. Suddenly, the fact that I imagined a bloke had no face becomes yesterday's news.

'Sheila? What the –?'

She sighs, takes a bottle of water out of her bag and sits in the seat next to me at the till.

'He's over from Kingston on a catering course. He's twenty-two and talented and his mother worked very hard to make sure he had a bright future. She sent him here to study and escape the violence at home. Within minutes of him sitting down I saw a gun in his cards. A bloody gun.'

'WHAT?'

'Exactly. Some distant cousin of his who lives in Tottenham offered him a different option to working hard at college. He came here because he's going to court soon

196

and he wanted me to tell him it would all be all right. He hid a gun for his cousin and it won't be bloody all right at all. He's an idiot. I told him that, plus things about his mum and his life that a stranger shouldn't know and it's put the fear of God in him. I hope it's scared him enough to make this the last thing he does for this cousin. There's every chance he'll be going down. I told him he's made a terrible choice and now he has to put it right. I hope he will. I don't like seeing guns in the cards: it scares the hell out of me. I'm going out for a fag.'

She exits through the kitchen to the back door. I feel unsafe suddenly, like I'm surrounded by faceless men and gun-toting criminals. I wonder if this is one of the 'dark energy' days that Sheila talked about? I take a can of cherry Diet Coke from my bag and opened it. I pull out a card. Death. I know about the Death card. It's all about change and a new way of life coming in. I wonder if the card is about me, as everything in my life seems to be changing right now.

I pull out another. The Falling Tower? Ooo-er. There's no good way to look at that card, not when it's next to Death. The Falling Tower looks like a catastrophe and it involves Death? No thank you. I shove them both back into the deck and try to think about something else as the shop door pings.

MUNCH'S SCREAM AND THE SCARY CREEP

As if I'm not freaked out enough, the faceless man has just come through the door with the hardest woman in England.

My stomach hits the floor.

There's something weird about both of them; the atmosphere in the shop is immediately thick and treacly. But, in better news, the tiniest shaft of rationality begins to creep in for me. Closer up, the bloke is definitely made of solid flesh; he's small enough to bash over the head with a lamp-stand if I have to and his eyes, nose and mouth are in roughly the right place. I'm now sure that the light on the café window caused an optical illusion. Without staring too hard I manage to ascertain that he's around fifty, with thick, dark hair and round, slightly droopy, basset-hound eyes. I remember a cartoon with a character who looked like him. What was it now? *Deputy Dawg*. That's it. He's shortish, stocky and fit-looking in a well-cut suit.

As for her, she's taller than him and younger. She's

wearing a red jacket with a black pencil skirt and patent court shoes. She has long, wavy, auburn hair and extremely manicured eyebrows. She looks like she might be part Filipino, but obviously not a massive part, as Filipino women are not generally known for their height. Also, the make-up and the expensive haircut cannot begin to hide the fact that she's a granite-faced cow and her energy's as cold as a witch's nipple.

I force a smile as she approaches me.

'I have a reading here in two minutes.'

Obviously better things to do than say hello, then? Her voice is a bit Essex, though she's trying to hide it. Being an actress, I'm quite good with accents. I check in the book.

'Mrs Beck?'

'Yes.'

The husband looks uncomfortable. Books about angel healing and little pottery fairies on branches don't appeal to everyone. Sheila appears and I introduce them.

'All right, Mrs Beck, if you'd like to come through.'

She turns to her husband. 'Dan, pay now. I don't want to have to hang around after.'

Charming.

'Right.'

'Go and get a coffee or something till half past.'

'Right.'

She follows Sheila and I'm left with him. As soon as the door closes he looks at me and smiles like a fucking snake. Oh Christ. He pays in cash and I feel a wave of discomfort when his hand brushes mine. He absolutely reeks of aftershave; there's a cloud of it around him that's so thick I can almost chew it. When I've given him his receipt he goes over to the bookstand and pretends to study the titles. I sit sipping my drink, getting more and more uncomfortable. His 'energy' is all over the place, completely unreadable. The shop actually feels darker now; maybe the sun went behind a cloud or something, but I just wish another customer would come in.

'Nice little shop.'

His voice is quiet and light. He has a Somerset burr, I'm surprised to note. I'd assumed he was from London. I try to look him right in the eye so he doesn't think I'm scared of him.

'Thank you. It's not mine, I just help out.'

He breaks my gaze. Ha, one to me!

'Not really my sort of thing, I have to admit. Would make a good little bar, though. Nice size. Carmen would do the interior, my boys would sort out the cracks in the ceiling.'

I look up. It is a bit dusty and cracked up there. 'Sorry? Carmen? Is that your wife?'

He's closed. That's what it is. I get this horrible feeling he's full of secrets that I'd never want to know. 'Sort of.'

I want him to go away; these attempts at small talk are weirding me out.

'If you do fancy a coffee there's a lovely little place over the road. They do a mean cappuccino.'

'Thank you. I was in there earlier. I might just go for a wander.'

Then, thank fuck, he takes the hint and exits. There is something wrong with that man. He scares me with his absolute wrongness. I want to talk to Frank, but before I

201

have time to demand he speaks to me about *Deputy Dawg*, I hear a woman's voice inside my skull.

'Oh God, oh God, oh God... Help me, please help me... Oh God. Oh God, oh God...'

There's a sickening desperation to the voice. I have no idea who she is. I try to ask, but I can't break through. I just hear the same lament over and over.

'Please... Help me. Oh God, oh God, oh God...'

It is an eerie and lonely cry. I try to 'see' her. All I can picture is dark, thick hair and terrified eyes. I want to talk to her, but I can't smash through the train of horror careering through her brain. What the hell happened?

My breath has started to quicken. This is not fun. She is now weeping copiously. I do the only thing that I can.

'FRANK!'

To an outside observer I'm sitting behind the till in a hippy shop staring into space. In reality, inside my brain, I am screaming for my friend's help.

'FRANNNNNNNKKKKK?'

Finally, he speaks. Far more calmly than befits the situation.

'Hey there, cheeky. What's up?'

'CAN'T YOU HEAR HER?'

'Of course I can. The poor woman's demented.'

'Calm her down!'

'I can't. You and Sheila will have to sit down together. It's very hard to talk to someone who's as panic stricken as this one.'

'She sounds alive. Is this a living person, trapped somewhere? Crying out for help?'

'No.'

202

'For God's sake, who is she then?'

'She's been murdered. She needs someone to talk to about it. She's a bit upset.'

'WHAT THE FUCK?' I always swear too much when I'm scared.

'You and Sheila have to work together to calm her down and get it out of her. Go somewhere quiet, the two of you, and sort this out. She needs to be released.'

It's funny how I have spent the whole of my life interested in the psychology of murder and the minute I come across the spirit of someone who seems to have been killed horribly, I am absolutely crapping it.

'Oh God, Frank. She sounds agonised.'

Suddenly the door swings open and the weirdo's 'wife' comes storming out, followed by a troubled Sheila.

'I'm really sorry, it sometimes happens.'

'Well, it isn't good enough. I drove all the way from St Albans, for this? You can't take people's money then tell them you can't read for them. What the hell happened?'

'I'm really sorry, I don't know. Please, of course, have your money back. Tanz?'

I open the till and take out the cash her husband handed me not ten minutes ago. She grabs it from me.

'Your husband has gone for a walk down the High Street.'

'I *think* I know how to find my own husband, thank you.'

Oh, so now she learns how to say thank you? What is her problem? Brick-faced harridan.

As soon as she's gone, pulling out her mobile phone as she slams the door behind her, I turn to Sheila who looks ghastly.

'Are you OK?'

'I need a bloody fag, right now. I've had enough.'

I put the 'Closed' sign up at the door for the second time today, turn the latch and follow through the kitchen to the yard. There's a parking space out here for Maggie's car and then a back lane that leads out on to a side road. Sheila's hands are shaking as she lights her Regal. Mine are also shaking as I reach into my bag and take out one of my emergency menthols and spark it up. What a pair.

'What happened in there, Sheils?'

'A bloody nightmare happened in there.'

She takes a long drag on her cigarette, and clocks my panicked face. 'What happened to you?'

'You first.'

She takes another puff. 'I need a bloody vodka. As soon as I saw that woman I knew I didn't want to read for her.'

'I don't blame you. Aggressive cow.'

'Exactly, love. Face like a slapped arse. Anyway, I started and I told her there had been some trouble in her past. Difficulties with her mother and all that. She stopped me, said she hadn't come to hear about her mother, she wanted to know about her business. He isn't her husband, by the way. She wants him to be, but it hasn't happened. I couldn't get any further than that because she told me she wasn't here about her relationship, either. Basically, she wanted to know about money.

Anyway, I then started to get feelings about her house, but as soon as I mentioned it I saw this face. It was a woman. She was in shadow and also in agony and she was screaming so much she looked like an Edvard Munch painting. It was really traumatic. I could hear her – not loud, but I could – and I could see her pain.'

She takes another drag, closing her eyes for a second. I am gobsmacked.

'I heard her.'

'You what?'

'She was crying in my head, Sheils. It was horrible. My friend Frank says she was murdered.'

'I thought as much. It's tied in with her…'

'She's called Carmen, that's what her fella said. And he's Dan. Speaking of which, he is one terrifying creep. I didn't like being on my own with him. Frank said we should sit down together later and try to communicate with the murdered lady properly. She's too panicked to speak to right now. He said if we combined forces we'd probably have more success.'

'I like the sound of your Frank. Sensible.'

I feel pride on his behalf. Ever since the dream on the aeroplane, I have been speaking to Frank a little more each day.

We make our way back into the shop and I almost have a coronary when I look towards the window and Dan Beck is standing there with his nose pressed against the glass like a pint-sized Joe Bugner. Sheila jumps when I yelp. I quickly smooth down my fear as I don't want him to see it. I take off the latch and smile.

'Sorry, Mr Beck, cigarette break. Is everything OK?'

'Filthy habit, that. You'll ruin your looks.'

I try to laugh. Bill Hicks he ain't.

'Can I help you?'

205

He steps forward so I have to move to let him into the shop. Immediately I am caught in the cloying death-grip of Issey Miyake (I can tell that aftershave from a mile off anyway, but in this case he must have bathed in it before he came out.) He wanders in with his hands in his pockets and looks at Sheila.

'I just wanted to apologise for my... erm... wife. She gets a bit stressed sometimes and I think she was upset that you couldn't do your cards for her.'

Sheila nods.

'I'm sorry. I don't meet many people I can't read for.'

'Oh?' he stares. 'What usually causes it?'

'There's not really one cause, Mr Beck, it's just that some people have defences up and I can't get past them. Others... others don't want to hear what I have to say, they just want to hear what they want to hear.'

He lets out a high pitched laugh then swivels his dark tunnel eyes towards me. 'That's Carmen all over. Anyway, just to say, to both of you, I'm very sorry if she caused any offence. I don't know why she wanted to come here at all... superstitious, I suppose. You women. Always needing someone to tell you you'll get everything you want. But that's not always possible, is it girls?'

I don't like his tone; I can't help replying. 'Some people get what they want. Others get what life gives them.'

That laugh again. It's unnerving.

'Too true. Right ladies, I'll leave you to it. Don't work too hard. And stop turning customers away or you'll make no money. Just tell them what they want to hear. Nice to meet you Sheila and... erm...?'

I don't want to tell him. 'Tanz.'

'Tanz. Interesting.'

I don't breathe again until he leaves.

Sheila sits and massages her temples. I run and lock the door.

'He is the scariest man I have ever met. I want to go home.'

'I think we should, love.'

'What? Really?'

'I think they bumped off that poor lady, Tanz. And I don't know what he's up to, but it feels very bad that he came back in here. Like he wants us to figure out what he's done.'

You see, I don't like that kind of talk. It makes sense. From years of exhaustive reading, I know that loads of murderers seek attention and get caught, when if they'd just kept schtum they would have got away with it. It's their ego or something.

'Shiels, what are we going to do?'

'Well, I can't read for anyone else in here, I know that much. They've left evil in the shop. I'll get the smudge sticks out when I'm next in, but right now we need to go home and work out who that poor woman is and how we can help her. Let's cancel everyone else's bookings and go.'

We always take a number from clients and put it with their name in the appointments book. Fortunately, the three customers this afternoon are local and regulars. They are quickly informed of Sheila's horrid 'sickness bug' then we shut up shop and leg it.

I like my murderers to be safely locked up in prison or

already executed. This is petrifying. As we speed towards Sheila's house, her clutching her keys as a makeshift knife, me gripping my can of hairspray like a poor-man's tin of mace, I realise that we can't even tell a policeman if we see Dan Beck behind us – 'Excuse me, Sheila here was about to tell a woman called Carmen's fortune when we realised she and her fella had killed a woman. The woman's ghost won't stop screaming and my dead friend says we've got to help her. Can you please arrest Carmen and her creepy "husband" for murder? That's him following us!'

We are all alone in this. Well, in the land of the living we are.

THE MAGIC CARPET

I buy us a bottle of red. A good Merlot. We're both shaken up, but once we reach Crouch End Broadway we feel less intimidated as there are lots of ladies pushing uber-expensive Bugaboos and tons of coffee-shop hoppers popping into Waitrose. Saying that, neither of us are completely comfortable until we're in Sheila's flat with the door locked. I open the wine immediately and pour a large one each into purple goblets, while Sheila opens up the French doors and lets in the smell of greenery and road-dust.

After half a glass, a fag for Sheila and a few wasabi peas for me, we both feel a bit better. A pig-headed part of me always refuses to be intimidated by bad people. Sheila doesn't 'do' bullies. But we're both shaken up.

'What now?'

Sheila takes another mouthful of redders.

'We chat to that poor girl. Call your Frank. He'll tell us what to do.'

Frank arrives when I say his name; I feel him like a glow in my chest. I nod to Sheila. She sits still and closes her eyes.

'Hello. She's called Monique. Calm her down and ask her direct questions.'

'Frank, slow down. Why doesn't she stop crying?'

'Thing is, she's utterly traumatised by what happened to her and right now time has absolutely no meaning. It might as well be the same moment she died. You'll just have to get her to speak to you. I can't do it. Oh – her nickname might help. Everyone called her Mona...'

'Thank you.'

'No bother.'

I relay this to Sheila. We sit at the table with topped up glasses of wine and ask for Mona. Eventually we both hear her cries, as pitiful as they were before. I decide to speak to her first.

'Mona, we want to help you and make you feel better. But to do that we need to know where you are.'

Her sobs carry on as though she can't hear.

'Mona. Come on, we just want to know what happened to you. Where do you live?'

She stammers out a reply. *'Just outside... St Albans. We built it together, it's my dream... our dream.'*

I get a picture in my head. A large property on plenty of land. There are stables and at least one horse. I tell Sheila, but she's already seeing it.

'Mona, your house is beautiful.'

'Thank you.'

This calms her a little.

'How long did you live there with Dan?'

I'm taking a risk here, but I'm betting she was married to Dan Beck.

'Twelve years.'

I tell Sheila, who's pretty much getting this anyway. Neither of us is surprised.

'So Mona, what changed?'

She sobs again. *'Our business. He went into the office and I stayed at home with the horses. I love animals. There was a girl there. His secretary —'*

Both of us are appalled, but not completely surprised by the secretary Mona shows us. She resembled Mona in hair colour and figure, but was younger, tougher, angrier and ready to take what she wanted.

Carmen.

As Mona gasps out her story, we learn that she knew Carmen was after Dan – or, more precisely, his money – but she didn't believe for one minute that Dan would bite. Dan could be a shit when he was stressed, but Mona saw this as part and parcel of marriage after experiencing her own father's fury when she was a little girl.

When I ask exactly when things went wrong, she shows us a calendar in the office of Dan's work. Apparently Carmen came into Dan's life about two years ago. Mona whispers that she thought they might be 'dabbling', but she hoped Dan would get bored of her like he had of the others. But he became obsessed and, as far as Carmen saw it, Mona was in the way.

When I ask her what happened when she was attacked, there is a long pause. Sheila tells her not to worry and to take as long as she wants. The sobbing starts again as Mona begins to describe a night on her own in front of the TV with a glass of wine. I see pictures in my head of the wine glass, the table, the big comfortable room. Then I see Dan coming into the living room. I see her jumping up to kiss him and him pulling back. To my absolute horror his right hand emerges from behind his back holding a large wrench. It's such a shock, even just seeing it in my head, that I jump in my seat and nearly knock Sheila's drink over. I can't believe anyone could be so cold. Mona herself couldn't quite comprehend what he was doing until the wrench connected with her head. The crunch of metal on bone is excruciating. Suddenly it's as though I'm actually there, and it is the single most shocking moment of my life when I feel the reverberation of a giant spanner smashing me over the head, wielded by the man I love. And make no mistake, I feel it. I'm in the room. I look into his eyes to find an answer. I see blankness. I see a stranger in those empty eyes. And as I fall to the floor, bleeding and screaming, I see a woman entering. The hard-faced usurper of my husband's affections, looking triumphant.

God, it's nasty. I can't stop the tears running down my face or the shaking in my body. Carmen's hatred of Mona is overwhelming. It's coming over me in waves. When I try to link in with Carmen's energy at that time, I just get a wall of malice. Mind-boggling when you think Mona's only crime was existing. Carmen and Dan were poisonously in love and Mona had to go. I try not to think about it, but it occurs to me that Dan and Carmen's sex life must be bloody terrifying.

I speak to Mona as calmly and lovingly as I can, trying to keep her fear from exploding into panic again. 'Mona, listen. You have been brilliant at telling us your story. Amazing. But you have to tell us what happened to you next? Where are you now? Do you know where they... took you next?'

I don't know how else to put it, how to lessen the outrage of her murder. Now I hear her screaming again. I know Sheila is experiencing this as some kind of film show. Sheila, being clairvoyant, sees everything as a kind of mime. She hears little snippets, but mostly she sees pictures of what's going on. And whatever she's seeing is making her wince.

'Mona, listen to me love, stop screaming... Tanz is telling the truth, it's all right now. We're going to help you, but please, just show me. You don't have to tell, just show. After he hit you, what happened next?'

That wine is disappearing fast. This is as intense as it gets. My head is spinning from Mona's distress and that smack on the head with a wrench. She wants to help us, I know she does, but she is still so shocked and traumatised by what happened, still reliving it every second of every hour, that she's finding it difficult to think straight. Suddenly she bursts out, *'The rug! The rug.'*

Sheila gives a little gasp. 'They rolled her in the carpet!'

'Fuck off!' But now I can see it. Rolling the living room rug around her like she's a tortilla wrap. She is semi-conscious and trying to struggle. She is calling Dan's name. When she is completely bound tight in the carpet, a rope securing it round the middle, Carmen picks up the heavy wrench and begins to rain blows down on the material, where Mona's head would be. She keeps swinging and hitting like she's trying to obliterate her. I am completely aghast and can't hold back the sobs.

Sheila grabs her wine. 'Oh God.'

'Stop. Stop, Mona. Don't keep replaying that. You don't deserve to be still living this nightmare. Let's find a way to make it stop.'

'Pleeease... pleeeease help me. Make it stop. Help me.'

I can hardly get the words out through my own tears. 'We will. We promise. We will, won't we Sheila?'

'Of course we will, darlin'.' She makes her voice even more calm. I couldn't do it right now: I'm too upset.

'Just think. Calm down and think. When was it? When did it happen? That night. Can you show us?'

I can feel Mona's confusion. It was such a terrible time, maybe she's lost some of the detail because of it? But then I hear the TV. She had the TV on. I hear the theme tune to some shitty soap. I hate soaps. That could be any weeknight, or it could be a Sunday afternoon. But it isn't, because it was night-time, I know it. The curtains are drawn, the lamps are on... Mona can't remember... I try to jog her memory.

'Mona, did you buy a magazine or a newspaper that day? That month? Can you remember?'

'I don't know... Oh God... I don't... Oh... Wait...'

I can see a magazine. *Grazia* or something. She's holding it in her hand.

'Look at the date! Look at it, Mona... What does it say?'

Her reply is quiet but distinct. *'It's November. NOVEMBER.'*

As she speaks I hear a bang. Then there's a crash and another bang, from the past. Was there a storm? Was it gunfire?

'Sheila, it was November last year. She's been dead

less than a year. And I think there were fireworks going off.'

'Oh. Well, that narrows it down, doesn't it? Brilliant, Mona. Brilliant work. Now darlin', stay calm and think hard. What happened to you after? What happened to the carpet?'

Mona's voice is diminishing now. I wonder if she's had enough. I'm not feeling her presence so strongly, she's becoming less and less distinct. I pick up one last snippet before she completely disappears.

'They put me in the ground. I was still alive.'

RUN FOR HOME

There's something so fantastic about driving at five o'clock in the morning. Yeah, baby, you heard right. Five a.m. Hardly a car on the M1 (still plenty of lorries though, the massive, murderous, metal fuckers), sun still not up and a whole new day dawning on the righteous. And the wrongteous. If I ever feel out-of-control I drive up north. It's my default.

Sheila and I were not at our most comfortable after that performance last night. Sheila said she'd rarely come across such a distressed spirit. She said we should try to tune in to Mona another time and find out where they buried her.

Sod that for a game of soldiers. I wasn't feeling like tuning into anything ever again. I left in a taxi. Usually I'd walk, but no way José. Not with Deputy Dawg Dan and his evil, killer-bitch secretary on the loose. The fact that he'd come back to the shop kept playing on my mind. The fact that he was being incredibly sinister was also playing on my mind. Which is why I double-locked my front door, closed all the blinds and checked under my bed before I got in.

I was jumpy as hell. If I'd not already had that half bottle of wine I'd have leapt in the car there and then. I didn't feel drunk, but I knew that I'd get sleepy an hour into the journey and have to drive another three hours in the dark. I was discomfited, not suicidal. So I put on a film. Some schmaltzy Sky movie that turned out to be funny and took the edge off. I had a strong vod and ate a whole packet of seafood sticks with houmous. (Do not knock these unless you've tried them. Some may argue I eat too much fish. I would counter that seafood sticks are so processed they contain *no* fish whatsoever. But they're lovely and comforting and they don't make me fat.)

Near the end of the movie, about nineish, my phone went off. For a minute I just looked at it, like it might bite me, then I checked and a strange number was flashing up. Not strange as in a numerical alphabet I didn't recognise, just a number that wasn't logged into my phone.

Deputy Dawg had found my number!

That was my first thought. But that was impossible. I couldn't keep freaking myself out, so I picked it up. It was a girl's voice.

'Tanz?'

I didn't know who it was. 'Yes?'

'It's me, it's Ruth!'

'Sorry, who?'

'Ruth! Ruth from Spain!'

Spain's shenanigans had escaped my mind in all the palaver of the last day or two. Suddenly it came pinging back, like a frog on a stick.

'RUTH! How are you, lass? Recovered all right?'

'Yes. Yes, I'm fine! How are you?'

On our flight back, Rog and I had found ourselves sitting an aisle apart at the front and, mercifully, Ruth and her new beau had been many seats behind us, nursing hellish hangovers. I'd pointedly taken out my novel, forcing Rog to amuse himself with his iPod and several large Jack Daniel's. I couldn't in any polite way refuse to give him my mobile number just before we landed, unfortunately, though I was tempted to change a digit. Anyway, I didn't mind hearing from Ruth. She was very magnanimous about the bruised scab on her ankle and she was touchingly grateful about our little talk.

'I'm OK, thank you. Could do with more money, but couldn't we all?'

She laughed at this, like a little bell tinkling. 'That's kind of what I'm calling you about. Where are you?'

'I'm in Crouch End.'

'I'm in East Finchley tonight, that's really close! Do you want to hook up? I've got something to tell you.'

'Errrrm. Actually, if I'm honest, I'm not really in a position to come out. I'm not like you young 'uns; once I've nested, I don't put my face back on, not at this time of night.'

That's not necessarily true. I will come out if it's pre-planned, but I certainly couldn't be arsed to put proper clothes back on after slipping into my jim-jam bottoms and my slipper-socks. Plus, of course, I was sort of in hiding.

She laughed that laugh again. 'Fair enough, I like to get my early nights in, too, keep the skin looking good… I'm dog-sitting tonight, that's why I'm here. But listen, you know you said I had a job coming in the next six months? You remember?'

I did, vaguely, though I do spout this stuff without really thinking about it.

'Well, it was even better than you said. After we landed I slept for a day and a night. I woke up feeling like a different person. All of that stuff about Rog, it had eased. I felt better. And that's when I got the phone call. My agent had put me up for this big telly drama, *The Siren* it's called. I've done virtually no TV so I usually only get seen for bit parts. Anyway, I auditioned, and today I found out I got the part of the daughter. It's a lead!'

Actor's jealousy aside, this is fab. 'You're kidding me! Oh Ruth, that's great!'

'It is, and what's hilarious is it starts shooting in a month for five months! Your six-month prediction was spot on. You are a genius and I love you and I want to take you out to celebrate.'

Actors are always telling people they don't know very well that they love them. Still, it was kind of heart-warming.

'So, are they making you rich?' I couldn't help asking. How could I resist?

'Compared to how I've been living since my accident, they are making me a millionaire. My agent says it's shit money for telly, but I don't care. I'm just over the moon that someone wants to employ me and I can have a rest from cleaning pubs for a living.'

Oh, bless her.

'I am so pleased for you Ruth, and I would love to see you. Tonight's just a bit –'

'No! Honestly, that's fine. I'm back next week for two nights. We can do it then. I want to take you for a tasty dinner and drinks. I'm now hopelessly addicted to Zubrowka, you know! Better than hopelessly addicted to Rog, though, eh?'

She really did sound better. A bit of affirmation, a bit of success. We've all been there.

'That's a date. Speaking of which, how's the new fella?'

'Who? Oh. No. That's not... he told me he loved me when we landed in London. I'm afraid that's a bit much after a day, even for me, so I told him I was still upset over someone else and couldn't commit the way someone as wonderful as him would need. He started sobbing and I sped off in a cab before he could fall to the ground and grab me by the knees. I mean, who can be bothered?'

Our call ended so amiably; I felt cheered. I still felt cheered as I crawled into bed and Inka got up beside me and curled up on the pillow, purring and touching my face with her pink paw-pads. Cheerily, I drifted off to the strains of my bedtime compilation and a tree whispering out the back.

Less cheerily, I woke up with a silent scream on my face having dreamt a very realistic dream that Dan Beck was knocking on my bedroom window. Oh, how much less cheery was I to find a *bat* on the pillow next to me, in my confused half-awake state. A pointy, black bat? A bat that was actually Inka's tiny head, the rest of her under the duvet as she attempted to emulate my own sleeping position. Still less cheery was the realisation that someone really *was* knocking at my window. A terrified peek through the blinds revealed a crow banging a snail off the corner of the pane like something out of the bloody *Omen*.

That was enough to catapult me out of bed and into the shower at four a.m. I chucked everything I needed into a bag, opened the cat flap and filled up Inka's feeder. A quick note through nice old Steve's door and I was away at four thirty-five a.m. A new world record, I reckon.

Now, safely at the beginning of the M1 with Aretha Franklin lulling my ears, I feel I'm leaving that dark stuff behind me and barrelling towards safer territory.

Hallelujah.

SCARY MAMMY

When I arrive, at nine a.m., my parents are already pottering. Dad's in his shed, probably having a fag and listening to his little radio. He must be on lates today. When I get through the door, my mam comes in from the kitchen and stops dead. She hasn't combed her hair yet and she's all in apricot. She looks like a baby chick.

'Eee, hello. What are you doing here?'

'Welcome home, Tanz!'

She clutches me awkwardly. 'Eeeee. I didn't mean it like that. Are you not working today?'

'No. I'm, err, I wasn't feeling very well.'

'What's wrong?'

'Nothing! Just couldn't sleep; think I wanted to see you two nutters.'

She's looking extra anxious this morning. What on earth is going on here? She hasn't even offered me an unwanted cup of tea yet.

'Right.'

'Mam, you're being shifty. What's going on?'

'Nothing. I just...'

'What?'

She gives a dramatic pause. Sometimes I think my mam should have been the actress, she's a master of the dramatic eye-blink and the martyr's sigh. That'll be me in fifteen years.

'If you must know, I've been very worried. I want to know what's going on.'

'Eh?'

'With that psychic stuff you've been messing with.'

'What? Mam, *I'm* not messing with *it*. *It's* messing with *me*!'

'Well whatever it's doing, you've got to stop.'

'Why?'

'I had a dream.'

Bloody hell. For the first time since the oven-chip incident, my mam just sent a shiver up my spine.

'I had it the night before last. It wasn't a very nice dream. I've been fretting ever since.'

I don't know if I can take any more scares, but I'm now intrigued. 'Go on.'

'Oh, I don't know...'

She's definitely the master, this one.

'Mam, come on. I'm very interested in this stuff, you know that.'

'All right. If you're sure...'

'Mam!'

'All right!' She sits on the rock-hard two-seater and clears her throat, like a regular Hans Christian Andersen. 'I dreamt that I was in some woods. It was night-time and there was a big hole. A woman sat up in it. I got the fright of my friggin' life. She had long, brown hair and she was holding the sides of her face and screaming. She wouldn't stop. And she was bleeding, Tania. Bleeding everywhere. Then it was daytime and I was still in the woods. There was a fallen tree, like a big hollow stump and there were flowers. Bluebells.'

Holy fuck. Bluebells again. And Mam really does look freaked.

'You were sitting on a rug next to the bluebells and the stump. It was sunny and the birds were singing. I thought you were on a picnic blanket, then I saw it was one of them posh-looking rugs and it was covered in blood. You were on this blood-soaked carpet and the sun went dark and I looked over your head and there was this black angel floating over you. I started screaming at it to go away, but it just hovered over your head like the angel of death. It had no face apart from these scary, droopy eyes. I was sweating when I woke up. I didn't ring you straight away because I didn't want to frighten you.'

Oh my Lord. I have absolutely no way of computing this. I'm glad she didn't call me as I'd have had an embolism. I was already terrified yesterday and now my mam is describing stuff I've told nobody. Bluebells and droopy eyes and blood and rugs and MONA. Mona's energy is so strong, she's even reached into my mam's dreams. This is beyond incredible.

'Is there anything you need to tell me, Tania?'

If I tell her what's going on she'll be beside herself. She looks so frightened already.

'Not really, no. Do you think maybe you're just worried about me being involved in spiritualism, after what your mam said about your nanna, with the ghosts and everything?'

Her face changes. She doesn't like being patronised, my little mam.

'No, I don't. It felt *very* real and I don't dream wrong.'

She is indignant and earnest when she says this. What the hell else has she dreamt? I decide a half truth is the best way to diffuse this for now.

'I can't lie. I've been having nightmares Mam, and the dream you just described is very like one I had myself. That's why I'm a bit shocked. Maybe we're both tapping into the same thing. But I don't think I'm in any danger or anything, I'd tell you if I was.'

I have my fingers very tightly crossed behind my back as I say this.

Just then my dad enters, Zorro following at his heels like a love-struck shadow. Dad's wearing his overalls, so DIY must be on the cards.

'Tell her, Bob!'

'What are you doing here?'

Mam jumps in, nodding knowingly. 'She didn't feel well. She's been having nightmares. Didn't I tell you? There's something going on.'

'Mam!'

He crosses his arms and looks me up and down. 'We've been talking and we're worried. What's happening?'

'Erm, how about hello, Tanz?'

He remembers himself and opens his arms. 'Hello, come here.'

So I jump up and he gives me a big hug. I want it to go on for ages: that familiar smell always makes me feel better. But if I cling on for too long he'll know I'm out of sorts.

'Now. What's been happening?'

'Nothing? What do you mean?'

'Well… it's just, if you're not in any trouble, then I don't want you to get in any trouble. You're our daughter, all right? You don't usually come home out of the blue. Would you tell us oldies if you were in trouble, or scared or worried?'

'Of course I would.' Wouldn't.

'Because if you're ever up the proverbial without a paddle, come straight home, we'll look after you. We'll pay for the petrol. Or the train.'

'Dad. That's lovely. But honestly, there's nothing wrong.'

He's making me feel like I might be in trouble. They both are. So much for the safety of Gateshead.

'OK. But no woods, all right? She's never wrong, your mam.'

Boy, he's serious. I really, really love him for supporting my mam in her spookiness. I had no idea he had such faith in her. Just once in a while I get a glimpse into a part of their relationship that I don't know much about.

Mam looks at him and nods. He goes back out. That's the most words I've heard him speak at once in years.

'Did you hear him?'

My mam's hilarious. 'Of course I heard him.'

'Well, just be careful. It's got me worried, this.'

'I promise I'll be careful, Mam.'

'Good.'

I spring up and put my jacket back on.

'Where are you going?'

'For coffee. I'm going to buy the biggest cappuccino in the world with a vanilla shot. Then I'm going to see Milo.'

'All right. If you pass Marksies will you get me some crinkle-cut beetroot?'

'Yup.'

The only food she'll buy from a 'posh' shop. She loves it like I love my seafood sticks and houmous. Bless.

'Errm. Mam. Lots of love, right?'

'Uhuh.'

Back in the car, Van the Man is crooning 'Sweet Thing'. Good old Van Morrison. We don't go in for 'I love yous' in my house. We also don't usually go in for conversations about deadly portents in dreams, especially not ones in which my dad gets involved. This is dark stuff. Not only did my mam dream about Mona, she dreamt about the carpet. She hit so many nails on the head, it's almost impossible to believe, and I don't even want to *think* about that black angel. My only hope is that it's not a warning, it's simply my mam tuning into my fear.

I call Milo, it's ten a.m. None of my other friends would be around, even if I wanted to see them: they've all got day jobs. They put me to shame, the lot of them. But it's Milo I need, anyway. He doesn't answer the first time. He does the second.

'What the fuck's happening, Tanz? It's the middle of the night! Did your mam die or something? She better have, or you're finished in this town.'

'Milo! Don't wish death on my little mam!'

He coughs a groggy cough. 'Fair enough, I'll just wish

it on you. Are you all right, sweet cheeks? I was up till the wee hours. I've been writing a play about a family of dwarves who live in a cave on Whitley Bay beach and kidnap unsuspecting American tourists to make into sexual zombies and send off to rob the Esso garage. It's called 'Yankee Doodle Tanker Wankers'.

He's made this up on the spot, of course. Right now he still happens to be slaving on that TV script, trying to become part of a stable of 'reliable' writers and earn some proper money. And it's driving him nuts. I sometimes wish he was an actor, as Bill and Joe, my agents, would lap him up. Gay, pretty, clever, northern and warped like a 45-vinyl left on the windowsill in summer. He would make a splendid Thespian if he wasn't so crippled by his own introspective demons.

'I'm getting a gargantuan cappuccino, you want one?'

'Get in!'

'Muffin?'

'Ahhhhhhh. *Marvellous*. Skinny lemon poppy seed, since you ask, you cheeky little so and so!'

That's my Milo.

DUVET DAZE

Two duvets piled on the floor, settee cushions, pillows, blankets – we are lying there like Cleopatra and Mark Antony, both sipping coffees the size of Egypt, muffins already munched. Never has Milo been this quiet. He is simply too freaked to speak. Milo loves a bit of drama, but not if it's real and especially not if it's about ghosts. He likes pretend-y stuff. Twice, during my summing up of Mona, Dan and Carmen's tale he grips my wrist so hard it causes actual pain.

Eventually, when I tell him about my mam's dream, he shrieks.

'Oh my God, Tanz, you have got to forget this ghost. I'm sorry she's upset and all that. Scary, spooky lasses are terrible things, but you can't have anything to do with it.' He stares over my head. 'Dark angels are *not* good. Don't you watch horror films?'

'I do, Milo. But I think her dream was about the badness of the killers. Until I help Mona, that darkness is going to be hanging over me. So I'll have to go and help her. Then it'll clear. But that doesn't mean I'm not scared. I'm pooing myself.'

231

His eyes are like dinner plates. 'I think you're mental. You didn't know her. Why get involved? Why's she involving you? It's selfish. She's a selfish spook.'

'She needs someone to be there for her. She's lost.'

He puts his hand to his chest and he clears his throat. 'Look, I'm no psychic medium, but I'll do what I can to help. Just don't leave any dark angels at my flat: it's hard enough keeping this place tidy.'

'I won't.'

'How long are you up for? You fancy a wee tipple across town tonight?'

'I can't, I'm working tomorrow in that bloody shop. I don't want to, but I promised. I really, really want to get out of it, though.'

'Are you telling me you're driving back the same day you came?'

'Yeah, but not straight away. I'll have a little sleep first at my mam's, then I'm off.'

'Why would you do that?'

'I just wanted to pop up. Wanted to see you.'

'Now I'm worried. You never come up here without enough time to drink alcohol.'

'Hmmmmmm.'

'I can come back down with you, you know? I can bring my laptop and work at yours just as easily as working here. We can listen to my new compilation and buy a massive bucket of sweets for the journey!'

That is so nice. For all of his naughty banter, Milo is one of the kindest, gentlest souls I've ever met. And if I say I'm talking to ghosts, then I'm talking to ghosts. He would never doubt me. Despite the coffee, my eyes flicker as I snuggle into the duvet nest.

'That's lovely, Milo, but you've got a deadline and you've probably got a million things to do.'

I know he's having his own nightmare with this script commission and I don't think me distracting him will help. However, were he really writing a film about smaller-than-average zombie makers living in caves, I'd be happy to load him straight into my car and take him to my place. He could describe ideas for plot twists and stay up all night writing and I'd supply him with nice bottles of red wine and a bowl of gobstoppers. It still amazes me that two mates from a normal comprehensive became an actress and a writer. We are just so glamorous.

As my eyes flicker I feel a blanket being lightly draped over me.

'Have your sleep here, why don't you, and I'll make us some tasty pasta when you wake up.'

I'm asleep before I can reply. He makes fantastic spaghetti with spicy meatballs, so I nod off knowing I'm in for a tongue-tingling treat.

THE ANGEL OF THE NORTH

Of course I over-stayed at Milo's. Two hours' kip then the best, tastiest food. We decided I would drive back up north in the next fortnight, as soon as his script was finished and dispatched, and we would have one of our legendary all-nighters in the Toon. We then giggled about nonsense until I realised it was three o'clock and I'd have to go and see my parents for an hour. In the end, I drove back to London at peak time. I'm an idiot. And I didn't even go to see my nanna, so I'm also an idiot who's going to hell.

On top of all this, I got a call from my agents, Bill and Joe, which held me up a bit before I left. Mostly it was Joe's call, but Bill piped up here and there, bellowing Scottish obscenities about the producer being 'a fucking bellend'. They were very, very pissed off because they'd put me up for a job and it had been offered to some vacuous pretty girl whose Geordie twang was as convincing as my Martian accent. The first ep had aired and she sounded like she was Danish or something. I wasn't surprised; the acting world was never fair, but this one was particularly galling.

'OMG Tanz, the part was made for you. It said thirty-four-year-old, gin-soaked, fast-talking Geordie! I mean, *come on*! And it's an all-Geordie show with hardly a northerner in the bloody cast.'

'Are you calling me an alcoholic, Joe?'

'Of course not. I've never even seen you with a drink in your hand.'

I could hear Bill roaring with laughter behind him. Pair of gits.

'Anyway, I wouldn't usually call you about this stuff, but I wanted you to know how hard we work for you and how ridiculous it is out there at the moment. What are they all doing?'

'They're doing what everyone else is doing. Promoting telly faces and ignoring has-beens like me.'

'Fucking bollocks, we will have a great job for you soon. Promise.'

I felt very sorry for them, actually. They really thought I had that job in the bag at the time. I don't dare think things like that any more.

Fast forward to my flat, ten o'clock at night, and I'm travel-weary, dreading work tomorrow and needing a shower. Inka comes and sits on my lap, purring like a freight train, which is usually a great comfort. At least she hasn't taken a dump on my duvet today. Bonus. Carefully, I pick her up and lay her on her favourite fluffy cushion.

'Ten minutes, babelicious, I'll be back.'

My shower head is super powerful. It splooshes away the worst of the fear and weariness from the last twenty-four hours, especially when I douse myself in grapefruit shower gel and allow the water to get a teensy bit too hot. I emerge like a citrus lobster and return to my silky feline, scrubbed, moisturised and wrapped in a six-inch-thick bathrobe.

I light a nice white candle on the side table next to me. It smells of figs. I grab my phone charger and look for my phone. I eventually locate it in my coat pocket. Two texts. One from Elsa and one from Pat.

Elsa's says, *What you doing this weekend? Would love to take you out. Lots to tell xxx*

She's probably got a bloke. That's what she means when she says 'lots to tell'. It must be easier without an umbrella-wielding, dead pensioner looming over her flat. I don't want to live through another one of Elsa's doomed romances though, so I ignore that one.

Pat's says, *Help me! X*

Both of these texts are cryptic, I notice. Pat's seems to be demanding an immediate response. He sent it half an hour ago. I'm sure he can wait a little longer. I actually can't be chewed with a night of shagging tonight, shocking though that is. I'm too worked up about the shop tomorrow. I am *not* a tarot reader. I don't know what I am. I quite like the word 'sensitive'. I'm that all right, usually with the word 'over' preceding it. If anyone asks, I'm *a* 'sensitive'. Until I come up with something better.

With the candle casting a lovely, calming scent about the room and Inka reinstalled on my lap, warmly revving her engines as I tickle her ears, I close my eyes for a second and let the aroma envelope me.

Without thinking much about it I ask for protection

from my 'angels'. Immediately Frank says hello. Not quite an angel, but he'll do. He hasn't piped up much in the last twenty-four hours.

'*Hiya.*'

'Hey, Frank. How are you?'

'*Better than you. What's with the driveathon? Nearly six hundred miles in a day?*'

'I wanted to go home.'

'*Were you scared?*'

'Of course I was. After yesterday, who wouldn't be?'

'*We're looking after you, you know.*'

'Well that's very nice, but there's not a lot you can do if that nutter Dan gets hold of me, is there?'

'*Fair point.*'

'Should I just drop it, Frank? The Mona thing? Should I let it lie?'

'*What do you think?*'

'You sound like a blinkin' therapist, throwing my questions back at me. Look, I don't want to let Mona down, but Milo wants me to drop it and my mam and dad want me to drop it, and they don't even know what's going on. I think I just need to know more about the situation. Forewarned is forearmed and all that. What can you tell me?'

'*I can't help you with this, but I know someone who can. Do you want to meet her? She's here now.*'

I'm scared. But always overriding 'scared' is 'nosey'. 'Only if she's nice.'

'*She's very nice... Now, still your mind, slow down all your thoughts and then ask questions. Direct, non-ambiguous ones, please. It can all get a bit literal over here. She'll help you, though. She's great.'*

I do as I'm told. I pick up Inka and put her around my neck, sit on the floor on a cushion and put the lit candle on the floor in front of me. I don't know why I do that, but it feels right. I empty my mind and breathe, while watching the flame. Soon I feel a 'closeness'. Someone has stepped forward, so to speak. Wow. She is blue, flippin' sparkly *blue*. If I unfocus my eyes I can 'see' her to the side of me, just behind my shoulder. She's bigger than any human I've ever met and she tells me she's Jemimah. She is very tranquil.

'Ask me a question. I shall try to help.'

'Who are you, Jemimah?'

'I am a friend.'

'You're a very big friend! And beautiful.'

'Thank you.'

I don't know what else to say. She has a shimmer to her, or that's how it looks in my peripheral vision. I wonder why I can never see things square on, but then, as Sheila says, it's probably because I'd flip out. Her voice is androgynous and soft, yet I can hear every syllable.

'I want to ask you about Mona, if that's all right? I want to help her.'

'What do you want to know?'

'Why did Carmen and Dan kill her?'

'Money. Divorcing costs a lot of money. Carmen wanted the house. The lifestyle.'

I'd guessed this, but I just want to make sure. 'Why haven't Carmen and Dan married yet?'

'Mona is dead. They have done many sneaky things to cover it up, but if he files for divorce, people will look for

her and discover their lies.'

'Why did Carmen come to Sheila yesterday?'

'Carmen is desperate to be very rich. She thought Sheila could give her the answers she seeks and also put her mind at rest that Dan will stay with her.'

'Why did Dan come back to the shop?'

'You interest him very much.'

Oh God, I've always been a loony magnet. I've certainly dated plenty of them. 'Would he hurt me?'

'Possibly.'

Oh shit. I plough on. 'This one is really important.'

'Yes?'

'Will I be able to find Mona's body?'

There is a silence. *'If you so wish.'*

'I do so wish. I don't think the police will take us seriously unless we find where she is.'

'Perhaps.'

'So what should I do?'

'You will be led.'

'Thank you.'

She is utterly still. The whole room is silent. It's like I'm in a trance. Slowly, I feel her large presence fade into the background, but I know that if I ask her she will come back immediately. That's a good thing.

'Thank you so much, Jemimah.'

Suddenly, Frank pipes up. *'Jemimah's one of your guides.'*

The spell breaks. Now I'm sitting on the floor of my ordinary room with a candle burning in front of me and the TV on pause. Inka, who has been a statue until now, suddenly climbs down and approaches the candle. Two whiskers are on fire before I manage to pull her away. What a doofus. I scoop her up and cuddle her. She now smells of scorched hair and is shaking her head about trying to get rid of the stink.

'Frank, she's amazing.'

'Isn't she just! Toodle pip!'

And he's gone. I blow out the candle, before Inka can burn off her whole head, and place it on the side table again. I pick up my phone and call Pat. For a while I think he won't answer, then just as I reckon it's going to answerphone he yelps, 'Hello!'

'Hi, Pat. What's with the SOS?'

There's noise behind him, he might be in a pub. He might be at work. When he speaks his voice is lowered.

'I'm now outside the kitchen at my sister's. A minute ago I was inside the kitchen. She's got some of her schoolteacher friends around. She's not usually a major socialiser so I'm very pleased for her, but talking about six-year-old children and OFSTED for three hours is not my favourite thing. Plus, most of them are usually stuck in the house with their own kids in the evenings and now they're off the leash, I have become their pet for the night. I'm starting to feel sullied.'

'That's not great.'

'No, it isn't. Please tell me you're calling because you want me to come over? I don't care what we do, I will happily watch a documentary on the history of vacuum cleaners or help you paint a yak, as long as I can get out of here. Plus, you are probably the only excuse on the whole planet that my sister will accept, seeing as she thinks the sun shoots rainbow lasers out of your arse.'

I groan a little, inwardly. I am such a fickle cow. I think Pat's gorgeous, but it's already late and I don't want to wake up tired tomorrow. I am always worried about this 'not getting enough sleep' thing. I am a monster when I'm tired. Conversely, he's asking a favour and I can't say no.

'OK. I have a yak here waiting to be emulsioned. I shall allow you a sympathy visit. Just so you can escape your sister, of course.'

'Of course! Would you like me to bring you anything? Zubrowka?'

'No, thank you. I have plenty. But I can't be staying up. I need to sleep.'

Half an hour later I hear a tap on the door. Outside is a grinning Pat, wielding his bike and a backpack.

'Sorry it took so long to get here; trying to escape a bunch of wine-filled primary school teachers is not as easy as it looks. Plus, I stopped to get you this.'

He delves into his backpack and presents me with a big box of truffles. He probably got them from the all night Tesco, but it's still basically a box of chocolate heaven. Now I seriously have to let him off the fact that he's arrived at my bedtime.

'They look delicious. You're not getting any!'

'How kind. Should I make us a cuppa and we can dig in?'

When we're nicely ensconced on the sofa with the open box of chocolates and a vodka each, (*a cuppa?*) I relate the past couple of days' adventures in absolute skeletal form; I make it sound less scary and I miss out anything about blue, sparkly angels or black, doom-mongering ones. There's such a thing as overkill, even with someone as open-minded as Pat. Then, very quickly, the day's driving catches hold of me and I'm nodding.

Pat has to literally carry me to bed. I hope he didn't come looking for a night of naughties – he's more likely to be painting a yak.

MYSTERY POT
MENTALISTS

I'm so reluctant to be in this bloody shop today. Especially as a 'reader', something I'm grossly under-qualified to do. Last night I slept like a rock and I woke up thirty minutes before I was supposed to be here and had to abandon Pat with barely a kiss. It isn't very long before he leaves now, so I suppose it's good that we're not at it like rabbits every day. He is not, and will not be, my fella, so spending too much time together would be bloody stupid.

My tiredness from too much driving has turned into a headache this morning, despite the night's sleep, and I'm in a right strop. I hate doing things I don't want to do. Plus, because Maggie is on the till, I have to be on my best behaviour and not swear or take the piss. I feel very much like swearing. I've set up the room like I've seen Sheila do, but it doesn't feel the same. I'm basically a fraud.

I drag my moody arse in there and close the door to sulk. Ten minutes later, Maggie pops her head in and, with jolly hockey-sticks enthusiasm, tells me I have a walk-in customer.

I try to look professional and straighten my card-deck as a woman lumbers to the table. She's a big lass, not so much fat, just big-built and clumsy. She's in black. Black trousers, black jumper and black trainers with greasy, mousey hair. I wonder if she always dresses like she's headed to a down-market funeral. I know I shouldn't be nasty, but she is a slob and I'm in such a mood.

'Hello.'

She speaks like a sack of potatoes. The one thing in her favour is a pair of violet eyes, the trouble being that they are vacant and set in a doughy face. She is watching life from a planet in her head. After she sits, she produces a double pack of Jaffa Cakes and proceeds to shovel them into her face like there is definitely no tomorrow.

I smile. 'I'm Tanz, hello. I'm going to shuffle the cards, then I want you to do the same and hand them back to me.'

Probably covered in Jaffa Cake residue, for fuck's sake...

'If there's anything you'd especially like to know about, just bear it in mind as you shuffle the cards.'

She shuffles, still chewing, and hands the cards back to me. I lay eight of them down on the table, carefully placing them, hoping it looks like I know what I'm doing.

My first impression is that her dad is ill. I tell her this, but she shakes her head.

'I'm not here for that. I have a love problem. I love a man and he loves me, but we have troubles.'

I look at the cards, I wrack my brain, but there's no

man. I put the feelers out; I can't feel anything from this woman and I can't find a bloke. This is pitiful.

'So, I'm looking and I'm not sure who this man is. Is he your partner?'

'No. Not yet. But he cares for me, I know he does and I just want to know when we will be together.'

She speaks slowly, I can't work out if she's thick or mentally disabled. As I say, I'm in a rotten temper. I'm now flailing, because there is no sign of a bloke in the cards or in my head. And my instincts are telling me that this woman is not well. Obviously bringing this up is not the best idea. So I go for plan B. Talk to her. Forget the bloody cards.

'When did you first meet him?'

'He works at the deli.'

'And is he nice to you?'

She puts another cake in her mouth. 'We don't talk. We look at each other. I know that he wants to be with me, but it will take time. How long do I have to wait?'

I want to bang my head on the table. 'I'm so sorry, I don't want to upset you, but I don't think he feels the same as you do, this man at the deli. I think he has a family and a life. In the cards I don't see an involvement at this moment for you. I see other things. I can see that your dad hasn't been too well and I can see your mum wasn't the most supportive... and I see that you get very down, sometimes.'

Actually I can't 'see' these things in the cards so much, but I can feel them and it hits me that my first impression was bullshit. She's not just some thicko who dresses badly. She suffers from chronic depression

247

and… what? Something else. She glances at me vacantly; I'm wondering about that glassy look now, I think it may be medication. Strong anti-depressants, or sedatives, or anti-psychotic drugs – maybe all of them? I don't know. There are things, big things, I could get from holding this lass's hand and concentrating. But I doubt she would be stable enough to talk about them. Or she may be too doped up to care.

'What's your name?'

'I'm called Vella.'

'I've never heard that name before. Nice. You like Jaffa Cakes, I see?'

'It's my breakfast.'

I nod encouragingly. I don't know what I'm nodding at. If she's on medication it would probably explain why she's so hungry and it could have caused her to gain weight. Now I feel awful. I'm so bloody horrible.

'Where do you live, Vella?'

She indicates vaguely with her head. 'Just a place. Up the road.'

I am well aware of open facilities in the area for people with mental issues. I wonder if any of her carers know what she's spending her money on.

'Well, Vella. The thing is, I think you have to feel stronger in yourself before you get yourself a boyfriend. The man you like, even if he's looking at you, I think he's just being friendly. It feels like he already has a wife. And you can't go taking other people's husbands, can you?'

'When will we be together? I know we will.'

'Vella, I'm sorry, but I can't see it.'

'Thank you.' She stands up, clutching her Jaffa Cakes,

now dwindling in number.

'Vella, you haven't had your full half hour you know?' Sheila told me that when Maggie is on the till, people have to pay upfront for readings. 'You should get some of your money back.'

She isn't even listening; she is leaving the room. I follow her into the shop; she doesn't look back.

'Thank you. Thank you.'

She lumbers off. My stomach is clenched with nerves. That poor lass. How could she even afford this?

'Maggie. She is mentally ill and drugged up to the eyeballs; I shouldn't have been reading for her.'

'Oh, don't worry, you probably perked her right up!'

'I doubt it.'

There's no point arguing. Maggie is a business woman in her own topsy-turvy way and a client is a client. I don't know how Sheila does it. I'm pretty sure with a customer like that you just have to put down the cards, find out what they want and try to be understanding as you explain it's not going to happen. Or lie. Just a white one. I doubt Vella will remember anything about this reading in a few hours. She might even imagine that I told her, 'Yes, yes, he loves you. You'll get married soon'. This kind of stuff scares the hell out of me. This is the second time in a week I've been completely uncomfortable in this shop.

I go and sit back in the reading room. I remember Sheila saying the shop needed to be smudged after the other day's shenanigans. I wonder if she's done it already? Maybe not. Maybe that's why my first reading was such a disturbed one. I sit, hold my head in my hands and speak to Jemimah.

'I don't like doing readings like this, in a shop. The money's a great help; it's not like I'm rich. But it doesn't sit well with me. How do I get out of it?'

I don't hear anything for a moment or two and then comes a calm, androgynous voice. Clear and succinct. *'All will be well.'*

'All will be well' isn't exactly the same as, 'the roof will cave in in five minutes and you'll be able to go home', but it will have to do.

'Thank you.'

I decide to go to the coffee shop to escape this place. I'll pop to the one across the road where I can spy on who's coming in and out of the shop. I'm still freaked out about Dan Beck, but I can't tell Maggie about the murder scenario. There is no room for that kind of nonsense in her head. She'll tell me I'm being silly and dramatic. This, ironically, from a woman who claims to be able to converse mentally with her stabled horse from her living room.

Maybe she can... See? I'm open-minded.

Anyway, I slip out, waving my phone to show her she can reach me if I'm needed, while she serves a couple of black-clad, teenaged waifs with matching purple hair. As I'm crossing the road, I spot a tiny, bespectacled figure coming towards me. It is miniature Rose West, looking very anxious.

'Excuse me?'

Her voice is extraordinarily timid and accented. I stop walking.

'Is Martin working today?'

'Erm, I'm very sorry, Martin doesn't work at the shop

any more.'

Her face caves in at the edges. 'Oh no. That's my fault. Oh no. Who's reading instead?'

'It's me, supposedly, but I'm just off for a cappuccino.'

She bites her lip. 'Could I talk to you, just for a minute, while you have your coffee?'

Oh, for fuck's sake. I can't even drink in peace without some Mystery Pot mentalist dogging my tracks. She has an interesting accent, though. I'd put my money on Croatian. 'Erm. OK. I'm just going in here.'

We walk in together and I order my usual, while she gets a little bottle of orange juice. We sit at a table a foot or two from the window, which has a wonderful view of the shops opposite and the constant, endless traffic.

She doesn't say anything for a minute or two. I'm not sitting having my escape coffee next to a midget mute, so I clear my throat.

'So, ermm…?'

'Nada.'

'Nada, I'm Tanz. What did you want to talk about?'

'The other day. I had a reading with Martin.'

'I know. I was on the till.'

'Yes. Well, we had a chat. He was very understanding about things. I needed to talk.'

'Is that why you extended the reading to an hour?'

'Yes. He was helping me think things through. He is a good man, Martin. Very shy, I think, but kind.'

'When you left, you looked alarmed. I thought Martin had scared you.'

'No! Martin gets it right. I like to get a reading once a

month, just to hear what he has to say. He was frustrated with me because I couldn't take his advice, even though he was completely accurate.'

Oops.

'Wow. I am now confused.'

'I don't want to ruin your coffee break, but I have to say something in Martin's defence because my husband is a big bully. And I can't talk to that woman in there. What's her name?'

'Maggie.'

'Yes, her. She's another big bully. I don't like bullies.'

I'm warming to Nada.

'The thing is, my husband is a very difficult man to live with. He is bossy and controls everything in my life. What I wear, how I have my hair, who I talk to.'

I look at her dowdy clothes and nondescript hair. She dresses like a fifty-year-old nun. I'd stab any man repeatedly who even *suggested* I walk the streets in sensible brown shoes like that. She begins to chew at her thumbnail and sighs.

'He works from home twice a week, but three days a week he has to go into his office building for four hours. He gives me lists of chores to do so I don't go out, but once a month I come and see Martin. My mother pays because my husband doesn't let me have money and she thinks it does me good. We moved here when I was a teenager and she thought I had met a good, hardworking man. Now she wants me to leave him. The problem has always been, I don't have a job. I'm not qualified to do anything.'

And I'll bet her husband likes her to think she's

useless. My blood boils for her. She's probably an A1 quality cleaner, the poor cow, with his lists of bloody chores. Half of North London employs cleaners. Even the women who don't work still employ cleaners; she could make a bomb.

'He only lets me have a front door key if he needs me to get some groceries, so I have to see Martin on a grocery day.' She smiles at me conspiratorially. 'Though sometimes I climb out of the kitchen window to visit my mother and climb back in before he gets home. He doesn't know that.'

Her tinkling laugh is such a pretty surprise. Oh my God, I want to go round there in a mask with a baseball bat! This bloke sounds terrible.

'Anyway, when I came here last grocery day I was only meant to be here a half hour, but I had a problem. My husband goes out on a Wednesday and Saturday night and leaves me without a key. Says it is business. I was tired of it, so I did something I am not supposed to do and switched on his computer. He thinks I don't know how, but knowledge is power! I learned how to go on the internet and use the PC at the library; he allows me to go once every two weeks for new books. I checked his emails. He has a woman. She has a wonderful life. They go to restaurants and the cinema. They are planning to go on holiday soon. He is a bastard.'

That word out of nowhere almost has me honking coffee on the table.

'When I first saw this I was devastated. He had all of my youth and now this? So I came to Martin. Martin told me I should leave and I said I couldn't; I have no life away from him. But then he made me stay and talk to him more. Said I didn't have to pay extra, but I said that wouldn't be fair! So I listened to him and he told me about the future I could have. He told me money was coming shortly and I could change my life. He said I would find out in the next week.

When I left I was anxious because I knew I was late. When I got home, my husband was waiting for me. He shouted and screamed until eventually I told him where I had been and he was very, very angry. He accused me of having an affair. He didn't hit me because he tried that before and I bashed him with a frying pan on the head. Instead he said I was a slut. I told him this wouldn't be possible as Martin is gay and he got even more angry. He locked me in my room. I heard him on the phone and I know he lied to this Maggie. Everything he said was a lie. He is a coward, and now I really want to talk to Martin. Do you have his number?'

'I'm sorry, I don't. But Maggie will. Do you want me to go and get it?'

She looks at her watch. Takes out some paper.

'Please. I have to go now, could you write your number and I will call you to get Martin's? He was right, you see! My uncle died and he has left me money.'

I write down my number as she talks. It's phenomenal what goes on in the real world. Much madder than telly.

'I found out yesterday. Enough to rent a small place for a whole year! My husband doesn't know about the money or that I can use his computer. And now I have a plan! I will call you from a telephone box; I have no mobile. I want to thank Martin. I must go. Thank you for this.'

I grab her hand as she's about to run.

'You are amazing.'

'Thank you. I like your clothes. Soon I will stop dressing like my grandmother!'

And she's off.

It never ceases to amaze me how ridiculously judgemental I am of people I don't even know. Midget Rose West just turned into the mighty Boadicea in front of my eyes. And she has a plan! That glint behind her specs was dangerous. She could take over the world. She is completely right. Knowledge is power.

The smell of mozzarella and tomato paninis is starting to get to me. I order a cheesy treat and sit back at the table. There are magazines to read and I idly pick one up and look at the cover. It shows three 'celebrities' who are a little heavier than usual: 'Girls Celebrate their Curves'. All of them are unflattering angles and all of them are supposed to make us think 'Jesus, look how big her arse has got'. We are a world obsessed with the superficial. Not only that, it is women who are pillorying other women like this. I'll bet if we all had proper problems like my new mate Boadicea has, then we wouldn't be flapping around calling other people fat bitches and complaining about things that are basically fuck all in the grand scheme of things.

I've eaten precisely half of my panini, and overheard the whole gynaecological history of a blonde woman with endometriosis in a 'private' phone call that is delivered as if through a loud hailer, when I glance across at the door and do a double take. There's a man looking through the window over there. He's in an expensive sweater and slacks, not a suit, but I know his build and his hair, I know those Deputy Dawg eyes and, most importantly, I know he brutally murdered the woman he was supposed to love.

Dan Beck is entering the café.

Never has my appetite abandoned me so suddenly before the end of a meal. Not since I was five and was given tripe and onions. I jump up and my seat scrapes loudly. I grab my bag and jacket. I turn desperately to the waitress and hand her a tenner even though I only owe her five.

'Keep the change.'

'Thank you!'

My breath is now speeding up. I look at her name tag. Peta. 'Erm, listen, Peta, I know this sounds weird, but do you have a back exit to this place?'

'Oh, yes, but it's not supposed to be for the public.'

I groan inwardly, panic mounting. 'Look, I... I just saw my ex-boyfriend hanging around outside and I wondered, could you help me escape? Just this once? He can be a bit unpredictable.'

She looks at the tenner in her hand, then lowers her voice. 'Just go through to the loo and take the door on the left that says "emergency exit".'

'Thank you soooo much.'

I am off like a rocket. Once outside, I take every back way I can, cutting through side paths and snickets that cars can't use. My phone has rung twice by the time I get to my flat, slam the door behind me and lean against it. I have two messages, both from Maggie, the second one sounding pretty furious. There is a man, it seems, waiting in the shop for a reading. Arrggghhh! I can't believe he came back. Not only that, but Mona's back. I can hear her crying and begging for help again in my head. *Fucking hell.*

I try calling Sheila, but I know she has some home-readings today and might be working. She doesn't pick up. With no other choice I call Maggie back.

'Maggie, it's me.'

'Where are you? A man has asked for you specifically, for a reading. He's having a cup of tea across the road, then coming back.'

The hairs on my arms prickle. He'd have walked in on me if I'd stayed a second longer at the coffee shop.

'I'm so sorry. I was sick twice after my coffee; I've had to come home. I think I might have caught that bug from Sheila.'

Her voice noticeably rises in pitch. 'You were fine this morning!'

'No, I wasn't. I was out of sorts this morning.'

'Well you could have rung me instead of just sloping off.'

'I'm so sorry Maggie, but I think I'm going to be sick again...'

'Well just so you know, he's asked for your number, but he's not getting it. If he met you here, you do the reading here. You're not poaching customers from my shop.'

'Oh my God, don't give him my number. Don't give *anyone* my number. I don't do readings from home.'

'Well, good. And I shall hope you're over this silly business ASAP, you're back in the day after tomorrow.'

'I know, I know. And I'm really sorry. Please don't hand my personal details to anyone.'

'I *won't*!'

God, she's stroppy. The receiver goes down. Now I think I actually am going to be sick. This is too much.

I'm tempted to drive round to Sheila's and bang on her door, I'm so shaken up. I try Pat's number. Male protection is always nice when you're feeling threatened by a bloke, but he's not picking up either. So I call Milo.

'You're making a habit of this.'

'Sorry Milo, have I called too early again?'

'Why are you hyperventilating?'

'I'm not... I'm... well actually I am. I just ran back from the shop. That bloke, Dan, turned up there, wanted me to do him a reading...'

'Dan who's Deputy Dawg? The *murderer*?'

His voice just climbed through several octaves and stopped at mezzo-soprano.

'Yes, well, suspected murderer. It's not proven yet, is it? Anyway, don't worry, he didn't see me and he doesn't know where I live.'

'How do you know? He might be torturing your boss as we speak.'

'No. He's having a cup of tea at Dino's.'

'Oh. Well I'd lock your doors, anyway. Do you have lots of tins of beans and plenty of vodka? Just stay in for the next four weeks. Resign from work and don't go out. Or come home. That's it, come back here right now. I just got the boxset of *Horrible Histories*. We can stay in together and sing folk songs to keep our spirits up!'

'Stop it, will you? This is serious.'

'I bloody know it is, I am serious. Why don't you call the police?'

'And say what? Any way you look at it, he showed up at the shop to buy a reading, which is what we sell there. He didn't do anything bad and screaming ghosts calling him a murderer probably don't wash with policemen. By the way, I can hear her again. Mona. She defo follows him wherever he goes.'

'Tanz, this is *so* scary. What are you going to do?'

'I'm going to have to try to find her, Milo. If her body's found, Dan will have bigger things on his mind than getting tarot readings from me.'

'God! Please be careful. Will you call me later? Take a weapon with you.'

'Eh? What weapon? Do you think I have an arsenal in my spare room?'

'A penknife will do. Come on, all northerners have penknives.'

'Actually, I do have a tiny Swiss army knife. It's really pretty, with flowers on the handle. It has a nail file and a bottle opener. It was one of my mam's bizarre stocking fillers a few Christmases ago.'

'Your mam is nuts.'

'Leave her alone. She was just trying to be original. Oh, wait, Milo. Sheila's ringing, I need to cut you off... I'll speak to you later.'

'Tanz, please be careful. You're like Jessica Fletcher and that kid out of *The Sixth Sense* all rolled into one. You're my little Dan Aykroyd.'

'Thank you, Milo. Bye, bye byeeeee... Sheila?'

'Hiya, love. You OK? Mona's shouting in my ear

again. I was just cleaning the bathroom.'

'You can hear her too?'

'Yes. Started up half an hour ago. Are you OK?'

'Dan Beck just showed up looking for me at the shop. I took off like Usain Bolt. I think I broke three world records getting here.'

She whistles. 'I hoped he wouldn't show his face again.'

'Have you got phone readings today?'

'I've done 'em. One at nine, one at nine forty-five.'

'You fancy a drive?'

'You mean to look for her?' Sheila is uncharacteristically quiet for a bit. 'I'm not sure, Tanz. I just wish we could read for ourselves as well as other people. I've got a bad feeling.'

That's not good.

'OK. I'm going to take a drive and I'll let you know what I find. I probably won't even get out of the car, I'm too much of a scaredy-cat, but I do feel like I'm being pushed to hurry up and sort this.'

There is another pause. 'Oh, sod it then. I'm in. Come and get me.'

I'm not going to lie. I'm pleased she's coming. We're a good team. Truth is, I want this all over with. And if this is one big flippin' delusion, then I can stamp it out and get on with my life.

WELL, THAT WAS A
CLEVER IDEA, WASN'T IT?

I pick up an apprehensive, bleached blonde medium in a purple, crushed-velvet jacket that I covet enormously, just after one p.m. She clambers into the front seat and her eyes are so wide I almost change my mind. If she's nervous then we definitely have something to be worried about. But she also now seems determined to see this through.

'She said St Albans, didn't she, love?'

'She did indeed. Let's hit the M1.'

I slip on some calm music. Heavy rock is not right today.

When we eventually reach the motorway after a typical blip on the A406, we both fall silent. We need to tune into Mona. As we pass junction 5A Sheila turns to me.

'We're coming off at the next one, aren't we, love?'

My heart is beating faster. 'Yup.'

We do just that and drive towards St Albans. The countryside is very lovely and the skies are a warm blue with soft cloud. In the distance there's a bank of grey coming, though, and I wonder how long it will be before it rains. This lovely weather is not making me feel any less odd. Something is going to happen. Really. I know it. I don't know whether to ask for help from Jemimah or Frank. Frank pops into my head immediately.

'There's going to be a sign soon. You'll see it and know. So will Sheila. Follow it until the next right turn.'

I don't say anything to Sheila. Then we come to a sign for Mersham and Bancroft.

Her head whips round. 'Mersham? What do you think? Mersham?'

'Yup. Definitely. The M hit me in the face like a shovel. Oops, sorry, no pun intended.'

She chortles, uncomfortably. 'You are *terrible.*'

We take the turn. The road is narrow and rendered a tunnel by trees. Quite fitting, really. A scary tunnel leading to somewhere unknown. We drive for about two miles then come a sign for Mersham and we turn right.

What now?

As we reach Mersham village, I slow down. We pass cottages, then a school; all very picturesque. We're about to leave the village completely when a large pub looms into view. The Bluebell. Its brickwork has been painted white, the name is in bold black lettering and there's a large pub sign with bluebells on it. My heart does that fluttery thing it always does when I'm excited or nervous, the one that makes me think I'm having a heart attack.

'Fuck a duck!'

'What, love?'

'The Bluebell! We have to stop.'

We pull into the pub car park. The lovely day contrasts

completely with the pressure in my temples, the kind of tension I feel when a storm is brewing.

'Bluebells bloody everywhere. I've been dreaming about them, my mam's been dreaming about them. It can't be a coincidence, surely? Anyway, I can feel it, can't you?'

'I feel dreadful, Tanz. I'm scared.'

She puts her hand on top of mine. It's cold and clammy, which freaks me out because the car is warm. Sheila is not given to histrionics, as far as I know, so this winds me up more than the distant screaming that has flared up like tiny tinnitus.

'Mate, we need a drink.'

She concurs simply by grabbing her bag and reaching for the door handle.

The pub is enormous. It has swirly brown carpets, original beams and three different areas: a snug with an open fire (unlit), a large bar area with a little stage, and a great big restaurant area. We go to the bit of the snug overlooking the pub gardens. There's a huge expanse of lawn and at the end is a tall wooden fence with trees behind it. That is where my eyes are constantly drawn as the bar girl places down two glasses of wine and a menu.

'Just in case you fancy a spot of lunch, ladies.'

She's in her late thirties with a bossy air of confidence. Her hair and make-up are perfect and she has a perm with red highlights. I could as much eat as juggle Fiat Puntos at the moment, but the drink is extremely welcome. I point down the garden.

'I love the greenery.'

'Oh, thank you. We host events if you're ever

interested? Weddings, birthdays…'

'I'll bet they're great. It's so tranquil here. What about the end of the garden, what's down there?'

'Oh, that's our famous bluebell wood. That's why we're called The Bluebell. This place was called The Woodsman until we took over, but I think The Bluebell is prettier, don't you?'

'Much prettier.'

Satisfied with this, she wanders off to another table where two wiry old ladies are just finishing up their lasagne and salad, which, to be fair, looks like a nice portion.

Sheila is staring out of the window. 'She's down there, isn't she?'

That fluttering in my heart again. Distant sobs in my head. Dread and adrenaline combined. Does it make me a pervert that I'm vaguely excited as well as terrified by all of this? We could actually help solve a murder. One that, so far, nobody seems even to know about. It's very cold wine. I approve, wine is never chilled enough in pubs.

'Yup. But now that we're here, I'm wondering about going in. I mean, chasing a moody spook around a bungalow is one thing, but looking for a burial site? Plus, we haven't brought a spade and we can't go around digging up the woods willy nilly. On top of which, are you prepared to see a decomposed body? Worse, are you prepared to find out this is all bullshit and we're a pair of fantasists?'

'Tanz, stop talking so fast, you'll be sick.' Sheila picks up her bag and pulls out a garden trowel.

I'm so shocked I inhale my wine and my laughter is

peppered with throaty coughs, like an injured seal.

'Stop laughing. You can't come to a burial site and not bring a trowel. There might be evidence, a ring or something; I'm not proposing digging up a whole decomposing body with this, you nit. We could destroy evidence doing that. We're not in *Silent* bloody *Witness*.'

Sheila is so cool. She believes in what we're doing and she has no doubt that Mona is real and that she's buried nearby. That is the confidence I haven't quite developed yet. Now I'm beginning to understand that 'development' is also about learning to believe wholeheartedly in what you're doing. Healthy doubt is always good, but not being a total doubting Thomasina like me. Part of me really wishes we'd called the police by now.

We look at each other. Next move: drink off our wine and visit the loo. It's business time.

DARKNESS DESCENDS

The strip of pavement on the side of the country lane that passes for the main road through Mersham is rather thin. I don't like those little pavements. Even when the sign says thirty, in my experience, country people drive like they're steering Learjets. They seem to have cars that don't go slower than seventy. They are basically mad. That's why I don't live in the countryside: it sends people bonkers.

Just down from the pub, twenty feet after the end of the garden, we come across a small lay-by with a wooden turnstile that leads into Bluebell Wood.

'Are we really going to do this, Sheils?'

'Look, if we don't, we are not going to shake off Mona. This way we can at least show her we're trying to get to the bottom of this. If we don't find anything, we don't find anything. Anyway, wasn't this your idea?'

I look at my phone. Virtually no reception. I reckon once we get under the trees there'll be none at all. That's B-movie stuff. Why don't they build better phone masts around here, the total Neanderthals? Sheila uses the turnstile first, the damp wood offering a little resistance before it gives and allows her to pass. The accompanying creak would make Vincent Price proud. If he wasn't dead. I am not liking the feeling that I'm currently the star of my own shit film.

Sheila stands a few feet along the path, where the canopy of trees has already made it darker and cooler. For all of her conviction, there's a sheen of sweat on her top lip. She is obviously edgy and as I step up to join her the trepidation is hanging heavy on me, too. I've tried to speak to Frank a few times since we got to the pub and he's not been more forthcoming than, *'Be careful'*. I don't like him saying that; he should know I'm going to be fine, shouldn't he? Isn't that his 'job'? I link arms with my scared mate as we begin to tread the foot-worn path.

'Help me, please. Oh God, oh God. Why? Please, help me, someone.'

Change the record, Mona. I can't see the sky now, just branches and leaves. I imagine the night it happened, being lugged into these woods like a sausage roll in a blood-stained carpet. I know it wasn't just one person carrying that roll. I can hear the breathing, the footfalls. There were two of them, in the dark.

Sheila grips my arm harder.

Suddenly I can hear Jemimah, as calm and steady as always. *'It's to the left. Look for the hollowed-out trunk.'*

'Sheila, I think it's through there.'

To the left there is a very faint, less-trodden path that seems to lead to nowhere but a thick bank of bushes and trees. Sheila takes a deep breath.

'I can see her, love. Mona. Her face is... never mind. She is beckoning to us from that tree over there.'

Oohh. Now I feel faint. A ghost beckoning to us is just

268

old-school Hammer Horror. I look towards the tree she's pointing at, then approach it. It's actually an optical illusion that the bushes and trees are impassable. Once you reach them there's quite a gap between the first tree and the one behind it.

I slip through and am surprised to find another little path. Sheila steps in behind me. I don't want to move. I can see a bit of sky and it's greyer than it was. I pull my jacket around myself. I am now wishing I hadn't come here. Mona's crying has become a keening wail and I am overcome by the worst, most all-consuming sadness I've ever experienced. It is crushing. She is nearby, I know it, and my legs don't want to take me there. Sheila holds my arm again and gives me a firm little tug.

'We've come this far. Let's just take a peek.'

There's a clearing just through the trees ahead. I hold my breath, count to five, then walk towards it. In very few steps we are past the oaks and willows and there it is. A patch of bracken and earth. The clearing's not that big, fifteen feet across maybe. It's dominated by a large, hollowed out tree trunk lying on its side and has a small patch of bluebells growing on the periphery. I am no gardener, but even I know bluebells are spring flowers. There shouldn't be bluebells growing wild in June. And yet here they are. That freaks me out as much as the hollowed out trunk that Jemimah told me to look for and that my little mam saw in her dream.

The energy here is horrendous.

Sheila has walked over to the trunk. All at once she squats down and starts pushing at it. What the bloody hell is she doing? It obviously isn't embedded in the ground, as her shove rocks it. She motions me to join her. She whispers, even though there's no one else around.

'Look over there. That shape in the ground. It's faint, but it looks pretty much the size of this trunk. I think this has been moved. I think it was embedded over there and then a while ago someone moved it a couple of feet.'

'Kids?'

'Maybe.'

Neither of us is convinced. There's no litter or sign of human visitation and apart from distant birdsong this clearing is eerily quiet. All at once I'm dizzy.

'Here! Here! I'm here, all on my own.'

I hear her. I drop to the ground again, by the trunk. Sheila joins me.

'We have to move this.'

We both put our palms flat on the trunk and give it another shove. It moves without much complaint once I put my shoulder into it, uncovering a mass of fleeing woodlice, shrinking worms and agitated grubs, unappreciative of their sudden exposure to air and light. Then Sheila takes the trowel from her bag. I'm not laughing now. My heart is hammering. There is a pulsating, throbbing black hole in the middle of my forehead and my chest is constricted by the pressure of being in this place.

Sheila has arthritis in her hand. I hold out my own. 'Here. I'll do it.'

I dig a few inches down. It's loose-ish soil. 'How far should I dig?'

'I don't know, love. Mona's here, pointing a few inches to your right there.'

I dig where I'm told. The smell of damp soil reminds me of being a child in Saltwell Park, when they'd dig up the large flower beds and overturn the soil, ready for the new spring planting. About a foot down I think, 'maybe I should stop now'. A fresh pressure on my forehead tells me I shouldn't. I take another large scoopful out and dig the trowel in again. I come against resistance. My heart stops hammering and skips.

'Sheils, there's something there.'

I put down the trowel and we pull more soil back with our hands. Carefully. It could be anything. I dig more and we clear more.

Then. Right in front of our eyes, in front of my sceptical, scathing, sarcastic *subconscious*, is the thing I never truly expected to find. The thing that I suspected to be true, but couldn't quite believe.

There, becoming more and more uncovered as we clear away dirt with our hands and that tiny little spade, is the corner and side of a rolled-up carpet.

Fuck.

It's all I can do not to burst into tears. The emotion (and fright) could be mine, or it might be Mona's. It's probably both. Sheila is suddenly a whitish-green colour and I hope she's not about to puke; the smell from the carpet as a few more trowels of earth are removed is already bad enough. We don't need to dig any more or attempt to look inside the carpet as that stench tells us everything we need to know. There's only one thing it can be. I step away from the hole. Sheila does the same.

We just stand there quietly for a bit.

'Mona. You did very well. Now we know, love.'

Sheila takes my hand and instinctively we both close our eyes. We attempt a prayer each. Sheila starts.

'Mona, I hope now that we have found you that you can find peace and remember the beauty in your life and not just the horrible ending.'

'Mona, I'm sorry you suffered so badly, lass, but now I hope you can be the special person that you truly are and not dwell on the hurt that others caused you. Safe journey.'

This is truly emotional. I reckon she was released as soon as we found the edge of that carpet though, because the weeping in my head has stopped.

We both check our phones. No signal on either. My teeth are chattering.

'Do we need to do anything else, Sheils?'

'No. That's enough. We can perform a little ceremony for her after she's been given a proper burial if you fancy? Right now I'd like to get back to your car and call the police. I don't like being here at all.'

No. The feeling of peace that descends after a spirit has been helped is being superseded by the unease at being in this place, on our own, with phones that don't work.

I let Sheila walk ahead, as she's slower than me and I don't want her to feel left behind. In reality, I want to leg it out of here and all the way down the M1 back to London without stopping.

I'm just wondering how the hell we'll explain this to the police when a hand, followed by a whole body, like a cheesy trailer for a slasher movie, shoots out from behind the tree ahead. My emotions are already heightened because of what we just found, but suddenly seeing Dan

Beck in his casual jumper and slacks grabbing Sheila by the hair is enough for me to disbelieve my own lying eyes while simultaneously spasming like I've stuck my hand in a live electrical socket.

And worse than him grabbing her is the fact that the other arm, currently around her neck, has a sharp-looking blade in its hand. And when Sheila tries to struggle it is brought quickly under her chin and draws blood. She goes still as a statue and he looks straight at me.

'I'd stay still and be quiet if I were you.'

That accent. Like being murderously threatened by one of the Wurzels. I look at the cut on Sheila's neck and I want to chop his liver out. Fucking coward.

THE HOUSE OF DEATH

Before being in that situation where a crazy person might murder you in cold blood at any given moment, you think you'll do certain things to save your own life. You think you'll fight and scream and kick and tear. You think you'll use your ingenuity and wiles; you won't be a victim and you'll *definitely* fling yourself out of a moving car rather than risk murder or rape or both.

But when a dangerous man puts his knife against my friend's throat, most of my options are completely buggered; especially when he bundles us into the back of his blacked-out 4x4 and ties us together with a skipping rope from the boot. He could slit either or both of us from ear to ear in a few seconds, the mad twat. Plus, Sheila is not the kind of girl who leaps out of moving vehicles, not with her arthritis, and – seeing as she's tied to me – if I jump, she jumps. So I'm staying put, because I can't let Sheila be harmed today, not a flippin' chance. It's my fault she's here and I'm getting her home safely, and that is that.

He only speaks once and it's to me, just before he pulls away from the wood that he recently dragged us from.

'That cut on her neck was a small warning. If I'd meant to cut her properly she'd be dead.'

I look at the back of his neck and wish I could give him a Vulcan death grip or kick him in it, so I damage his spinal cord and cripple him. That's how pissed off I am. And that's the problem with films and TV. They make us think we're all Hong Kong Phooey. In my head I cry out to Frank.

'Frank! What the FUCK do I do now?'

'Keep calm.'

'Is that it? Thanks for nothing, mate.'

We've only driven about four minutes when we reach security gates and find ourselves on the gravel frontage of what is presumably his home. And with iron gates closing behind us I have no idea what will happen next. It's the most bizarrely menacing predicament to be in.

He stops and exits the car. As he walks round to let us out, Sheila whispers to me that we're protected.

A tear rolls down her face. She's obviously not feeling *that* protected.

'I'm sorry, Sheils, for getting you in to this –'

Just then, Dan's hand shoots in and drags us out into the daylight.

'No conferring, ladies!'

He laughs a hyena laugh that gets right on my fucking nerve endings.

He bundles us clumsily through his front door into his hallway. This house has high, beamed ceilings. Mona's dream home, the one she helped build, the wife he killed.

This line of thought is not helpful. He bolts the front door, then unties us and leads Sheila to another door. It is a big coat cupboard. It contains various bits and bobs, including a small wood and leather stool shoved in the corner with a Barbour coat hanging down behind it. He pushes Sheila onto the stool.

'Sit down and behave yourself and life will be very easy for you. Make a fuss and you'll have more than a little shaver's cut to contend with. OK?'

Cool as a cucumber, he brandishes the knife again. She nods, not even looking at him, and sits on the stool. Her eyes lock on mine. If she can be that centred then so can I. He closes the posh, stripped wood door on her and puts down the wooden latch. There's a lot of wood in here. It looks like they built a house from scratch and filled it with old, reclaimed stuff. Right now it's difficult to appreciate its beauty, terrified as I am, but I can feel there was love in these walls and I draw whatever strength I can from that as he takes me by the elbow and leads me to another room.

It's a television room, with large, comfy-looking (and expensive) sofas. The curtains are open, letting in huge amounts of light; the window looks out over fields and a rose garden with what looks like a stable to the side. There is a table in the corner with four chairs that I imagine to be the 'dine while you watch TV' part of the room.

On the dark wood coffee table in front of a sofa looks to be the remnants of last night's dinner, an Indian take-away by the smell of it. And several empty cans. Carmen must be away, as there's only one plate and I cannot for the life of me imagine a money-hound like her drinking tins of lager. He puts his arm around me and I try not to

277

stiffen as he leads me to the table and sits me in one of the chairs.

'Do I need to tie you up, or are you going to be a good girl? Maybe you like being tied up? Yeehahahah.'

Keep laughing, mate. Until I'm angry enough to smash a chair over your head. 'No. I don't like being tied up.'

'Shame. Well, I'll let you off for now. But one false move and I'll gut your mate like a rabbit.'

To illustrate his point, he brings his face to the same level as mine and waggles the glinting knife. If he tries to kiss me, I will vomit. But he doesn't. He just sniffs my hair like he's trying to work out what shampoo I use, an action that freezes my blood, then sits down and stares at me.

'How did you find out about Bluebell Wood? Did Carmen tell your friend out there?'

What do I say? What? I want to tell the truth, but how do you judge how to play it with someone like this? His hangdog eyes are pools of blankness. How do I work with that? But Frank is here. To my relief I hear him, bold as brass. *'Be exactly like Jemimah. The truth, the literal truth. He'll feel it.'*

This is a film. This is a movie and I'm playing a massive, blue androgynous being called Jemimah. A blue being that has suddenly acquired a Geordie accent. I assume an absolute calm that I don't feel.

'You know she didn't.'

He flinches slightly. 'I didn't think she would. Good at keeping secrets, Carmen. And anyway, if she had, you'd have called the police, wouldn't you?'

'Maybe. People who come for readings can be

complete nutters, so she might have been lying.'

This catches him off guard and he laughs that high, inappropriate laugh.

'I bet you do get some nutters! I expected everyone at that ridiculous shop to be cuckoo, but was pleasantly surprised. When your mate couldn't tell Carmen anything, there was no charge. Instead of making something up she sent her away with her money in her hand. Why would a faker do that?'

'Sheila is an amazing woman.'

'She's not the only one. You looked into my soul.'

I swallow hard. The words of a true mentalist. How am I supposed to respond to that?

'You met my eye in that shop and for a second there I felt something I'd not felt in a while. I was scared.'

Talk about irony.

'That's a surprise.'

'Oh?'

'I'm not usually classed as scary.'

'You know things. Like my mother did. It was like my mother was looking straight through me. My mother wouldn't be very pleased with me at the minute, I'm afraid.' He rubs a hand over his perma-tanned face. If his eyes weren't so weird he'd be a handsome bloke. I'm sure Carmen and her ilk think he's gorgeous, this cologne-drenched creep with pots of money.

'Tell me what's wrong.'

He looks so troubled, it just slips out. I mean, Jemimah would ask, wouldn't she? Anyway, I'm improvising.

'You see, that's what my mother would do. She's dead now, but she would care about the other person. You ladies are up the creek without a paddle and you're asking what's wrong with me? Will you just tell me, be honest, how did you find that place in the woods? I need to know.'

'You might get mad at my reply.'

'I won't. I asked you.'

That is so easy for him to say while he brandishes a cutlass at me. Actually it's nowhere near the size of a cutlass, but I think I'm allowed to be slightly dramatic in the circumstances.

'Your wife, Mona, told us where she was buried. She was very upset.'

He blinks at me then looks away. He believes – I see it plainly in those unguarded two seconds. This man has more complications than a quantum Rubik's cube.

'What do you mean? My wife's not buried. How could she tell you she was upset if she was buried? She'd be dead. That makes no sense.'

I feel sick again. This honesty lark is a risky business.

'She was screaming in my head. Screaming and crying, when you and your second wife came into the shop.'

He lowers his head. 'Screaming, you say?' He places his hands on the table, as though to compare finger sizes, then pulls himself together. 'Carmen is *not* my second wife.' His lips tighten at the corners. He gets up from the table, goes to a draw and returns with a photograph in a frame. He shows it to me.

'*This* is my one and only wife.'

I bite my lip. It's Mona, but not screaming and not in shadow. The two of them have their heads together in the picture; her eyes sparkle with life. She has expensive, shiny hair, much like Carmen's, but her face is softer, older; she probably wasn't as toned and provocatively dressed as Carmen, but she certainly looks prettier. And Dan? His smile seems real and happy. But then he's a freak, so God knows what he was thinking even then.

He stands it up on the table where we can see it. 'A year ago on holiday. Then Mona suddenly disappeared last November. It was a terrible time. She found out I was having a stupid bloody affair and she went. Took a lot of money out of our account. Took some more in France. Sent me a postcard in January, haven't heard a word since.'

I have no idea what to say next, because that is a crock of poop and he knows it.

'What I want to know, Tanz, is what you found down that hole you were digging?'

'Nothing. Some old carpet.'

My eyes well up without warning. Damn them. I can't help it, that poor woman is down a bloody hole.

He reaches into his pocket and produces a packet of paper tissues and he offers me one. He then pats my hand.

'You are a very caring girl. Look at you. I don't function well around cold people.'

What's he talking about now?

'My wife disappearing wasn't good for me. Not good at all.'

I'm not sure what to do. Humour him?

'So you were having an affair with Carmen? And your wife found out?'

'She did.'

281

'And she just upped and left and disappeared?'

He covers his face with his hands. 'We used to walk in the woods. She said it was like fairyland. I don't believe in bloody fairies, but it made her happy. She found that little place where you were today. Took me to have a look. Put a rug down and we had some of her homemade bread with cheese and a bottle of Château Margaux.'

'She made bread?'

'Of course. And she could bake a great cake.'

'Could?'

'Before she left.'

I don't want to push this. 'So… why have you brought us here, to your house?'

His eyes are confused. Probably deciding on his next lie. 'What were you digging for? In Mona's special place?'

'She appeared to me and Sheila. That's why Sheila couldn't read for Carmen. She kept seeing Mona.'

He shakes his head like there's a bee between his ears. 'Carmen and her ideas. You'd think a cold-hearted cow like her wouldn't be superstitious, but there you go. She wanted to hear that our new business was going to make millions, that's what she said. Her bloody mate suggested Sheila. Made me drive all the way with her, like her chauffeur.'

'How come you moved her in if you don't really like her?'

He laughs a laugh with no mirth. 'If you lose your wife over another woman you've got to try, haven't you? Or it was all for nothing.'

I can feel Jemimah at my shoulder. Fuck it, I'm going

to go for gold. 'Mona said you wrapped her in a carpet and buried her. Did you know she was still alive when you put her in the ground?'

At that he's up and out of that seat like greased lightning. It scrapes noisily over the floorboards as he jumps back, brandishing his knife and breathing heavily. I push my seat back and jump up ready to run, but he doesn't come closer, just starts screaming.

'Don't you dare! Don't you fucking *dare* say that! I'll slit your fucking throat for you! What kind of *monster* do you think I am? I wouldn't *do* that to Mona!'

He bursts into tears, but keeps waving that bloody knife.

'I didn't say you did it on purpose!'

He takes a step towards me and, just as he does, the most extraordinary thing happens... the photograph of him and Mona, with its heavy gilt frame and glass cover, flies off the table and lands on the wooden floor five feet away with a crash.

I've never seen anything like it. Evidently neither has he as he lets out a loud shriek and jumps back several feet, looking at me, then wildly around the room.

'What the...?'

After the initial shock I want to laugh. That is the first time I've seen an object fly across the room like that. It has to be Mona. I shout encouragement in my head.

'Woo hoo! Go girl!' She must be one powerful lass now that she's been released, to move a heavy frame like that.

Dan's Deputy Dawg eyes are suddenly bigger than the rest of his face. Despite himself, he cries out, 'Mona?

Mona?'

I relax totally. Words are going to come and I won't have to think about it. This is new to me, but I know what to do. A warm energy rushes through my body.

'I knew about the women, Dandan. I knew about them all. I forgave, I forgave you all of them... you could have left Carmen, I would have forgiven you. You could have left me, I would have forgiven you.'

'Oh my God. Mona? Is this Mona? Or are you just messing with me?'

The hand with the knife is shaking now. I keep talking. It's my voice, but not my speech patterns. I'm intrigued.

'I loved you, Dandan, and I would have done anything for you. Why would you hurt me? I would not have made things hard for you. You know it.'

Now he's sobbing and holding out his hand in supplication. 'Mona, I got bored, that's all, but I didn't want to leave you. She was a dirty, dirty witch. She put a spell on me. She tricked me. She got me addicted to her, then she said you'd make things hard and take all of the money. She said me and her were soulmates and we couldn't be together with you about. She fucking messed with my head. She nagged and nagged and nagged, then one night I just couldn't take it any more. I brought her here and we did it. I knew it was a mistake when she was bashing you over and over. I knew it was wrong when we were burying you. I knew I'd done something terrible. And I miss you so much. For her, it was all about money and going out and holidays. I just wanted you and the horses and dinner and wine in front of the telly again. Why do you think I've been visiting the woods every

284

single day?'

'You are not a good man. I always thought you were in pain and I could help you. But you were just spoilt and arrogant and now you've spread your nastiness again! You're doing it now. It has to stop. You have to make it right! Make everything right, Dandan, or you will have to deal with me. Do you hear me? Make it right!'

As I stop speaking, the telly turns on. His head whips round. It's some kind of afternoon drama. A young couple arguing. Then the radio comes on. 'Wake Me Up Before You Go Go' by Wham!, at full volume. Admiration, as much as bone-shaking fear, takes my breath away. Dan is screaming like a woman when three drawers pull out of the bureau all on their own and begin to rattle up and down. Then, as a final nail in the coffin (so to speak) a huge portrait of a chestnut horse (probably Mona's) that is mounted over the mantelpiece falls with a dramatic crash to the floor. To my absolute astonishment Dan takes in a huge breath, as if to scream to high heaven, then promptly faints. He goes down like a sack of shit.

Without a second thought, I've vaulted him and I'm in the hallway. I grapple with the latch to the door which Sheila is now banging frantically, and grab her arm as she tries to question the racket that she heard coming from the living room. As we reach the front door, I see a button panel.

'The red one and the keys.'

It's Frank. I hear him loud and clear. The red button has 'gate' printed on it. I press it and scoop up the keys I saw Dan throw carelessly in a wooden bowl as we came in.

As we both run out, I am scared to look back in case he's chasing us. I press the little button to unlock the car and scramble into the driver's seat. Sheila opens the passenger door, but the shock of what's just gone on makes her clumsy as she tries to get in so I reach over and yank her as hard as I can.

'Owwwwwwww.'

'Sorry, Sheila.'

'Forget sorry, just drive!'

The car starts immediately, but the first time I try to move it I spin the wheels. I pull the seat forward and check the rear-view mirror; and suddenly, there is Dan emerging through the front door. I yelp when I see him, causing Sheila to swivel round in her seat and wail like a banshee. Without further ado I find the biting point and roar off, straight through the now open electronic gates as Dan begins to run down the drive after us. I have never stolen a car before. I have never been held at knifepoint before. And I have never seen a spook give such a demonstration of power before. What a day! Two of those things, I never want to happen again.

My biggest thought as I bomb down the lane like a 4x4 Intercity 125, is that Dan looked so scared, I didn't think he was chasing after us to kill us, I think he was trying to come with us.

THERE'S A WHAT BURIED
IN THE WOODS?

It's strange how fate works. Sitting back in my flat at two a.m. with a giant mug of camomile tea and Milo at my side, curled up on the sofa like a sleepy puppy, I can't help musing on the absolute fluke that was me speeding off down the road in Dan's big car, trying valiantly not to be sick on myself, as we bemoaned my phone's lack of signal. (I'd had my little bag hanging off me for the whole ordeal, whereas Sheila had dropped her purse in the woods.) And just as she fought an impossible battle to call 999 on my phone, those *very same* boys in blue emerged from a leafy little parking spot and flagged us down, lights flashing, for doing 58mph in a 40mph zone.

When I say boys in blue, I actually mean *boy* in blue. PC Markus. Later just Neil. Lovely, smiley, out-of-his-depth Neil. *How funny.* The poor lad probably thought he'd caught a middle-class boy racer getting a bit overenthusiastic in the country lane.

His first surprise was us two spilling out of the 4x4,

hyperventilating and speaking in tongues, pushing our way into the back of his vehicle, basically begging him to take us to a police station. His next one, before he could even issue a ticket, was realising we were claiming we'd been kidnapped and held at knife point. The biggest surprise of all was when he caught the tail end of what Sheila was bellowing at him as I tried to apologise for being in a (as yet unreported) stolen vehicle.

'I'm sorry, madam, could you repeat that? There's a *what* buried in the woods?'

It was Neil's second week as a traffic cop and suddenly he was looking at kidnap and murder on his patch. He seemed doubtful, to say the least. We weren't greatly concerned with his mistrust of our credibility at that moment though; we just wanted to get to a police station and hide in it. Dan Beck could be anywhere and neither of us wanted to meet him again.

PC Markus obliged and soon we were drinking absolutely appalling coffee and giving our statements to him. It took a long time. Mostly because the statement-giving was peppered with questions like, 'And then you heard a screaming in your head, Madam? Are you sure that's what you want to say?' and 'Then the TV and radio switched themselves on independently after the picture flew across the room, you say?'

I was acutely aware of how crazy my story sounded and I kept wondering if Sheila was OK, telling her side of things in another room. I gave them a detailed description of where we had found Mona. I was sure Sheila must be doing the same. Two officers were dispatched to check it out and another two were sent to call at Dan Beck's house. They knew who he was, it turned out. PC Markus knew him personally because his parents had bought a Beck-built house. PC Markus also knew Mona and had been as surprised as anyone when she left Dan and disappeared.

This he told us, as he drove me and Sheila back to London, his mate, Spike, following behind in my car so I wouldn't have to retrieve it tomorrow. Never have I been more relieved at getting a lift; I was too shocked and overwhelmed to drive my car safely. Sheila and I held hands all the way.

Neil had told us plenty of other things after they released us, at just after 11.30 p.m., to go home. Sitting here now, car parked safely outside and doors securely locked, I try to arrange the information I do have into bite-sized chunks so it doesn't overwhelm me. The whole thing is so ugly and sad, I can only cope with it in bits. It seems it runs like this:

1) The police originally thought Sheila and I were on drugs when Neil brought us in.

2) Mona was exactly where we said she'd be. The general consensus being that they'd probably find a dead dog or other such pet wrapped in that carpet. On the sly, Neil told us that an officer had vomited when they unwrapped her. Murder isn't that common a crime on the borders of St Albans, apparently.

3) While I was sitting on a chair in Dan Beck's TV room, trying to make reasonable conversation with a total psychopath, upstairs in a spare room Carmen was lying dead, and had been for at least twenty-four hours. Neil was not at liberty to say how she died, but the way his

boyish, clean-scrubbed face crumpled disgustedly when he spoke of it made me suspect that gutting Sheila 'like a rabbit' was maybe not just an idle threat, but a *modus operandi*. This is something that will haunt me for a while.

4) Dan Beck was not in his house when the police found Carmen. They looked everywhere for him. Eventually, some bright spark thought to search the stables at ten o'clock at night and found him in there, hanging from a beam. (Now I know why I dreamt of a noose. This bit has really freaked me out.) He had a note next to him. I don't know what was in it. Neil said he'd call me if and when he was allowed to tell me what it said. Without wishing to blow my own trumpet, I think Neil likes me a bit. I have no idea what it is with me and these young lads.

5) It turns out we won't be charged for speeding or car theft, there were too many extenuating circumstances.

I stroke Milo's floppy fringe. He opens an eye, then sits up. I made him a cup of tea just before he nodded off. He reaches for it.

'You all right, Tanz?'

'I am. Thanks to you.'

Inka has wedged herself between us and is lapping up our warmth. Milo yawns loudly, and scratches his head. 'You seem very calm considering what happened, Tanz. I feel like I just lived a day-long episode of *Tales of the Unexpected*.

He gives my arm a clumsy stroke. He's a bit like my mam when it comes to too much physical contact, but today must have been terrifying for him. I can't believe he's here, but thank God he is. I'm feeling so disorientated. It's only after an event like this that you start thinking of how close you may have been to losing your life.

'Milo, I want to thank you again for coming down. How much did the train cost? I'll get the money back to you. I'm worried that I've disturbed your work.'

'Don't be daft. Fuck the money. And I can work here, I can work on the train back home. It's fine.'

I kiss him on the forehead. He strokes my hand. I've obviously given him a fright. Apparently he tried to call me until tea time, then started freaking out and jumped on a train. On the way to London he'd had the fabulous sense to think of calling police stations in the St Albans area. There's actually only one so there weren't many calls to make, and fortunately, the desk sergeant, Colin, told him I was there 'helping with enquiries'. I don't know if he should have done that, but his honesty meant that Milo elicited the promise of a phone call from me as soon as it was possible. So yay for Colin! And yay for ninety-year-old Steve who took Milo in and regaled him with stories of the war until I got home. I shall get him some whisky.

At this moment I love Milo like the truest brother. I feel blessed and shaken up and grateful and sad all at once. Everyone should have a mate as good as him.

As for Pat the Cat, I found his phone, out of juice and in my bathroom when I got home. Plus, a note through my door asking me to call him via his sister. He must have left it here after sleeping over. I'll drop it in to Minnie's when I can actually bear to leave the house.

Probably sometime in 2057. I hate that my life has been touched by death like this.

Ironic, I know.

LOOK TO THE SKIES

It's taken me five days to be ready go into Mystery Pot again. It took Sheila no days. That woman is made of reinforced steel. She got back home after our ordeal and – always paranoid about bag-snatching – let herself in with the spare key hidden under a rock near her front door step. She then went to bed after a few stiff amarettos and went in to work next day. Reckoned it was better than sitting at home. Her only major comment about the whole nightmare was, 'Next time we go looking for a murder victim, I'm taking a gun with me. If I ever meet another Dan Beck in the woods, I'll blow his bloody face off.'

I think she's still mad at him for the indignity of being locked in a cupboard, even though he's dead now.

Neil the policeman called me on day three and asked how I was. Then he swore me to secrecy and said that Dan's note was an admission of guilt and an explanation of how Carmen's mum withdrew funds, pretending to be Mona in France, and also sent a forged postcard from abroad. (She's in big trouble now.) After a few self-pitying (but still, maybe true) sentences about his own abusive childhood, he suddenly finished with an apology to me and Sheila and the bequest, to me, of his car. I mean, how random? Why would I want the car he kidnapped us in? The car that is currently evidence because there are traces of blood and rug fibres in the boot? He really thought I'd want the murder car? Bloody men.

Neil asked if I wanted to go for a drink. I said I'd think about it when I was feeling better. Me and a copper? How the hell would that work?

I saw Milo back on to the train this morning. He's been my total rock since the 'happening', but he doesn't like being out of his routine and my bathroom will never be clean enough for him. It made him very twitchy. So I thanked him profusely, told him I needed my space and made him go home. As he boarded, I handed him a giant-size bag of retro sweeties and I swear I saw tears in his eyes. I also hugged him for ages, which he took quite gamely, then waved him off as he tried his best to hide the relief on his face. Milo is not a natural traveller, he likes to be at home, which just makes it even more spectacular that he jumped on the train to London in the first place.

I take a deep breath before I walk into the shop. Maggie has kept my position open on the till. She didn't really have a choice as no one else seems to want the job. No one that she likes the look of, anyway. I'm not supposed to be here today so she's a little confused when I enter.

'Hello, stranger.'

'Hiya, Maggie.'

'How are you feeling?'

This is a rhetorical question; she doesn't have a lot of

truck with human feelings and she thinks I should be fine by now, I can tell.

'A bit better, actually. Can I have a word, please?'

'Ohh. Sounds ominous. What is it?'

'Martin.'

She turns her nose up.

'What about him?'

'He didn't do it. He didn't tell that lady that she was married to a gay man. Her husband is nuts. She is actually very fond of Martin. As I'm sure quite a few of your less conventional clients are.'

'Well, that's as may be, but he doesn't do enough readings and he doesn't come to work on time.'

'What if he bucked his ideas up?'

'I've sacked him now. And I'm not apologising.'

'No, but he might apologise to you, if you give him a second chance.'

'Hmmm. What about you?'

'What if I get another acting job? You can cover the till, but you can't cover the readings. You need someone more reliable than me... Anyway, I'm not doing it. You can't make me and I won't.'

Maggie takes honesty better than I'd expected. 'I'm not calling him, Tanz. If you're ducking out of your post, you can sort it out.'

'Ducking out of my post? I could have been killed the other day.'

'Well you weren't, and neither was Sheila and she's in that room right now earning her bread and butter with a serial monogamist from Peckham.'

There's a sense of humour buried beneath that Maggie

Thatcher exterior, I know it. Sometimes it clambers close to the surface then it sinks again, into the murky depths. I smile at her – just a little one.

The whole St Albans debacle has threatened to properly mess me up, it has to be said. I'm still very tearful and shaky and I'm going to miss Milo's presence at night more than I would ever let on. The only way to get through it is to climb back on the horse of life. Or in this case, the Northern Line towards Morden.

The walk from the Tube station is a venture into alien territory. Grey buildings, no greenery, lots of cars – depression on a stick. I doubt blue skies ever reach here; it was invented for steely grey vistas. When I reach Martin's flat it's three floors up and has a balcony that smacks of Mike Leigh films and drug-estate dramas. I have no idea if he'll be in, but I have to try because I'm not doing this over the phone. The front door is black and the windows are small. There's no door knocker so I ring the bell, then rap with my knuckles. I wait a good couple of minutes before the door opens.

There stands a tiny, frail woman in a frilly, pink blouse and brown trousers. Her slippers are pink and beige tartan and her hair is like candy floss spiders' webs. She's one of the cutest things I've ever seen. When she sees me she grins and holds out her hand.

'Come in. I'm building my nest! OO-oo, OO-oo...'

I have little choice other than to follow this tiny, cooing woman into her humble home. Everything in the living room is in a state of disrepair. The television is so big and square it looks like cavemen made it out of stones and chewed bark. The walls have pretty, peeling wallpaper and the carpet has black age-marks on it. It doesn't smell nasty in here; it just smells unkempt. And it's too warm.

'Helloooo! Helllooo!'

She seems delighted to have a guest. I'm pretty convinced I'm at the wrong house, but she is so adorable, I sit on her rickety sofa and pat the space beside me. She 'flies' over, flapping her arms, and sits by me. Roosting, so to speak.

'What's your name, sweetheart?' She stares at me, friendly but confused.

I take her hand. 'I'm Tanz.'

'Hello, Tams. I'm DeeDee. OO-oo, OO-oo.'

'Are you a bird, DeeDee?'

She is inordinately pleased at the question and giggles. 'Oh, yes. That's me. I'm a birdie. My son won't let me open the windows because he thinks I'll fly away! He's probably right. I want to escape and not be trapped here in these ruins.'

Her eyes well up. Joyful to tearful in five seconds! She just beat my personal best.

I'm guessing Alzheimer's. It's not a particularly intelligent guess. I take her tiny bird-frame into my arms and hug her close. She begins to coo contentedly, her tears melting away. She smells of oldness and sweet, papery skin. She starts to hum a song in a tremulous alto. Just then I hear a key in the lock and Martin enters, with bags like rubbish sacks under his eyes, wearing a more moth-eaten cardigan than usual and carrying a two-litre carton of milk. He stops dead, confronted by the sight of his arch nemesis cradling what I can only assume is his mother.

297

'What's going on?'

'I just met DeeDee. She's beautiful…'

She looks up at him and waves. 'Look, Martin, I found a mermaid!'

'I'm sorry to bother you, Martin, but I really need a word.'

'Have you come to evict me from my flat as well as my job?'

DeeDee senses discord immediately and whimpers. I stroke her spider's web hair and attempt the tune she was just humming. She joins in. I place her carefully on the sofa, much as I do with Inka, and squeeze her bony hand gently. She continues to croon to herself. I follow Martin to his kitchen. There's a Formica table for two with foldaway chairs in there, green checked lino and the cupboards my mam and dad had twenty years ago. It's so old-fashioned it's almost cutting edge. I sit down without being invited.

'I got in a bit of bother last week.'

'What?'

'I've been off work. It doesn't matter why, but it means I'm doing this now when I should have done it already.'

'What are you talking about, Tanz?'

'I had a coffee with a client of yours. Nada. A couple of days after Maggie let you go.'

His eyes moisten and the corners of his mouth begin to drag down. It occurs to me that he has been devastated by this job loss. I doubt he had much confidence to start with.

'She said that you are a wonderful reader.'

He wasn't expecting this. 'Did she?'

'She said her husband lied to get you sacked. He was jealous.'

'He's such a controlling idiot. I don't know how many times I've told her.'

'Well, everything you told her this time was right. She came into some money. She rang from a call box early this morning sounding very pleased with herself. She poured bleach on every item of his clothing yesterday after he left for work, then climbed out of the kitchen window with her suitcase. She then jumped on a coach with her mum and has moved into a flat next to her cousins in Hove. She says if her husband comes looking for her, they will throw him in the sea.'

Martin can't help a chortle as he switches on the kettle.

'You did that, Martin. She's desperate to thank you. She wondered if she could have your number?'

He looks a tad disappointed. 'So that's why you came?'

'No. That's only part of it. You need to come back to the shop.'

He takes mugs out of the cupboard. They look like heirlooms from the seventies. 'I got sacked, remember? Maggie wouldn't listen.'

The petulant look is back on his face.

'I know you did. But that wasn't just because of a mad husband complaining, Martin. You must realise that?'

'No, it's because you came and stole my place.'

This gets my back up. 'That is bullshit. I don't want to be a tarot reader in that shop. I got the job to earn a few quid sitting behind the till. That's all.'

'You could have fooled me. Sitting there like Gypsy

299

Rose Lee, getting bunches of flowers and making people weep!'

'I didn't say I couldn't do it. I said I don't want to do it for money. I happen to be *extremely* talented!'

My joke is rewarded with a stony glare.

'Come on, Martin, the customers scare me. I don't know how you and Sheila do it.'

'Do you want a cup of tea?'

Oh God, if I turn him down he'll be offended. 'Just a little one please; I already had a coffee.'

'OK. Has Maggie said she wants me back?'

There's such hope in that voice. He actually looks up to Maggie. Bless him.

'Well, the thing is, she's not *averse* to you coming back. But she feels you've been... well, taking the piss a bit. You know, with your erratic business hours.'

'Taking the piss? You've met DeeDee. She's a full-time job.'

'She is so adorable.'

'Not when she's weeing in my yucca plant, she's not.'

This is not said without affection. On cue, in clacks the woman herself, resplendent in a kimono-style red dressing gown and silver high heels. She's put a cupid's bow of red on her lips and looks thoroughly proud of her ensemble. I start to laugh and give her a round of applause. She bows down low.

'Mum! What are you wearing? Off out, are we?'

'I decided to dress for tea!'

She's giddy from the attention. She bows again, then takes her tea and carefully carries it out of the room.

'She watches *Laurel and Hardy*. I got her the boxset

last Christmas. It cost an arm and a leg, but it keeps her happy for hours.'

'Does she have a carer?'

'Yes, me. Plus, she goes to a place down the road three days a week. It's got all of these activities, dancing and whatnot for the elderly. She loves it. It starts at ten and finishes at five. The lady next door picks her up for me sometimes and gives her a sandwich. But it's not easy juggling it all.'

'It sounds like having a child.'

'It is like having a child. But a child that used to be my mum.'

He looks so wistful suddenly. It must be very hard. I doubt there's much scope for romance in his life.

'Why didn't you say?'

'It's nobody's business. I don't want sympathy. She's my mum.'

I see him in a slightly different light now.

'Martin. You are going to have to ring up Maggie and say sorry. Sorry that you show up at noon and leave at three.'

'But what if I haven't got a reading? Sometimes I want a minute to myself when DeeDee goes to her day centre.'

'I understand. But come to work at ten, say hello, then have your "minute" in a caff by the shop. Just so you look willing. And stop being so bloody miserable with the customers.'

'What? I'm not.'

'Nada says she thinks you're shy and that's what people take as you being unfriendly.'

'I'm *not* unfriendly.'

301

'Martin, you look like you're curling your lip all of the time. If you like doing the cards then at least be a bit more positive when you're in the shop.'

'You haven't worked there five minutes, how would you know?'

'You have hardly any bookings. The proof is in the pudding. I'll bet you could double your clientele if you just smiled. You obviously know how to read. Or that's what Nada says, anyway! Why waste it? Just call Maggie, make things right and try again.'

He pouts. 'Why are you doing this, Mrs Goody-Two-Shoes?'

'Because life's too short and I'm trying to be nice. But don't push it.'

FUCK IT

Pat is having food with his sister and her boyfriend at six o'clock. Tomorrow he leaves for Bangkok. I saw him in Minnie's a couple of days ago when I delivered his phone, but haven't had him at my flat overnight since the St Albans nightmare. Cait would have liked me to come round tonight, but I'm still not up to socialising, really, so I say I'll meet Pat later for a bit.

Then I call round Sheila's. We've spoken on the phone, but I've not seen her since the happening. I should have waited for her to finish her reading at Mystery Pot today, but I just wanted to get back to my place and cuddle Inka. She's already opened a bottle of wine and set it out on the table with the goblets and Doritos when I get there. She looks radiant in a long white skirt, shirt and suede waistcoat.

'You all right, love?'

I give her a hug and sit. She passes me my wine. My eyes spring with tears. Why am I always tearful these days? 'Sort of. Still sorry, you know, about nearly getting you killed.'

'Will you stop saying that? You've said it a hundred

times and it's just not true.'

'We would not have been in St Albans in that bloody wood if it wasn't for me. That's what bothers me.'

'No, we wouldn't. And we wouldn't have released Mona or solved a bloody awful double murder. We did well!'

'I don't know if it was worth the risk.'

'Bollocks. There wasn't a risk.'

'Why do you keep saying that? Of course there was a risk.'

'There wasn't. Really. When I was in that cupboard, it all became clear. One of my angels came forward. He's not one that speaks to me that often, but he's a very high protector and he knew how scared I was that Dan Beck would hurt you. In the dark, when I tried to meditate to halt the fear, he spoke to me. He said that we were on a mission, you and me, and that it needed to be done. He said there was no need for fear because they would protect us and we wouldn't be hurt. He said you were as powerfully protected as anyone could be and that you would say the right things. He said we were being guided every step of the way. He laid a hand on me. It was a wonderful moment.'

'What, so while I was sitting in the TV room with a knife waving in front of my face, hoping I wouldn't be raped to death, you were having wonderful moments with your angel mate in the cupboard?'

'Something like that.'

She starts to giggle. Then so do I and soon it becomes uncontrollable and the tears rolling down my face are real tears and I have a cry, and then drain my glass. She tops me up.

'It was a big test for someone new to this, Tanz. I have never ever been in a situation like that, you do realise that, don't you? All these years and it never got that dangerous. It doesn't get any worse than what happened to us. It was an exception.'

'Was it, or do I just attract the extremes? Because I don't want that shit.'

'Have you enjoyed our ghost-busts so far?'

'You know I have.'

'Have you enjoyed making people happy by giving them useful messages?'

'You know I have.'

'Right. So chalk up what just happened as a one-off. Protect yourself every morning, keep doing what you've been doing, and quit dwelling on it. That man wasn't well. He would never have been happy after what happened, after what he did. He's better off where he is than in prison. And we really did help Mona.' She raises her glass and winks at me.

She has no idea how scared I am at this moment of ever 'dabbling' again. I feel more upset about what happened every day, not less. 'I'll take your word for it, Sheils.'

She comes over and gives me a smoky hug. We chat until the bottle is empty and I have to go to meet Pat. As I'm getting my bag and coat to leave, Sheila looks at her watch. Twice. What's she up to?

We hug on the doorstep and she closes the door after quickly glancing up and down the street. Just as I'm walking off my phone pings. I stop and read the text. It's from mad Ruth wanting to take me for dinner next week. I take a deep breath and text back, *Sounds good x*

As I do, a handsome, young black dude passes by me, carrying a couple of carrier bags. I recognise him, but can't quite place him. Then he walks up Sheila's path and knocks on the door, and suddenly it hits me like an Exocet missile. It's that lad! The one she did the reading for in the shop, the one with the gangster cousin! What the hell is he doing here? I push myself into the hedge so Sheila won't see me, and listen to the door opening.

'Hello, sweetheart.'

There's the sound of a kiss – on the bloody cheek I hope – then the door closes. Oh my God! He looked so scared when she told him off in the shop. Maybe he begged for a private meeting, a more in-depth reading, the chance to talk to a real life witch... or maybe... just maybe... he had a Pat moment and fancied the woman who could tell him things about himself!

Either she's nicking the shop's clients, which would drive Maggie insane, or she's getting it on with a very handsome young man who can cook. Or both. As I walk away I can't help chortling to myself. I won't ask her about it, not for a while. Secrets are great, but speculation is almost more fun than finding out the truth.

PAT THE CAT

I meet Pat at Purple Haze and I order my now habitual raspberry mint martini.

'You look perkier tonight.'

'Sheila put things into perspective for me.'

'Good. She seems like a top woman.'

'She is.'

We sit in silence for a bit. Then he reaches over and kisses me on the lips. It's a little awkward.

'I'm not sure if I'm allowed to say this, but I'm going to miss you, Tanz. A lot.'

I've allowed things to drift over the past week, what with one thing and another, but it's still lovely to be liked by someone so gorgeous. 'If you weren't leaving the country I think I could have become a bit over-attached, Pat.'

He takes my hand. 'I bet you'd be a great travelling partner.'

I sigh. 'I don't have the money. And I have to be a grown up and work. I can't just run off.'

'Thank God for Skype, then!'

I look at him and smile. I am genuinely pleased for

him, because he's a wonderful lad. He deserves to see the world. But there are a lot of people and a lot of adventures out there and I doubt he'll be thinking about Skyping me after about a fortnight of the 'new' him.

'I reckon we're better off thinking about tonight than the future, Pat. I've got you for six hours or so. Let's make it a good six hours.'

He beams and pulls something out of his back pocket, offering it to me.

'It's from Cait. She says she hopes you're not offended.'

I unseal the plain white envelope with my name scrawled on the back. She writes like a teacher. It's a letter.

Dear Tanz,

You have been so lovely to me and my brother and helped us immensely in our grief. I don't know if Pat told you, but we have money in a trust from Dad. It wouldn't dent the pot at all to get you a return flight to Bangkok any time over the next month with a connecting flight to Koh Samui. We would love to do this as a token of our appreciation; a word from you and it will be booked. Just so you can spend a week or two on your favourite beach. Please tell me at your earliest convenience if/when you would like to go. My phone number is enclosed.

Love, Cait x

I stare at Pat. I'm shocked.

'I told her about your love of Thailand. She says you gave her something precious so she wanted to do the same back. She says it's a gift from Dad.'

'Pat, I can't accept this.'

'Please don't be alarmed; it's not me trying to make you be my bird or anything. You can come as my friend, you can come as my beautiful Geordie lady or you can ignore me totally for the whole time. But I – we – just want you to have a nice time on holiday. We hope you'll accept the tickets as a thank you.'

I'm gobsmacked. 'This is the nicest thing anyone has ever offered to do for me.'

He smiles and puts his arm around me. 'Now you know what it feels like.'

I kiss him hard and wrap myself around him. I know there's no way I'll accept the tickets, for a multitude of complex and not so complex reasons.

'We're going home right this minute, Pat. I am going to sex you into oblivion.'

Mr Tricorn Hat, resplendent in full highwayman gear, snorts loudly into his pint, which splashes onto the table, barely missing his laptop. I smile over at him.

'Hello! And good night!'

Pat has to leave soon. His sister is taking him to the airport. Almost definitely accompanied by a waterfall of tears. For tonight, at least, I am going to forget the carpet and the bluebells and the smell of death and the droopy eyed murderer with his head in a noose.

I am going to savour Pat's gorgeous body and his lovely face and do whatever I want with him.

PHWOARRR.

ACKNOWLEDGEMENTS

Thank you Don and Flynn, my two stars. Love you.

Thank you Rebecca Lloyd for having the best taste in writers and for bringing me in to the fabulous world of Accent Press.

Thank you Caroline Smailes for being so helpful and for believing in my book from the start.

Thank you Roz for being so generous and helpful from the first draft. You made me take the next step.

Thank you Lee for being Lee, I mean Milo, I mean Lee. My dear and special friend who always makes things better.

Thank you to my family for giving me a wealth of material to work with!

Thank you Ross Collins for dedicating your totally wonderful book to me and not getting enough thanks at the time.

Thank you Philippa, for introducing me to all things 'other'. What an adventure.

Thank you Paul Burgess for being a fantastically talented fella.

And...

Thank you wine, sex and spooks. You've improved my life no end. (But maybe not in that order.)

JODI TAYLOR

THE NOTHING GIRL

A fairy-tale for adults

Getting a life isn't
always easy

And hanging on to it
is even harder …

For more information about
Tracy Whitwell

and other **Accent Press** titles

please visit

www.accentpress.co.uk